Best of All Gifts

Also by Sheila M. Cronin

The Gift Counselor Series

The Gift Counselor

Heart Shaped: a collection of short romances

BEST OF ALL GIFTS

SHEILA M. CRONIN

Chicago, Illinois

First printing, 2017

"Irish Lullaby," Anonymous
"Amazing Grace," John Newton

Cover design by pro_designer123 on Fiverr.com

Library of Congress Control Number: 2017916213
Publisher: Sheila M. Cronin, Chicago, Illinois

ISBN-10: 099604605-4
ISBN-13: 978-0-9960460-5-3

Publisher's Cataloging-in-Publication data

Names: Cronin, Sheila M., author
Title: Best of all gifts / Sheila M. Cronin.
Series: Gift Counseling Books
Description: Chicago, IL: Sheila M. Cronin, 2017.
Identifiers: ISBN 978-0-9960460-5-3
Subjects: LCSH Fathers and daughters--Fiction. | Family--Fiction. | Man-woman
relationships--Fiction. | Post-traumatic Stress Disorder--Fiction. | Love stories. |
BISAC FICTION / Contemporary Women
Classification: LCC PS3603.R6638 B47 2017 | DDC 813.6--dc23

Printed in the United States of America

In

memory

of

Frank Capra

For who has known the mind of the Lord

Or who has been his counselor?

Or who has given a gift to him

That he might be repaid?

Romans 11: 34-35

December 10, 1972

Chicago, Illinois

John Bloom crossed the lobby of the Pick-Congress Hotel, determined to beat the other departing conventioneers to the first available taxi. A glance at his watch told him to keep moving if he wanted to grab his little girl a birthday present at O'Hare before takeoff. He shifted his overcoat to his left arm. In his haste, he nearly toppled a placard on display announcing an upcoming high school sports tournament. He straightened the sign without reading it, jammed on his hat, and hurried on.

Nightmares had bothered him the whole trip which was unusual. He blamed the letter he'd received a week ago from an old Army buddy who asked whether they could get together. What for, he'd wondered, to reminisce about the war? Nonetheless, the sealed-off memories had begun to leak into his awareness—a fierce C.O., a .30-caliber Browning machine gun, ice choked rice paddies, trenches, body bags, hunger.

Korea.

Exiting through the revolving door, he slammed smack into a wall of arctic air. It momentarily closed his windpipe and blurred his vision. Overnight, the temperature must have plummeted twenty degrees. Gale force winds off Lake Michigan made it feel ten degrees colder.

The flag to the right of the hotel entrance snapped in fury. Moved by the sight, he didn't notice that he'd dropped a glove.

A doorman ran to pick it up. "Cab, sir?"

He shook his head in a fog. Meanwhile, a woman grabbed the doorman's arm and pulled him away.

The cold swept under John's clothing, through his skin, into his bones. The hairs in his nostrils froze so that it hurt to breathe. He didn't notice that his fingers had stiffened and loosened their grip on his belongings. Instead, he gaped at the unusual activity underway in front of him.

Three long, yellow buses were parked on the far side of the carport. Out poured wave upon wave of keyed-up Asian high school boys dressed uniformly in black pea coats. That spectacle, plus the shriek of a doorman's whistle racing up his spine, sent John back in time.

Back to 1951 and hill 205 where he was up against human wave charges on all sides with no end in sight, his machine gun barrel melting from non-stop use, the fear he'd run out of ammo dogging his every move. He would fall asleep in the bunker despite subzero temperatures and all-night shelling, only to wake up to the bugle's signal that the battle was underway again. Back and forth, the desolate heap of rocks changed ownership within hours, over and over, until days and nights became one frozen blur and the hill ran red with blood. He realized that each man there was fighting two battles: one with the relentless enemy, the other with his own sanity.

Braying car horns jarred him back to the present and his eyes blinked rapidly. The school boys now seemed to surround and engulf the three doormen. Laughing, jostling each other, mouths emitting vapor, shouting in their native tongue, they kept coming, until the whole carport was rife with black pea coats. The closer they drew, the harsher their voices sounded.

Then he recognized the language

John Bloom swayed and nearly fainted. He staggered away from the hotel entrance, past the idling taxis gushing clouds of exhaust, toward no particular destination. Left behind in a pile were his plane ticket, wallet, coat, suitcase, briefcase, and gloves. A panhandler who kept watch on distracted hotel guests absconded with the items, unseen.

At the first intersection, he ignored the oncoming traffic. His hat blew away but he kept going. He somehow reached the other side of the street intact. The man continued his odd bolt up Michigan Avenue two blocks to the corner of Jackson, where he collapsed.

Pedestrians stopped to assist him. An ambulance transported him to Cook County Hospital. Left alone in the emergency room after an initial evaluation, he shivered under a blanket and retreated from the bustle around him. When attention was finally paid to him, John could neither state his full name nor furnish his home address or phone number. Nor could he explain what had triggered his collapse. His belongings were never recovered.

Best of All Gifts

CHAPTER 1

Saturday, January 3, 1998 ~ Twenty-six years later

Venice, California

The sound of the kitchen wall phone brought her romantic daydream to a halt. Jonquil Bloom sighed audibly and closed the dishwasher before she picked up the receiver. Hearing her friend Annie's voice, however, made her whoop for joy.

"You're back. Wah-hoo! Let's do lunch."

"Let's eat at your place. Gal, I've got a surprise for you, and it's rather bulky."

They'd met ten years ago. Jonquil, a new mother, had moved from her tiny West Los Angeles accommodations to a spacious, two-bedroom apartment in the same building where Annie Berghoff lived in Venice Beach. The two women hit it off immediately. Annie used to run early each morning in the mist down the boardwalk. Then she'd jog back to the apartment building, see Jonquil's lights on, and cool down in the kitchen while Jonquil nursed her son, Billy. She'd make herself a fresh pot of coffee, and hours would pass as the women chatted.

Over time, they became more like sisters than friends. Jonquil confided to her how she came to be raised by her grandmother in Seattle. Annie described her more conventional upbringing in Bakersfield. Annie had never been married while Jonquil was a widow. After her husband's tragic death in a house fire in Seattle, Jonquil had relocated to Southern California. Annie had helped her dry many tears, and, in the process, became Billy's favorite babysitter. When her friend moved to a condo in Westwood two years ago, Jonquil had felt the loss keenly. By then Annie had begun to travel frequently on cruise ships and to posh resorts or spas as artist in residence. Her specialty was portraiture. Nowadays her schedule made it harder for them to get together. Annie had been away since Thanksgiving, so the they were long overdue for a good chat.

An hour later, Annie arrived in a Lakers tank top, cutoffs, and sandals that showed off her spectacular tan. Her hazel eyes sparkled behind gold-rimmed glasses. Her glossy brown hair was gathered in a ponytail that set off her round Germanic features. She lugged in a narrow package, roughly three square feet in diameter, wrapped in twine and brown butcher paper. It dwarfed the gaily wrapped box from Clyde's that Jonquil had waiting on the coffee table for her.

"God's teeth!" Jonquil exclaimed in the mock classical vernacular they teased each other with. Annie leaned the package against the sofa cushions before they hugged. "What's this? A piece of your artwork, I hope?"

4

"Happy Christmas, JB." Annie grinned from ear to ear. "Come on, open it."

Jonquil turned to grab a pair of scissors, but Annie neatly pulled off the twine with two tugs. The paper sprung loose, and together they removed the contents.

Staring back at Jonquil was a most exquisite portrait of her ten-year-old son. She recognized the pose from his recent school photo, the best he'd ever taken. Sketched on pale blue paper, Annie's spare use of color and skillful, bold light and dark contrasts had brought a flat photograph to life. The drawing, under glass, was double matted and framed in stained blond wood.

Jonquil couldn't take her eyes off of the rendering. Remarkably, it reminded her of her missing father, John Bloom. She felt close to tears.

"Oh, Annie," she murmured

"Sure you like it? You sound upset."

"I've never noticed before how much Billy looks like my dad. It's in the eyes." Jonquil gazed at the drawing with a mix of wonder, love for her son, and old resentment toward the father who had abandoned her in childhood.

She straightened up. "Let's find a spot to hang it."

"First, let's eat. Never thought I'd say this again after three back-to-back cruises, but I'm famished."

Just as they were about to have lunch, Billy ran in with Blackie, the newest member of the Bloom household, who greeted Annie with non-stop yaps. Annie offered the cocker spaniel her hand to sniff. He reciprocated with excited licks. She

5

gathered him in her arms and placed him on her lap like they were long lost buddies.

"His name's Blackie, Aunt Annie," Billy gabbed in a rush. "And Mom was on television 'cause of her new job at Clyde's, and I ran away, but then Claude and Mom found me and we had a real cool party on Christmas—"

"Slow down, buster," cut in Annie who'd sliced through Billy's tidbits for the morsel she found most enticing. "Who's Claude?"

"Claude Chappel," Billy replied impatiently as though anyone in the civilized world would recognize the name of his mom's new boyfriend. "He works on the building across the street. He helped me pass my fractions test. Then he took Mom on a date." He waggled his eyebrows at her.

"A date?" Annie's gaze shifted from Billy to Jonquil, who immediately found something to dry with a dishcloth.

Billy gathered up Blackie, snapped on his leash, and made a dash for the door. "I'm taking Blackie with me to Ramon's house."

"Aren't you hungry, sweetie?" Jonquil called. "Remember, we're taking down the tree later."

He turned to answer her and nearly tumbled into his portrait, still leaning against the sofa. "Wow!"

"Annie made a portrait of you," Jonquil said. Blackie barked until Billy firmly hushed him.

He studied the drawing intently. "It's perfect," he said. "Gee, Aunt Annie, you're the best artist I know, even better than Miss Emmanuel at school." Without informing his mom on the status

6

of his appetite, he ran outside with the puppy and let the screen door bang shut.

Annie swung around in her chair to face Jonquil. "Okay, the first cruise was rough going all the way to Hawaii. On the second cruise, I fell for the saxophone player, but the 'sax' was off key. It rained buckets in Sydney, Fiji was glorious, and I don't remember the flight back from Hawaii 'because I slept the whole way. That's my story in a nutshell. Now, start talking and don't stop until I say you can."

CHAPTER 2

Friend to Friend

Jonquil brought Annie up to date on her employment status. Her paid psychology internship at Children's Home had ended abruptly after Thanksgiving. She now worked as a gift counselor, a new term she'd coined, at Clyde's of Santa Monica. The family owned department store let her gather data for her graduate research on the psychodynamics of gift giving. Well acquainted with her friend's scholarly interest, Annie listened while they nibbled on shortbread cookies and shared a pitcher of iced tea.

"This is truly fascinating, gal, but when do we get to the main course?" She was not referring to lunch. When Jonquil started to respond, Annie urgently splayed her fingers. "Wait. First describe him in detail. Then give me the blow by blow."

Jonquil understood she was talking to a portrait artist who expected her to know how many moles the man had as well as the exact contour of his ears. Her brief description—tall, dark, handsome, French Canadian, early forties, melodious voice—was so unsatisfactory that she finally brought out snapshots.

That shut up Annie for several seconds.

"He's gorgeous!" she pronounced. "Look at dem muscles." So much for mole inventories. "And he's never been married?"

"No, he claims he never had time. He's originally from a little town near Montreal. But his family moved to California when he was nine. His dad's a housepainter and could work here outdoors year-round. When the Vietnam War escalated, they returned to Canada because he and his brothers were draft age. After college, he moved back here to start his own business. One of his sisters lives in Santa Monica, too. I'm meeting her tonight."

"Oh, wow! I take it your love life is good?" Annie said with a grin.

"I forgot how wonderful it could be." Jonquil refreshed their tea glasses without looking up but her face glowed.

"Oh, I'm happy for you, JB. And Billy likes him, too. I always knew you'd meet someone."

"I don't know," sighed Jonquil. "I could mess things up." Her tone grew edgier. "Trusting men is not my strong suit."

The room got still after so much banter. Annie was the first to break the silence. "Does having a puppy help? How did that happen?"

Jonquil smiled ruefully. "Remember how much Billy always wanted one? Even after I told him I was allergic? I got in the habit of buying him stuffed animals as decoys. It worked, so I thought."

"Right, right." Annie nodded, for she had purchased a few of those toys.

"But last month Billy started up again about wanting a dog for Christmas. Claude thought I should let him have one. We had a major fight about it. Then Billy found pictures of his dad and me and our setter," Jonquil murmured.

"Wait, *you* owned a dog?"

"Yes, back in Seattle. Sorry, Annie, I thought it best to keep that a secret. But as I said, Billy found out the same day I was on the Poppi Blair show."

"Wow!" Annie grabbed another cookie. "Why were you on television?"

"They moved the show from New York to L.A. that week and thought a gift counselor would make an ideal guest on the day before Christmas."

"I get that. So, then what?"

"Billy had the show on while he went rummaging through my closet for his Christmas gifts. Instead, he found some old photos. So, he dialed the show's 1-800 number and when he got on air, he called me a liar. I realized what had happened. I raced home but by the time I got back here, he'd run away with a puppy one of our neighbors let him have—little Blackie. Claude and I finally found him late that night in the park near the cliffs." Jonquil winced.

"Gawd!" exploded Annie, stretching out the one syllable into four. "You must have been so scared!"

Jonquil nodded. "It was time to tell him the truth. That when the house in Seattle caught on fire, his dad died trying to save our dog. Billy's so like his dad, I was afraid to let him have one." Her face relaxed. "Claude was a big help that night."

Annie reached across the kitchen table and squeezed her hand. "Wish I'd been here for you." Then, lightening the mood as she

10

tended to do, Annie said, "So now, Billy has a dog. That son of yours, he's a living doll."

She stood up. "Gotta go. Alas, can you believe it's already 1998? My search for a date for the millennium continues tonight at a party in the hills. Tom Cruise may be there."

Jonquil giggled. "Methinks you have cruising on the brain."

They left the kitchen and paused by the shedding Christmas tree. "Thanks for listening, Annie. Thanks for everything." Jonquil remembered the gift on the coffee table and handed it to her.

Annie tore off the wrapping and held up the Dior black silk blouse to her chest. "I adore this. It will go great with the new leather skirt I bought in the ship's boutique." She twirled happily. "Thanks, my friend. I'll drop by the store soon. I'm so proud of you!"

She located her car keys and something else. "Oh, I almost forgot to give you these."

She handed Jonquil a package of nails and instructed her to prop the drawing in several places before deciding where to hang it. *Ah*, thought Jonquil, *the complete gift!* With a farewell hug, Annie departed and hurried down the stairs to her car.

Jonquil perched on the arm of the stuffed chair across from the sofa, where the drawing was propped. Her mind wandered again to John Bloom and her New Year's resolution to find either him or his grave. He'd disappeared on the night of her eighth birthday, and soon after that, her mother had died of a broken heart. She'd never lost hope that her father might still be alive but had let the search for him lapse. Yet, now at age thirty-four, she decided that finding him was no longer for just her sake but also for her son's.

The phone rang and she jumped up to answer it, her pensive thoughts instantly banished by the sound of Claude's captivating hello.

CHAPTER 3

Katie's Party

Jonquil and Billy lingered over dinner, tired from having taken down Christmas decorations. The second-floor garden apartment had been the only home Billy had ever known. The kitchen faced the courtyard and pool area below. Opposite it, a snug breakfast nook by a window overlooked the street. The dining room held a breakfront, a matching cabinet, and an oak table that comfortably sat six. Built-in bookcases separated the dining room from the main room. Large, curtain-less windows filled one wall and offered plenty of light. Her desk took up a corner, surrounded by piles of papers and journals. Kitty-corner stood their entertainment center. A rocking chair and other furnishings were arranged around a hardwood coffee table.

Jonquil had made the place cozy by having each room painted a different pastel color, adorned with framed prints, family photos, or Billy's art work. Billy's bedroom, however, featured zoo animal-themed wallpaper. A hallway directly right of the front door led to the two bedrooms and main bathroom.

The stark transition from holiday cheer to post holiday pallor always, in Jonquil's opinion, required a period of mood adjustment.

Not Billy. On those occasions, he enjoyed his role as man of the house, and climbed the stepladder to remove ornaments, or helped her haul out the tree to the curb. Besides, every task involved his puppy, who found the dismantling process a source of endless excitement. Blackie now reclined on the floor between them, snout between paws, too pooped even to beg for scraps, while Billy stared at his empty plate deep in thought.

His head bobbed up. "Mom, are you and Claude going to get married?"

The unexpected question made her pause. It was much too soon to think about marriage, she just wanted to enjoy Claude's attentions. But Billy had begun saying he missed having a father to come to his Little League games, so she chose her words carefully. "You really like him, don't you, sweetie?"

Billy grinned. "Yeah, he's all right, I guess. Can I be excused?"

"May I...."

"May I?"

"Yes, you may. Don't forget we're going to early Mass tomorrow."

She watched him take Blackie down the hall to his bedroom, then cleared the table. The babysitter could do the dishes. Claude would be there in an hour, and she wanted to primp. Tonight, they were going to his sister Katie's house in Santa Monica. She knew the Ryans were members of her parish but had never met them.

14

What pressures on our new relationship lurk there? she wondered.

Jonquil wore a long, red plaid skirt and beaded black top. A new conditioner that Rita, her colleague in the store had suggested, removed the frizzes, darkened her auburn hair, and sharpened the gleam in her green eyes. Nothing took away her freckles but Claude assured her he liked them. The way Claude looked at her upon his arrival let her know her efforts had succeeded. She felt giddy as he bent to kiss her. *There're no duds in his sweater collection,* she kidded herself. Tonight's choice was charcoal cashmere covering a magenta-colored shirt. Smashing.

Blackie leapt up on Claude's dark trousers, his knobby tail wagging joyously, and Claude leaned over to give him a friendly scratch. Billy, keyed up too, mimicked a Little League game home run while Jonquil gave the baby sitter instructions before they left.

They held hands in the Jeep all the way across town and she fought the temptation to openly stare at the thick, dark lashes that fringed his eyes. He described his sister and brother-in-law and added that friends of theirs would also be there. Knowing he'd been adopted as a toddler, Jonquil was eager to meet Katie.

Ed and Katie Ryan both greeted them at the front door of their two-story stucco home on Euclid Avenue. After introductions, Ed took their jackets while Katie led them to their living room, where an electric fire burned in a glass enclosed fireplace at the room's far end. A baby grand piano stood in the opposite corner adorned with untidy piles of sheet music. Sofas draped with Native American blankets and assorted furniture filled the rest of the room. Family photos and seascape watercolor paintings adorned the off-white walls while soft jazz played from hidden speakers. Altogether, it was a most welcoming atmosphere.

Overhead, bumps and squeals could be heard. Katie tilted her head upward before announcing that the children would be down later to say hello and good night.

Katie was shorter than her brother, rounder, and fair. She was younger than Claude's forty-three years by about ten. Her thin light brown hair hung loosely down to her shoulders. Her small, quick aqua blue eyes matched the color of the floor length caftan she wore. The warmth between Katie and her brother was obvious.

Ed entered the living room and took drink orders. He was not remarkable in the looks department—neither tall nor short, neither thin nor heavy, yet appealing. Jonquil decided to break the ice with him when he returned with her wine.

"Who plays piano?" she asked, taking the wine goblet from him.

"Oh, I do," he admitted sheepishly. "A little. All the kids too, except Michael. He's only three but he tries. Do you play?"

"I used to when I sang. School choirs, friends' weddings, that sort of thing." Jonquil's voice trailed off. Not in their home even five minutes and already the topic of weddings had been broached by of all people, her! *Thanks for planting the idea, Billy,* she thought.

16

But Ed neatly ended her discomfort with a nod and then asked Claude what he thought about the Lakers' chances that night against Miami.

The doorbell rang.

It rang two more times announcing the arrival of guests who turned out to be the Ryans' neighbors. Jonquil was relieved. The other couples would keep attention off her and Claude. After the requisite settling in period, the men eagerly escaped to the den to catch part of the game while the women spread out in the cozy living room.

They got acquainted while sampling chili and assorted toppings that Katie had arranged on the side board. Jonquil learned that one of the women had a child in Billy's school, that one of their husbands knew Claude, and that she was the only full time working mom there. This surprised her but as she smiled across the room at Tawana, a stunning black woman about seven months pregnant, she realized that these other women were mothers of one or more toddlers and well off enough to be stay-at-home moms. The variety of perfumes in the air ran the gamut from fruity to musky and reminded Jonquil of the scents department at Clyde's, the store where she worked.

Katie asked whether Jonquil wanted a wine refill.

Tawana broke off the conversation she was having with Lucy, the woman seated next to her.

"Jonquil? That your real name, baby?"

The others twittered at Tawana's directness. "What, y'all?" she grumbled. "That's a fair question. I swear I've never met

17

anyone called Jonquil before. And you know we black folk do like to be exotic."

The others waited for Jonquil's answer.

"It's my real name, all right," she replied, explaining that when she was born in Minnesota in wintertime, her father had surprised her mother in the hospital with a bouquet of fresh jonquils, her favorite flowers. Their last name happened to be Bloom, so, in a totally uncharacteristic fit of fancy, her mother named her for the romantic gift whose mysterious source her father never revealed.

"I'm so glad you're here," whispered Katie as she bent to replenish Jonquil's glass and squeeze her shoulder.

Lucy, the ash blonde, snapped her fingers, her excessive bangles jangling furiously. "Jonquil Bloom! Oh my God, you're *her*! The one who ran off TV! God, I thought I recognized you from somewhere."

All eyes swung back to Jonquil.

Lucy continued to supply details. "I told you, about it, Rosemary, remember? How people were calling in with last minute gift questions and then some kid called about wanting a dog and this crazy chick just up and ran off the—"

"Lucy!" exclaimed Tawana and Katie simultaneously.

Claude, where are you? Jonquil thought tensely.

Dr. Mazziotti's words from a recent lecture at UCLA came to her rescue.

"Remember, people, there's crazy with a small 'c' and then there's crazy with a capital C. Big

18

difference. We all get a little crazy now and then, hm?" he asked in his provocative tone. "Listen up. Big C, small c—big difference."

The vivid memory receded. Her whole body relaxed.

"I was a little crazy that day," Jonquil admitted and added, "because the kid who called the show happened to be my son." Her listeners exchanged bug eyed looks. She gave them a tightly edited account of the circumstances and swiftly moved on to how understanding Poppi Blair, the celebrity talk show host, had been. Jonquil was even invited back on the show at a later date.

The women lapsed into mollified silence.

"Why were you a guest on the show?" ventured the slender woman named Rosemary.

"She's a gift counselor," said Lucy. "She works at Clyde's. She—what exactly is it you do, Jonquil?"

"I help people work through their issues with gift giving. It's the topic for my doctorate in psychology. I'm ABD—all but dissertation." Their puzzled expressions made her add a clarification. "It's a new, free service at the store."

"Can you give us an example of how it works?" asked Tawana.

Jonquil nodded agreeably. "So, a woman married ten years stormed into my office on the day after Christmas. She'd had high hopes that her husband would give her a fur coat for Christmas. He'd had a prosperous year and she'd been dropping hints for months. When she saw her husband sneak a long, beautifully wrapped box under the Christmas tree, she became so excited that

19

she invited their families and friends to their home Christmas Eve for a gift exchange. She purposely waited to open his gift last. But when she finally tore off the paper and removed the lid, she discovered not a fur coat but a shotgun!"

On cue, all of her listeners gasped. Their initial shocked reactions—"You gotta be kidding!"; "No freakin' way!";"For *Christmas*?"; "In front of their friends?"—rose higher, then descended into raucous laughter.

"But why?" Katie stammered, tears rolling down her cheeks. "Whatever was the poor man thinking?"

"He had her safety in mind. Seems they live in a remote canyon off the beaten path and he travels a lot, so...."

"Was it loaded?" Tawana demanded which set off another round of giggles. Once they subsided, Rosemary asked Jonquil how she had handled the situation.

"Well, it sounds funny now but the poor woman was deeply hurt. Turns out it wasn't the first time he had so completely miscalculated with a gift. With that information, we focused on her setting herself up for major disappointment by making assumptions and inviting guests over. We talked about the importance of direct communication versus hints. Men aren't mind readers. And then we talked about forgiveness."

At that point, the men rejoined them. Claude came over, took her hand and kissed it. She felt a thrill pass between them.

"Are you having a good time?"

"You bet," she said almost like a sigh.

Just then, the party was invaded by the younger Ryans. Little Michael already in pajamas bounded in ahead of his siblings to kiss his parents good night. The children stayed long enough to be introduced and then disappeared as quickly as they'd come. Katie then served up a savory late night supper of baked ham and scalloped potatoes, green beans, miniature rye bread, and fresh cut fruit, followed by tiramisu. Afterward, Ed got them singing around the piano until one o'clock. Jonquil felt happy during the singing especially when Claude put his arm around her or stroked her back. The desire to kiss him grew intense.

Toward the evening's end, Jonquil was leaving the bathroom when she bumped into Rosemary, who tapped her arm. In a low voice, she said, "Jonquil, would it be possible for my mother to come see you?"

"Certainly. I don't have any cards with me, but just have her call the store and make an appointment."

"Thanks!" She smiled with unmistakable relief, and then Jonquil went looking for Claude.

CHAPTER 4

Just One Kiss

On the drive home, Claude leaned over and said, "Fun, wasn't it?"

The wine, food, and singing, plus the Jeep's heater, made her drowsy. "Um hmm," she mumbled. "I like your sister. She's real sweet. Who does she favor more, your mom or your dad?"

"She's a dead ringer for our mother. They often get mistaken for sisters."

"That's cool. Have you ever searched for your birth parents?"

"Yeah, once. I soon gave up. I figured God gave me a loving family, so why tempt fate?" He glanced in the rearview mirror. "Have you started looking for your dad again?"

"Not yet." Jonquil yawned loudly. "Oh, pardon me, I'm a little sleepy tonight."

He removed his right hand from the steering wheel and squeezed her left knee, which instantly sent restorative shivers all over her body. "Katie likes you, too. She told me in the kitchen after dinner. And Ed thinks you have a nice voice."

"Huh, I did once when I really worked at it," she demurred, "but tonight I was all wind and croaks. Still, it felt good. You carry a tune pretty well yourself, Mr. Chappel." She nudged him playfully.

He grunted. His hand returned to the steering wheel to complete a turn, and they continued down a block in companionable silence. "So, what's on deck for the rest of your weekend?" he asked, peering again at the rearview mirror.

"I have to work tomorrow. I get Mondays off now."

"And tomorrow night?"

They came to a stop light, and she glanced over at him. "Billy and I are going to a movie. With my new schedule, now we have to make plans to spend time together."

He turned onto her block. "Maybe Billy might like to have me tag along," he said, pulling over to the curb and cutting the engine.

She nodded. Billy would, no doubt about it. But she wouldn't. Claude was too new in her life, too close, working on the construction site all week across from her apartment. She liked the dress up part of dating and she liked the dress down time away from work when she didn't have to look her best. Besides, she'd already reserved the time with her son, a time when he could count on being the center of her attention.

Or was it that she wasn't ready yet to share Billy's attention with Claude?

Claude wanted to steer their relationship into the fast lane, destination: commitment. It had been many years since she had dated and she wasn't about to be pressured into any complicating life changes. She kept her voice light. "Not this weekend, Claude."

Just as lightly, he kissed her. "Better get you inside."

That was quick, she thought.

They exited the Jeep and strolled toward her apartment door. A breeze lifted the palm branches overhead. The lily-like fragrance of night blooming jasmine filled the air. They leaned into each other as they walked. Reaching the front door, she opened her purse for her key. Then she looked up at him. "Good night, Claude, and thank you for a lovely evening. Why don't you come over for dinner some night after work?"

"I'd like that. Meantime, I'll amuse my old bachelor self as best I can. Maybe have a solitaire marathon or sort my sock drawer." He leaned down and swiftly kissed the tip of her nose. "Or roll pennies," he added, stepping away, a smile once more in his voice. "Or back up my computer files. Or maybe I'll spend the time counting the seconds till I see you again."

"Flatterer," she laughingly called out to him as he sauntered down the walk.

He called back, "One-one second, two-one second, three-one second...."

Jonquil unlocked the door and stepped inside thinking just *one* kiss? She shut the door and frowned. Why hadn't Claude been as amorous as last time?

CHAPTER 5

Clyde's

A week later, Jonquil arrived at Clyde's late. Rita Oglesby, her fiftyish red-haired assistant, was waiting for her, wringing her hands. Rita, in her Southern drawl, told Jonquil she'd been invited to the weekly executive committee meeting and to hightail it on up to the fifth floor.

Jonquil took the express elevator. Reaching her destination, she pulled open the frosted glass door to the conference room and scanned the faces already there.

Sy Saginaw, the store's beefy attorney, sported a darker tan, no doubt acquired over the weekend on the links of a Catalina golf course. The Burney brothers, Clyde's fifty-year-old twin accountants known as BB1 and BB2, looked red-faced as though they had been in the sun, too. Maybe they'd spent the weekend playing chess on the boardwalk. Iris Escanaba, the PR director and mother of four young boys, yawned unabashedly but managed a friendly wave. Cornell "Corny" Bramson, personnel director, and Big Al Yates, store manager, were huddled together

trading laughs in one corner. Rich Ridgeland, the newest member
of the team and director of advertising, hunched over his notes.

Leigh Usher's chair sat empty.

Jonquil served herself a cup of Clyde's roasted coffee at the
sideboard. She slid into a chair just before Mr. Merrill, the store's
president, entered from an inconspicuous side door. He bestowed
a curt nod on the assemblage and took his customary seat at the
head of the polished, oval-shaped wood table.

"I have some announcements," he said without preamble. The
small talk ended.

"Ms. Bloom has consented to be our in-house gift counselor,
hence her presence here this morning. We're still working out her
schedule." Hearty congratulations were directed her way. She
accepted them graciously.

Rich finally looked up, became aware of the empty chair next
to him, and asked, "Still seems weird. About Leigh resigning. So
sudden-like."

Rich's comment elicited a shrug here and there. Most around
the table appeared relieved with the head buyer's decision to
vacate her job.

"I'll be flying to Paris tonight with Emily," Mr. Merrill
continued smoothly. "Some of you may recall that my wife was
head buyer back when her father ran the store. We'll fill in
temporarily until a new head buyer is hired. I've appointed Al
Yates acting vice-president during my absence." Big Al beamed.
"Al will also continue as store manager for the time being, and
I'll stay in close touch with him. I know we can count on your
support during this transition.

26

"There's just one fly in the ointment, folks, and it concerns Leigh." He glanced around the table to confirm he had everyone's attention. "She wants to rescind her resignation."

Stunned silence was followed by a burst of angry reactions. Only the Burney brothers seemed above or not in tune with the fray.

"She can't come back," stated Al flatly.

"So that's why you're still holding onto her final paperwork," surmised Corny with dismay.

Mr. Merrill raised his hands to halt the reactions. "It turns out that the contract Leigh signed four years ago gives her exclusive control over several brand agreements she negotiated which aren't up until next December."

"She has to stay? Don't forget she wants your job!" exploded Al. "What makes you think she won't continue to undermine you or any of us to ...," he nodded in Jonquil's direction, "to get it?"

BB1 cleared his throat.

"Yes, Barney? Do you have anything to add?" Mr. Merrill was the only person who was allowed to call the twin accountants by their first names.

"Better the enemy you know—"

"—than the one you don't," finished BB2 without missing a beat.

Jonquil grew more uncomfortable by the minute. "Why does she want to come back here?"

Mr. Merrill threw his hands in the air. "In her words, 'This is home.'"

"Oh, for Pete's sake," grumped Al.

"Contracts can be broken. That's why we pay Sy here a fancy retainer. Clyde's is not that desperate!" Corny said defiantly. "We can promote her assistant or else hire a new one." The others were so busy expressing their vehement solidarity on this point, they didn't hear the door to the conference room behind them open.

"I'm surprised she'd want to show her face around here," Corny added with a snicker and then blinked when he discovered who'd entered the room.

"Aw, but it's such a pretty face, don't you agree?"

At the sound of the familiar purr, the others' heads jerked in the direction of its source.

There stood Leigh, minus her usual high fashion attire, yet still alluring in a fitted cherry red leather jacket, tight jeans, and shiny black over-the-knee boots, looking coquettishly woebegone.

Chapter 6

Conference Room Surprise

L eigh, this is highly improper," said Mr. Merrill.

The palms of Jonquil's hands moistened at the mere sight of her nemesis while her breath caught in her throat. No one knew that Leigh and Jonquil had had a nasty confrontation on a store elevator before Christmas where Leigh had threatened to sabotage the talk show the next day by publicly embarrassing her.

Leigh's flagrant ambition struck the gift counselor as bordering on pathologic. Jonquil also knew that her chosen field of psychology was an unwelcome reminder to the head buyer of a serious drug problem within her own family.

Leigh, with her blond precision cut, crystal blue eyes, and tall, winsome physique, claimed the room's full attention, but her eyes stayed glued to the president. "I just came by to see if you'd made a decision."

Fat chance, thought Jonquil. The manipulative blonde who knew the store's routine better than anyone had chosen her moment well. Would the prodigal daughter be allowed back home? Would the man so determined moments ago to make big changes now buckle under? Jonquil sipped cold coffee in an effort to show indifference.

Leigh spied the gesture out of the corner of her eye and whipped around to face Jonquil.

"Am I boring you, Ms. Bloom?"

Before Jonquil could respond, Mr. Merrill intervened. "The meeting is adjourned. Leigh, Sy, my office. Now."

"What happened?" asked Rita Oglesby as soon as her boss re-entered the gift counseling suite. Jonquil was indeed glad that morning that the suite was cut off from the rest of the first floor by a short hallway. She plopped into the chair opposite Rita's spotless reception area desk and stretched her legs.

"Leigh Usher showed up. She wants her job back."

"No way," cried Rita.

"Mr. M is meeting with her and Sy right now. Any calls?" Jonquil's tone indicated to Rita that what she really meant was whether Claude had called.

"No."

"Rita, can I ask you a non-work-related question?"

"Ooo—is this about you-know-who?"

"Uh-huh. We went to a party at his sister's house this weekend."

"Ain't he the fast mover! Was she as nice as he is?"

"Yes. But afterward he only kissed me once."

"Hmm. What kind of a kiss?"

30

"Not a lingering one, that's for sure. I may have dampened his ardor when I turned down his offer to spend the rest of the weekend together. I told him Billy and I had plans."

Rita rolled her eyes. "Sugar, you two need a road map."

Jonquil huffed. "Fine. I'm leaving early today. I have a meeting at UCLA with my faculty advisor."

"And I'll get the lowdown on what's up with Leigh," vowed Rita.

CHAPTER 7

The Mazz

The deal struck between UCLA and Clyde's of Santa Monica permitted Jonquil's gift counseling sessions at the store to count toward her degree at the medical school. However, since she was no longer working exclusively with children, her revised dissertation tutorial required a change of advisors.

It so happened that Joe Mazziotti had returned from a six-month teaching sabbatical at Jefferson Medical School in Philadelphia. His dance card needed filling up.

"The Mazz," as the students called him, was among the graduate school's most intense, literate, and attractive psychiatrists on staff. In his early fifties, he was a trim, dapper dresser of average height. He wore his slow-graying hair close to his scalp. His skin was the color of olive oil, yet there was about him an air of dry self-discipline. Under expressive brows, his dark eyes glittered with intelligence. His nostrils had a tendency to flare when he became vehement. A discreet mustache added to his allure, and his mouth was smile ready at the first hint of humor. He was as smooth as a nightclub entertainer. Had he been a force for evil, his cultured voice alone could have mesmerized the angels. Fortunately, Dr. Mazziotti was one of the good guys albeit, in Jonquil's opinion, distressingly sexy.

They spent the first few minutes getting reacquainted. He remembered she had a son and asked after him. She was fast succumbing to his charm, a strategic mistake.

She then launched into a summary of her project—the psychodynamics of gift giving—while he sank lower into his chair, ever smiling, ever Dr. Suave. She explained how initially, while gathering data in her previous job at Children's Home, she believed that all gifts came with strings attached. This theory, she now admitted, was based in part on a survey of the scant literature, personal experience, and intuition. But over Christmas, she'd seen the light.

"In conclusion, Dr. Mazziotti, my initial theory was unsupportable."

"Oh?" he asked, perking up slightly.

"Yes, and here Corinthians II helped me." She happened to know they were both Catholics, surely, though her loose reference to Saint Paul was unscientific, he'd know what she was getting at. *All's fair*, she thought. "There are many gifts, but true gifts are free!" Her voice rose to a crescendo of affirmation. Excellent! She'd said what she'd come to say and had incidentally proved that she was on solid ground spiritually if not yet academically.

"Come again?" he asked quietly.

It was not the reaction she'd anticipated. He lowered his chin, steepled his fingers, aimed his gun-barrel-like eyes at hers and waited. Oh, how she hated that confused look. When a student got that particular look from a professor, she may as well drop out of the program. Better yet, off the earth.

"Free—as in no strings attached. From the heart … uh, sincere, generous—um, no hidden agenda. Uh, with no expectation of a return gift. You know, like—like the Aztecs, the Japanese, the Aborigines? They had elaborate, reciprocal rituals. True gifts are free!"

Miserably she realized she'd broken every rule ever catalogued by his many students. 1) she'd resorted to sentimentality—from the heart—yuk; 2) she'd "ummed" him; 3) she'd invoked the pathetic "you know"; 4) she omitted any psychological terms; and 5) she'd failed to convince him, much less herself, that she knew what she was talking about.

She sounded about as desperate as a game show contestant.

"There's no such thing," he snapped. He leaned backward in his swivel chair after grabbing a number two pencil, his form of sublimation for a three-pack-a-day cigarette habit, and tapped it rat-a-tat-tat on the edge of his desk. "Every conscious action undertaken by creatures—be it human, animal or vegetable, if you will—has demonstrable self-interest at its core."

Mutely, she scoffed.

"If I exaggerate, it's for your own good. But I do so because I want you to succeed because as your advisor, *I* will benefit. I expect you to make me look good. *Capisce?*"

She nodded and then he said, "You have a son." The abrupt change of tone and topic were among his classic ploys. Warily, she nodded. She thought they had already covered that subject. Then he tossed aside the pencil.

"I have four children." The rapid eye blinking had begun. "And as a parent, I must give them more than they can possibly give me. What's my motivation? Simple. Cut through the hokum, the law, the church, the dictates of nature and society, oh, and let's not forget the mooo-vies, and you will discover that my reasons for being good to my children are basically selfish. Just. Like. Yours."

She stifled a protest.

He sat forward, the chair squeaking in protest. "We don't want to end up at a police station one night, do we? Or on the front page of the newspaper because your kid or mine screwed up? But let's put that nightmare aside. That's the extreme." He paused to stroke his mustache, a gesture she guessed was calculated to let her catch her breath before the kill.

"You obviously know your Bible, Ms. Bloom. May I suggest an earlier passage? I refer to the story of Cain and Abel. Both made gift-offerings. Abel offered the best of what he had and his gift was found acceptable. On the other hand, Cain tried to pawn God off with a lesser choice, and God saw right through him. But perhaps Man was so new to *making sacrifices*—hm?—God let Cain off with a warning. What did Cain do? Did he work harder? Learn from his mistake? Change his ways? He did not! Instead, he grew jealous and slew his brother. And that, my dear Ms.

35

Bloom, was the end of the free gift theory you're so eager to postulate.

"Abel was the true altruist—he alone met your criteria—but it was Cain who survived the first gift giving contest. Cain, the narcissist. And there's a trace of him in all our acts of generosity. Cain, Ms. Bloom, not Abel."

He swiveled in his chair and appeared to be deep in thought.

"It's the roots of his narcissistic character disorder that you must delineate, no? The origins of sibling rivalry. You can cite the Greeks, the Romans, the Egyptians, the East Indians, the nation of Islam, the countries of Africa, the tribes of the New World for all I care, or the hucksters on Madison Avenue who invented that slickest of slogans, 'free gift with every purchase.' A crock! *They* know the score. Even charitable donations are not immune—ever hear of tax deductions? It always comes down to this: What's in it for little ol' me? That, Ms. Bloom, is the true *quid pro quo* dynamics of gift giving.

"Oh, you can cry altruism till the cows come home. Getting the cows home or the town rebuilt after a flood, better yet, getting a life resuscitated via a heart transplant nets one *Time* magazine cover for the surgical team and one *People* magazine cover for the donor family. And you say free?" She blinked. "Wrong. There isn't a gift you can hypothesize that doesn't have its source deeply imbedded in the query—forgive the crudity—was it good for you, too?" Now his face relaxed with a triumphant smile.

Heat rose steadily up her neck and spread like red dye across her face. He was so Italian—opera and earthiness all mixed up together. And righteous—preaching to her his damned sermon.

36

How dare he be so sexy!

"I see I've shocked you. Forgive me. Now, prove me wrong for all the right reasons. Knowing how much you psychologists like to gather data, where're your metrics?"

She could barely find her voice. "I'm using a gift inventory I designed myself. It covers gifts given as well as gifts received."

"Fine. Let's review it next time. Now, scoot. I have at least six other wayward students to point toward reality before the rush hour. Oh, and Ms. Bloom, when we meet again, I want to hear from Freud et al. I'll even tolerate Rank, Maslov et al. But not Saint Paul, whom I may add, never once mentioned the word 'free' in the text you cited but did develop the concept of love, a curious omission on your part."

Stomping back to the parking garage, she seethed. He'd thoroughly trashed her presentation. He'd easily seen through her weak spiritual innuendo, then clobbered her with the Old Testament. He maintained that giving was inherently self-centered, a position she didn't consider worth pursuing.

Yet, at the end, he'd left the door open just a crack. Intentionally? Pausing to find her keys, it hit her:

He hadn't goaded her out of malice. Just the opposite. He'd raised the stakes and transformed her ordinary project into a full-blown mission. The anger faded. She felt aglow with fierce purpose. Finishing her dissertation was no longer just a career milestone, it was absolutely vital! Though not nearly as vital as proving the Mazz wrong.

Crafty buzzard.

Chapter 8

Teeth Rinsed, Not Brushed

They worked out a schedule. Jonquil, by habit an early riser, walked Blackie each morning. He'd become her new alarm clock, padding into her bedroom before dawn to lick her face or hand until she threw off her covers. Billy walked him after school.

First, she'd alert Billy when she was leaving. He'd get up to finish homework or more likely fall back to sleep until she got home.

Meanwhile, she'd trot over to the park. Blackie did his business, barked at the squirrels, sniffed out his territory for intruders and left his calling card. It took approximately twenty-five minutes, unless a confrontation with other dogs slowed them down.

She enjoyed this new morning ritual. She inhaled the tangy sea air that made living near the beach so desirable. From the south, small commuter planes flew over from Catalina Island, while to the east, the rising sun gradually burned through the fog, exposing the mountain peaks above Malibu like a protracted movie opening. Other people were stirring. The paperboy on his bike. Joggers. Roller skaters. Neighbors out with their dogs. Early sun worshippers. Claude's men on the construction site. Often his foreman, Fred, waved to her.

Some parts of Venice were rough and tumble, hangouts for dopers, dropouts, and chronic runaways—those she avoided. Others areas were kinder on the eyes, such as the canals that gave the city its name and the oceanfront. Jonquil kept on the move, relishing the time to herself, knowing the minute she reached home, her real day would begin.

That morning when she and Blackie ducked inside, Billy stood in his underwear, impatiently waiting for her. "Mrs. Phillips called. She can't carpool today. Mrs. Monaghan's doing it." He knelt and removed Blackie's leash.

"Okay," she said and went into the kitchen, Billy trailing her.

"Mrs. Monaghan will be here fifteen minutes early."

"O-kay," she said, this time drawing out each syllable.

She consulted the clock on the microwave oven. "I'll feed the dog and get breakfast started. What else?"

"I can't find a clean uniform shirt."

"Billy, no. Not again."

He shrugged off her irritation, keeping his focus on the time.

"You didn't lay out your clothes last night, did you?"

He shrugged again. "I forgot." His wily smile made his eyes twinkle in a way that totally disarmed her.

"Okay. Pull one out of the hamper and I'll plug in the iron."

Jonquil hated losing her temper with him. For one thing, he seldom gave her cause, his occasional bouts of stubbornness notwithstanding. For another, she happened to agree with Mary Poppins that the Golden Rule applied to children as well as to adults.

Swinging open the pantry door to fetch the iron, her mother came to mind. Pauline Ditmar Bloom had married years after her two younger, prettier sisters. A stern woman, she was fanatical about social conventions. *God knew what He was about sending a daughter to Pauline and not a son*, Jonquil mused. It took an appreciation of the ridiculous to successfully nurture a boy. Plus, stamina.

"Found one!" called Billy from down the hall.

Blackie was yelping at her heels, his tail twitching frantically.

"Right, Blackie. I hear you, boy."

She finished scooping out his dog food just as Billy appeared with a wrinkled shirt. Holding it up by the shoulders, then rotating it, she noted dark smudges in all the usual places. "Wear your sweater today, buddy."

She swiftly pressed the collar while humming to herself. She noticed she was humming everywhere now. Humming in the car, humming on Clyde's elevators, humming at UCLA, humming in the shower. Humming like she used to and she knew why.

True, singing at the Ryans' party had aired her vocal chords. That Ed Ryan sure knew his way around a piano.

"I play a little," he'd told her. Ha!

The real reason was Claude. Claude Chappel. *Sha-pell.* She loved the sound of his name. Her thoughts and emotions fused

40

into a vivid fantasy as she shoved the iron to and fro in order that Billy's hamper-freed shirt would meet school handbook compliancy.

"It's done, Mom. Mom! It's done!" To get her attention, he had to pull the plug.

An hour later, Jonquil folded herself into her VW Beetle, whose ruby red color hid rust well, still marveling that Billy had joined his carpool on time. Teeth rinsed, not brushed.

Her car was parked on the street because the garage keypad wasn't working. Triumphantly, she now turned the key in the ignition. Nothing. Again. Nothing. Again. Nothing. Again, again, again. Perversely, Jonquil tried again. The only audible sounds came from the job site across the street.

She pounded the steering wheel with the palms of both hands in vexation. She tried once again, garnering the same result.

She exited the car and gave the front left tire a swift kick. Behind the hood, she glared down at the motor, so she didn't see the man approach. He'd jogged across the street from the job site. Fred, the construction foreman. Up close, she observed how very tall and stocky he was, rather oafish in appearance but calm and genial. "Need a jump? Claude sent me over. I got cables in my rig. Back in a jiff."

So, she leaned against her worn out car, pulled out her new mobile phone to call work, and despite the delay, started humming again.

CHAPTER 9

Tryouts

L ittle League tryouts came up fast in late January. It so happened that Claude had been the utility player on teams all through school. He seized the chance to get Billy in shape, thereby securing himself a spot in the Bloom agenda on consecutive weekends. Jonquil gratefully accepted. She was proud of her son's courage and determination to play despite having fractured his arm the previous season.

Billy welcomed the help, too. His right arm tired easily; he needed to build up its strength. Claude took him out to the alley behind the Blooms' apartment building and tossed balls for him to hit, catch, and field.

Jonquil interrupted her studies to bring them Gatorade and apples. She stood on the perimeter watching them, observing Claude's patient interaction with the boy, in tandem with Billy's near adoration of the man. The ideal family scenario.

Romance wasn't all she wanted from Claude. She wanted more days like this one, easy breezy, getting-to-know one another time that might smoothly knit a new family together. The common experience the three of them shared, of missing one or both parents in childhood, brought with it the need to go slowly.

Typical of Memorial Park, on the day of tryouts the area was about ten degrees cooler than the rest of Santa Monica, though no one knew why. Jonquil made sure Billy wore his jacket. She checked in at the registration table, handed over a copy of the waiver he needed to play in Santa Monica, filled out required forms, and paid the fee. Billy was given a bib for the AAA division which she helped pin on his chest. He was then assigned to a group of about nine other boys, former teammates among them, as well as newcomers. Though the sky was cloudy, the air crackled with dueling expressions of excitement and jitters.

Billy's best friend, Ramon, cagily watched from the sidelines with Jonquil and Claude who'd arrived just in time. Ramon thought baseball was about as thrilling as hiking. He preferred racing on his bike and skate-boarding. Besides, many of the kids on Billy's team were also in his class. They were Billy's other friends. Ramon could claim one advantage over them—proximity. Both he and Billy lived in Venice.

Tryouts were held on one of the softball fields that formed part of the huge main field. Claude spotted the coaches and managers with their clip-boards sitting in a line of beach chairs behind the third base line and figured they were much like his former coaches, sizing up each player as well as their parents.

By the end of the day, many coaches had spent time consoling kids who'd swung and missed all five balls, or dropped the balls they hadn't properly fielded. Tears were shed and hugs were doled out. Billy, with Claude's help, had had a fair day. He hit four balls and caught all five. Only his pitching showed weakness.

He felt disappointed with himself until he was assigned to his new team. Coach Hillman welcomed him back to the game and promised a winning year ahead.

Bobby Hillman was divorced, his wife having left him two years ago for another woman. A man in his church had suggested he check out Santa Monica Little League—they were always looking for volunteers. He and his ex-wife had been childless. He gave his full support to the kids on his team and the league as a whole. Consequently, Mr. Hillman became a popular, intense coach.

Jonquil introduced the two men and mentioned to the coach how Claude had prepared Billy for tryouts. The men shook hands. Billy ran off to join Ramon.

"Jonquil," said Coach Hillman, in a Western twang, "your son's grown at least three inches since last year. You ready for another season?"

"You bet." Like most women, she found herself smiling back easily at the man.

"Wish more mothers were like you. We make every effort to avoid injuries, but we can't eliminate them completely. Glad you get that."

"It's Billy's passion," she replied simply. "I could try to stop him, but he'd find a way. He can be very resourceful. This way, he gets supervision."

Turning to her companion, the coach asked, "And you, sir? Would you have any spare time to help out here?"

"Let me think about it," said Claude a little too quickly. Other parents were waiting in line to speak to the coach. Claude steered Jonquil over to the hospitality table.

"Sorry, Jonny, coaching other kids is not my thing. Coaching my own kids, well …"

His eyes flashed with suggestion. When she gave him a puzzled look, he reached for her hand and squeezed it.

"Just a thought," he said, lifting an eyebrow.

CHAPTER 10

Mrs. K

One day early in February, Jonquil's afternoon began with a challenging new client. Seated across from her was a woman who looked to be about sixty years old. She had trouble maintaining eye contact. Her hands fiddled with her eye glasses, coat buttons, and the strap on the square vinyl purse in her lap. Her appearance and simple attire gave no hint as to her ethnic or socio-economic status. WASP? Domestic? However, there was no mistaking her frame of mind. Anger, fueled by resentment or possibly guilt, grated her speech.

"My daughter's life was too short. She died in a car accident a year ago. She was only forty-one and kind to a fault. I think her generous nature's what got her killed."

"Why is that, Mrs. Kingston?"

"She couldn't say no to anyone!" was the client's indignant retort. "Never stood up for herself, never complained. Always with Carol, it was 'Yes, I can stay on for another shift'—she was a nurse—or 'Sure, I'll bake ten dozen cookies' the night before

46

the school fundraiser. Not even my son-in-law could keep Carol from driving their elderly neighbors places at all hours of the day and night."

As much as this woman needed to vent, Jonquil felt obligated to either direct her back to the reason for her visit or recommend a psychotherapist to deal with her loss. "What brought you here today?"

"Oh, it's because...." The woman paused while her wandering hands finally latched onto her purse in a fierce grip. After noting her body language Jonquil kept her eyes peeled on the client until she met her gaze. "I want to do something for people to remember her by. Carol shouldn't be forgotten. But each time I go to do it, I'm so bothered by the way she died, falling asleep at the wheel after staying up all night with a sick patient—she wasn't the only nurse at that hospital—someone *else* could have held that hand that night! Such a *waste!*" Her shrill harangue broke off into bitter tears. "I miss her terribly."

Jonquil offered tissues and mentally stepped back to consider alternatives.

Here was a classic dilemma, a generous impulse checked by unresolved anger. She was becoming familiar with these darker aspects of gift giving. New research confirmed a negative component to many gift exchanges.

Mrs. Kingston, she imagined herself saying, *let's puzzle out the meaning of that last phrase you used. "Miss her terribly." Do you see how well you put it? Your anger is ruining your grieving. I speak from experience. My husband, Gerry, died trying to rescue our dog. I didn't do a good job of missing him—no, I missed him terribly! I blamed him and his love of animals for leaving me so suddenly. It stunted my love life and created a barrier with my son. That was the waste, Mrs. Kingston. Because Gerry's love of nature was the very thing that attracted me to him in the first place.*

Her associations seemed so transparent, she felt she'd almost uttered them aloud. But no, the client sat placidly gazing back at her, tears drying, waiting for her to speak.

Professional responsibility overcame her powerful urge to focus on the client's gift problem. *First things first,* the counselor side of her reminded the researcher.

"Perhaps you need to talk out your feelings about your loss with a therapist."

"Oh, I'm already in a grief support group, if that's what you mean," the woman volunteered. "I joined it before the holidays. My other daughter, Rosemary, met you at her friend Katie's party and urged me to come talk to you. When I called here, the woman on the phone said you could help me. Can you help me?"

So. Not only was it now permissible for her to explore this gift problem in depth, but Rita had sensitively handled Mrs. Kingston's telephone inquiry.

Feeling more confident, Jonquil asked, "How did you want to honor your daughter's memory?"

"I can't decide." Her hands still gripped her purse, an indication to Jonquil that Mrs. Kingston might not be ready to give.

"What do you want your gift to say or do?"

BEST OF ALL GIFTS

She frowned. "That's a funny question. What do I want it to say … or do? Um, I've never thought about gifts that way. You mean like … a message?"

"It's possible."

She thought the client might balk. Maybe gift counseling was coming across as too cerebral. But the woman remained as motionless as a statue. Jonquil reached over for a pre-stuffed manila envelope on the corner of her desk.

"Mrs. Kingston, I'd like you to take this form home with you and fill it out, if it wouldn't be too much trouble. It's called a gift inventory. I designed it to help me counsel gift givers and serve as my research instrument. After you complete it, could we meet again?"

Mrs. Kingston accepted both the envelope and a follow-up appointment, with long-suffering shakes of her head, each shake miming work, work, work.

CHAPTER 11

Valentine's Day

A stream of walk-ins, mostly women, as well as giggling teenage girls showing off their conspicuous makeup, stopped by the gift counseling suite in the days leading up to Saturday, February 14th. However, on the auspicious day itself, the walk-ins were chiefly men.

One of whom set Jonquil's teeth on edge.

"Doll, I need gifts for two very different valentines," Mr. Dimitri stated glibly. He appeared to be in his fifties, portly, with a bad comb-over, but the cut of his sports jacket gave the impression of someone younger. On purpose, no doubt.

"One's for my wife of twenty years, the other's for my girlfriend, who's about twenty years … old. Badda-bing, badda-boom, psssh!" He jabbed the air as if to strike an imaginary cymbal. Jonquil let him motor mouth about the women in his life until he eventually ran out of gas and chugged to a stop.

"Any ideas, ma'am?"

BEST OF ALL GIFTS

Her mind flipped to Billy coming home from school Friday with a stack of frilly-edged valentine cards. After letting her admire each one, he'd stuffed them into the waste basket.

"Why'd you do that, sweetie?"

"They're all from girls," he'd replied with disgust.

Now it was she who was feeling disgust with the new client's cynical attitude toward his surfeit of valentines. She dodged the issue by asking for more information.

"Please call me Jonquil. First things first. What's your total budget, Mr. Dimitri?"

He had a ready answer. "I usually drop a couple thou on the wife and about half that on the girl. That way the wife don't get suspicious and the girl don't get ambitious—*if* you know what I mean."

Was everything a joke to this guy? "The" wife, "the" girl, so detached. She considered one or two options, then opted to improvise. "Tell me first. What was the best Valentine's Day gift you ever received?"

"Me? Well now, that's tough to say. I've had my share, don't cha know." He continued in this vein a few more moments, then slumped back in his chair. His hands dropped to his sides, his chin sank to his chest. Time passed. Then, he sat up again, fingers snapping.

"Sally-Jo! I haven't thought of her in years. We were in 4-H club together. She once knitted me a long scarf using our high school colors, red and gray. It got damn cold in February back there in Boise." He nodded his head. "Sweet little Sally-Jo.

Wonder where she is now." He stood up resolutely. "I should give her a call. Just to, you know, say hi, catch up."

"But we haven't discussed your gifts yet."

"Some other time, lady. Thanks, thanks a lot."

He hastened out of the suite, leaving her to ponder the power of a gift from long ago. What had she done? The image of Pandora's box creaking open flashed in her mind. Was some poor woman in Idaho going to receive an ill-timed telephone call today on her account?

She dropped her forehead onto her balled fists and groaned.

Before lunchtime, a huge bouquet of red roses in a glass vase was delivered to the suite for Rita, who reacted with coy embarrassment.

"Sugar, it's not like Al's got gobs of money to fritter away on me," she chirped with obvious pleasure as she sniffed the fragrant blooms.

"So? Enjoy them, Rita. Isn't that what you'd tell me to do?" Yet, Jonquil returned to her desk wondering where her flowers from Claude might be.

Later, a note on her calendar reminded her to call Father Tim Moran. They'd met the night of Billy's birth. Father Tim, a hospital chaplain back then, had baptized her son. From that time forward, he'd kept close to them, watched Billy grow up, all the while keeping an eye out for marriageable prospects for her. It was the Blooms' habit to invite the retired priest, now in his seventies, to breakfast a couple of times a month after Sunday Mass. Jonquil telephoned Saint Monica's rectory and left a message for him.

Feeling out of sorts, she tried to anticipate the evening Claude had planned: dinner at an intimate French restaurant and dancing. She loved to dance, though she was not a fanatic like either Rita or her honey, Al Yates. But it had been quite a while since she'd kicked up her heels. Not comfortable with the prospect, she begged Rita to update her on the latest dance steps. Rita instantly paged Al, and before Jonquil knew what was happening, she was gliding around her office in the arms of the store's acting vice president.

Jonquil, in a sleeveless sheath, was glowing with excitement by the time Claude arrived that night. The missing roses were forgotten when he presented her with a jewelry box that contained a silver keepsake bracelet of colorful beads and dangling, heart shaped charms. Her delight with Claude's romantic surprise became a shower of kisses despite Billy's gagging noises in the background. She slipped the dainty valentine gift onto her wrist while Claude petted the dog, then collected her shawl and purse and they left.

Instead of his Jeep, he led her to a gleaming, black Lincoln Town Car and opened the side door. "What's this?" she asked, surprised.

"A rental, if you must know. More romantic, isn't it?"

"It's lovely. But I do like your Jeep," she demurred, folding herself into the spacious front seat.

He walked around the rear, opened the driver's door and slid in beside her.

"And I like you," he said, his black eyes glittering in the dark like two gemstones. He leaned in and kissed her.

"You smell *delicieuse!*" he exclaimed.

Her cheeks warmed with pleasure. "Thank you, kind sir. I've been experimenting with perfumes."

"I vote for this one. What's it called?" he asked, turning the key in the ignition.

"Gamine—like Audrey Hepburn for whom it was named."

"Gamine. I'll remember that."

She inhaled theatrically and smiled as a scent reminiscent of Christmas potpourri filled her nostrils. "Do I detect a trace of spice in the air tonight? Yum."

"Special occasion, *ma chérie, mais très discret.* My dad has a word for after shave lotion. Politely translated, it's 'smell'ums.'"

She giggled and said, "Mm, me like your smell'ums."

During dinner on the patio of an intimate Beverly Hills bistro, she said, "Oh, my gosh, I never thanked you for sending over Fred and his cables the day my car wouldn't start."

"Well, Fred's the one who saw you were having trouble. He's good like that—mindful of what's going on around him. To tell the truth, I'm lucky to have him on my payroll."

"He's very tall."

"Yeah, poor guy claims that's why he can't find anyone to date." He took her hand and kissed it. "Shall we go?"

When they'd made their plans, he had chosen the place to eat. Now, she got to choose the venue for entertainment. "I know a great spot in Santa Monica called The Beach House. We can salsa or play ping-pong or listen to live music in the bar."

"Salsa? I don't get out much. You'll have to teach me."

"You're on!"

Her refresher course that afternoon paid off. Claude was a quick study and gave himself over to the hot, flirty dances. She suspected he'd been holding back when he claimed not to know the steps. *He's probably dated his share of women*, she thought pensively, then grinned. *But I got 'im now.*

"Have I ever told you who you remind me of?" she whispered as he took her in his arms for a slow dance.

He kissed her shoulder and she missed a step. "No. Who?"

"The actor Hal Linden. You might know him by the character he played on television, Barney Miller," she said, her tone breathless.

"Don't know him," he said, "so he can't be as famous as our gamine. But I assume he's hot?"

"Mmm, yes, but not as hot as you," she murmured and held him more tightly.

Well past midnight, they drove home. She hadn't stayed out so late in years, and, though she might pay the consequences later that day, it felt good. They exited the Lincoln and paused in the shadows near her building's entrance. The night air felt cool and refreshing on their skin.

His free hand pressed the back of her neck as he leaned in and kissed her. Their clasped hands tightened, broke free as they explored each other. He held her close. "Jonny, my love," he whispered softly in her ear. She snuggled in his arms, and then they kissed again. Eventually, she pulled back and sighed reluctantly. "It's late."

The babysitter gave her the message that Father Tim had phoned to say that due to a bad cold, he regretfully could not join the Blooms in the morning for breakfast. *Too bad*, she thought, *just when I want so much to tell him about Claude.*

She'd drop off a fortifying carton of chicken soup from Polly's Pies to the ailing priest along with a slice of his favorite Irish cream pie. But only after she and Billy had first demolished their allotment of silver dollar pancakes.

CHAPTER 12

Rita Wants Out

The following week, a determined Rita appeared in Jonquil's office late in the day, softly closing the door behind her.

"Got a minute?"

Jonquil lifted her nose out of *American Psychologist* and sat back.

"Park it anywhere you like, Oglesby," she invited cavalierly, indicating, with a wide gesture, the various furniture groupings that dotted her spacious office. Clyde's star perfume sales associate flopped down in one of the arm chairs facing her boss and immediately burst into tears.

"Rita?" Jonquil rose, circled her desk, and planted herself in front of her distressed colleague. "Hey, Rita, what's up? Aren't you feeling well?" She patted the items on the desk behind her, located a box of tissues, and served up a clump.

"Oh, sugar," Rita began, eagerly taking the tissues with both hands, then letting all but one flutter to her lap. "I hate to complain after all you've done for me." She blew her nose thoroughly, then trained her red-rimmed blue eyes on Jonquil.

"Rita, spill."

Like she wasn't already.

"I miss my old job," she wailed, sounding so like Lucy Ricardo that Jonquil half-expected Ricky to rumba by any second.

"The Scentsations counter?" Jonquil asked.

"Uh-huh."

"Why?" Perplexity colored her tone.

Rita took a moment to compose herself while Jonquil's thoughts of the Ricardos faded into the ether. "I'm bored silly. I miss my fragrances, and I miss my customers."

Jonquil sat on the edge of the desk, folded her arms across her chest and studied the carpet's design. Three solid reasons. This was serious indeed. "Since when?" she asked.

Rita's involuntary reply took the form of healthy sniffles followed by a loud hiccup. Jonquil waited.

"Since Christmas.

"It's not your fault, Jonquil," Rita hastened to add. "You're really into this gift counseling thing-a-ma-jig. You have been ever since you stepped foot inside Clyde's. At the beginning, I was too. I was thrilled when you asked me to be your office assistant. After seventeen years of selling perfume, I thought it was time for a change.

"But it's not me. Folks come in here upset, or else they leave here upset, and that fries me. Another thing: I can't fit everyone into your schedule, and if I have to cancel and reschedule an appointment, the client gets mad at me! I'm nervous all the time, and I'm sitting down too much. Why, do you know I've gained five pounds?" She dabbed her eyes. "Al and I are getting married this summer as you well know. I can't look fat and spread out on my wedding day."

"Rita," Jonquil said, patting her friend's right shoulder, "I understand. I only wish you'd told me sooner. Even though I don't know how I'll manage without you, I hate to think you were so unhappy."

"Now, sugar, don't feel bad. 'The bear went over the mountain to see what he could see.' Plus, the extra money came in handy. As for filling the position, I don't think you'll have any trouble. Bet the minute the job's posted half the store will apply."

Jonquil wasn't so sure. Could Mr. Merrill's freakish agreement with Leigh Usher to reinstate her as head buyer only after she spent a minimum of two weeks in every store department include the tiny gift counseling unit?

Rita seemed to read her mind. "Leigh's been assigned to jewelry and she likes it there. Ha, does she ever. Don't worry about her."

So, Jonquil signed off on an immediate transfer request that returned Rita to the center counter in the scents department. Then the gift counselor decided to take her time selecting a replacement.

Rita's parting observations had alerted her about what to look for: someone comfortable with phones and desk work, someone who wouldn't cringe at the emotional side of gift counseling, someone, she now added to the job description, who could become an advocate of this strange new discipline.

As Rita rightly predicted, over a dozen Clyde's employees inquired about the receptionist position. Jonquil interviewed them between appointments. Personnel secured a temporary named Vanessa Ford from an employment agency to cover in the interim.

Vanessa arrived early Monday morning in the shortest skirt Jonquil had ever seen except on a mannequin. It showed off to full advantage her long brown legs (unencumbered by nylons) and strapless heels. Slightly taller than Jonquil, she wore her plum tinted black hair parted to one side. Large gold hoop earrings dangled from her ears. Under a black short-sleeved jacket, she wore a white camisole. Wearing the legal limit of clothing—and who wouldn't with those legs and that figure—seemed to be the secret of her wardrobe.

There was no secret to her charm, however; it shone through a ravishing pair of brown eyes, a dimpled smile as sweet as her disposition, and a voice that yielded at the least provocation to soft, infectious giggles. Vanessa had completed secretarial school and was twenty-six years old. With a minimum of instruction, she got to work answering the phone and greeting walk-ins in the waiting room. Five times that first morning she interrupted Jonquil between sessions to ask questions, after which she was able to work independently for the rest of the day. By the third day, she was entirely on her own, and their small department of two hummed with efficiency.

CHAPTER 13

Dealing with Leigh

ut within days, Vanessa spied a posting on the cafeteria bulletin Bboard for a sales position. She and her husband were buying a house, so, although gift counseling had captured her imagination, she needed a job that paid more. Jonquil overcame her disappointment and gave Vanessa an enthusiastic endorsement.

The day after she left to begin orientation, there came a knock at Jonquil's door. No appointments were scheduled that afternoon, so Jonquil glanced up, expecting to see a walk-in.

Leigh Usher! She gulped.

"I thought we should meet and clear the air."

"Oh." The gift counselor's gaze dropped back down to the piles of gift inventories spread out on her desk.

"Ms. Bloom?" The familiar pout in the visitor's voice made her blood boil.

"Call me Jonquil, Leigh. Only my faculty advisor and my son's friends call me Ms. Bloom." Leigh sashayed into the office, pausing in front of the desk. Though she refused to look up or invite the statuesque blonde to take a seat, Jonquil could not completely block out the other woman's chic attire or muted, expensive fragrance.

"Your name's a tongue twister. I can't pronounce it."

Jonquil exhaled loudly. "Put the emphasis on the first syllable." She wanted to, but refrained from adding, *Dummy*.

"JON-kill?"

"Excuse me?"

"A little paranoid, are we?"

"Oh, for heaven's sake. 'Jon' is the first part. Pronounce it like the name 'John.' Then 'Quill,' like the feathered pen. Jon-kwil." Bending forward to scribble a note, she made herself add, "Try it more slowly."

"Jon. Kwil?"

"That's better. I have trouble with your name, too. In print, it looks like it would be pronounced Lee. But I've heard people say it like 'lay' when they use your nickname. Which do you prefer?" Referring mischievously to Leigh's in-store nickname "Lady Leigh," she sat back and waited.

Leigh ignored the insulting sobriquet earned from her colleagues. "I was named for the actress Janet Leigh. I read somewhere she had a problem with people mispronouncing her name her entire professional life."

"Please answer my question."

"'Lee,' all right? Like the general. Just plain 'Lee.' May I sit?"

Jonquil gestured to her to do so while she gathered up the research papers. She quickly shoved them into her briefcase, mentally preparing herself for the blonde's belated apology or explanation for her past weird behavior—whichever had prompted her unscheduled visit.

"First of all, I am sorry for threatening you that day on the elevator before you went on the talk show last December. It will never happen again."

Jonquil regarded her in silence. She had no intention of forgiving or forgetting the incident. Leigh waited in vain for a sign of agreement.

"Second, I've done a lot of thinking about gift counseling and Clyde's. I may have been hasty in my initial assessment. It appears our valued customers want what you have to offer."

Jonquil's eyebrows rose. She wished Rita were present or Al or even Mr. Merrill. Anyone in fact who could verify whether or not Lady Leigh was being on the level.

"My sister's drug addiction seems to be out of control. Your presence in the store reminds me of her situation. I'm scared to death she'll do something stupid that will somehow jeopardize my career."

"Now who's paranoid?"

"I'm getting help with that. Look, I can't lose Clyde's, Jonquil, not now. This plan Mr. M and Sy concocted is brilliant ..." Jonquil let her drone on while she took stock of the amount of jewelry the nuisance was wearing. Pearl earrings, jade bracelet, slender diamond wrist watch yet her left ring finger was bare. For the first time, she wondered about Leigh's marital status. The nickname Lady Leigh could be a reference to her love life or a rich boyfriend.

She tuned back into the conversation in time to hear Leigh say, "So it seems an opportune time for me to come work in gift counseling and help out."

Jonquil hoped her involuntary body spasm telegraphed clearly *you must be kidding!*

"Wait. Before you say no, consider the time of year. There's no major holiday coming up, no major gift occasion in the foreseeable future. We're between Valentine's Day and Easter. It's quiet. I won't get in your way. I just want to get this over with, I mean—this meeting—and get started with—"

The telephone rang in the outer office.

"Got it," said Leigh, snatching up Jonquil's receiver, then expertly punching the receptionist's button.

"Clyde's exclusive Gift Counseling Department," she purred, turning her back on Jonquil. "How may we help you?"

Jonquil listened as the nuisance answered the caller's questions about gift counseling. Not for one second did she buy Leigh's story. Help out? Help herself out, more likely. It would be tantamount to having a terrorist chair a security summit. On the other hand, she'd have to accommodate the sidelined head buyer sooner or later. Might as well get it over with.

But never ride an elevator alone with her again!

Leigh's sour expression, aimed at her, seemed so familiar to Jonquil, she felt she could read the head buyer's thoughts. She'd wager a week's pay that Leigh's sneer had to do with Jonquil's frizzy hair, scant make-up, and off the rack suit.

But Leigh simply cradled the phone and waited.

Emerging from her thoughts, Jonquil said, "All right. Since it *is* quiet, you can do the required two weeks now. Just so you know, I'll be interviewing candidates. I want to find someone who believes in what I'm doing."

"When do I start my training?"

"As soon as I clear it with Mr. Merrill."

"I did that over lunch."

The outer office phone started up again.

Jonquil inwardly fumed at the woman's encroachment on her territory. What did "over lunch" signify? Was the nuisance back in Mr. Merrill's good graces? Or was she lying? She clamped down on her lower lip to keep from blurting out the accusation.

Leigh didn't wait for an answer. Her long legs ferried her out of the gift counselor's office in time to grab the other phone receiver before the third ring.

CHAPTER 14

Origa Tu!

"Claude, on your line," intoned Leigh an hour later over the intercom. The door to Jonquil's office stood ajar, affording a glimpse of the gift counselor's pleased expression as she reached for her receiver.

"Hello, what have we here?" Leigh said aloud to the empty waiting room.

She kept track of how long the call took. Seventeen minutes. She had no difficulty finding some pretext to enter Jonquil's office after the call ended.

"Who's Claude?" Leigh inquired airily as she placed a printout of the next day's appointments on Jonquil's desk.

"A friend."

"He sounds nice. I should probably know which calls are a priority, shouldn't I?"

"Leigh, you don't have to answer my private line."

"Good." She came closer.

"Was there something else?"

"You're aware, aren't you, that long personal phone calls are against company—"

The sound of sharp knocks on the doorpost cut her off. Two pairs of eyes peered inside the office.

"May we help you?" asked Jonquil.

"I apologize for the intrusion. We're looking for gift counseling. Are we in the right place?" asked the younger one. Leigh noted that the visitors, now framed side by side in the doorway, were Japanese.

"Yes, you are." Leigh started to walk out.

"Please don't leave on our account, miss. This will only take a moment of your time."

Leigh glanced over at Jonquil for direction. She wasn't eager to join the party but anything was preferable to the isolation of the reception area. To Leigh's surprise, she heard Jonquil invite her to stay, that it would be good for her to observe a session. Then, Jonquil invited the visitors to take seats around the coffee table. She indicated a chair off to the side for Leigh.

It took time for the younger woman to coax the older woman into the office. Leigh closed the door behind them, before dragging over her chair so she could better follow the conversation.

"I am Yuuko," said the young woman in a gentle voice. "I work in the housewares department on Five. This is my mother, Mrs. Shigeta." Mrs. Shigeta dipped her head several times toward both women. She seemed to prefer eye contact with the carpet.

"I'm Jonquil and this is my assistant, Leigh. How may we help you?"

Leigh dipped her head as the Japanese woman had done and murmured, "*Konnichiwa.*" She relished Jonquil's look of surprise so much, Leigh added a few more head bows for good measure. Mrs. Shigeta welcomed the unexpected greeting. She whispered in her daughter's ear.

Yuuko addressed Leigh. "My mother asks if you have been to Japan."

"Yes, several times for fashion shows in Tokyo and Yokohama. I bought this bracelet there." Leigh offered her wrist for their inspection, relishing Jonquil's obvious surprise. At this news, the older woman relaxed.

Their reason for being there, per Yuuko, boiled down to a family squabble over gift giving. Yuuko had been hired recently at Clyde's. Mrs. Shigeta, as was the Japanese custom, wanted to present her daughter's new boss a gift to show her parental appreciation.

Yuuko's tone took on intensity. "I objected, fiercely, and we have been fighting about it ever since. You see, gift giving in Japan has many rules. Mother expects me to practice all of the old gift giving customs even though I was a toddler when our family came to America. The old ways are too formal and confining. They aren't me. I go to USC, I'm an American."

Leigh nodded sagely. "Yes, of course." She bestowed a warm smile on Mrs. Shigeta who stared back at her. Mrs. Shigeta again whispered something to her daughter.

Yuuko then said to Leigh, "Mother wants you to know that she loathes airing our dispute in front of non-Japanese strangers, but because of you she has decided to stay and listen. She doesn't speak much English but understands it pretty well."

Before Jonquil could tease out a compromise, Leigh spoke up, explaining to the older woman that giving a gift to Yuuko's new American boss for hiring her could land her daughter in big trouble. The store's policy forbade it. Mrs. Shigeta looked disappointed, so Leigh added that Christmas was an appropriate time to give gifts to anyone. The older woman bowed her head repeatedly with relief. When the two visitors left, they both appeared to be in better frames of mind.

"You were very helpful today," said Jonquil. "And resourceful, mentioning Christmas."

"I enjoyed myself. Oh, phooey. I forgot to give them their parting discount coupons."

"Never mind that. Now, about my personal calls …"

"Eh, do what you like."

Leigh sashayed out to the reception area, a smirk on her face, knowing for once she'd gotten the upper hand with Jonquil Bloom.

CHAPTER 15

Claude Comes to Dinner

Jonquil began with the best of intentions. In the end, she threw up her hands and blamed a full moon.

That morning, she'd called Claude and invited him to come over at six that evening after settling on a fail-proof, man-pleasing menu of filet mignon, baked potatoes, steamed asparagus, beefsteak tomato and scallion salad, and soft dinner rolls, with ice cream sundaes for dessert. She would pick up the food at the Safeway on her way home.

But at six o'clock, Jonquil was just getting into the shower. The dinner she'd ordered at the last minute because she couldn't get to the store hadn't yet arrived. Billy, having first put Blackie in his crate, anxiously kept a lookout for the delivery man along with his friend, Ramon, a last minute addition to the guest list. The doorbell rang. Billy sped over to the door, tip money in hand, and discovered Claude Chappel standing opposite him, holding a planter of tulips.

"Hi, Claude," he said as he unlatched the screen door.

"Hello, Billy." Claude stepped inside and closed the front door behind him. He was dressed casually in a yellow polo shirt and slacks. His damp hair gave evidence that he had recently showered. Since this wasn't his first time inside the Bloom apartment, his eyes scanned the room for Gerry's photo and saw that it was still resting in its appointed place on the desk. Check.

Claude loudly cleared his throat, his habit when he wanted to change subjects, and thrust one hand out to Ramon who stood next to Billy. "Hi, there. My name's Claude, and you are?"

"Ramon DeWitt." The two shook hands.

"He's my friend," said Billy. "We go to the same school. I'll tell Mom you're here." Billy ran down the hall, shouting the news at the top of his lungs, while Claude placed the flowers he'd brought on the coffee table and took a moment to size up the situation.

Clearly, this wasn't going to be a romantic evening with two young boys in attendance. *Okay*, he thought as he let go of his fantasies, *have it her way.*

His attention turned to the other boy. Ramon appeared to be older than Billy, perhaps because he was inches taller. He had black, unruly hair, smoky black eyes, and a chubby build. There was a familiar untidiness about him. The boy reminded Claude of when he'd been that age and overweight. Ramon also seemed uncomfortable being left alone with a stranger.

Claude stood for a moment frowning, one hand massaging his jaw, the other parked at his hip. Loudly he sniffed the air. In a conspiratorial tone, he said to Ramon, "Smell anything?"

Ramon inhaled warily. "Like what?"

71

"Like dinner."

Ramon sighed. "It ain't here yet."

Billy caught the tail end of their exchange when he rushed back into the main room. He shrugged his shoulders and confirmed, "Yeah, dinner's late."

Just then the phone rang, and Billy dived out to the kitchen to answer it. "Bloom residence," he stated loudly, and, because the kitchen had no door, the guests heard him clearly.

Turning to Ramon, Claude remarked, "Women sometimes take a while to get ready, have you noticed?"

"Oh, I know," agreed Ramon heartily and rolled his eyes in a way that made Claude smile. They listened to Billy.

"Uh-huh … uh-huh … uh-huh … oh! Um, hang on." He left the phone receiver dangling as he sped out of the kitchen, straight past them, and back down the hallway.

Claude said, "Let's take a seat." He chose the cushioned sofa and let Ramon have the rattan chair opposite. A short silence followed and then Billy raced passed again. They heard him mutter into the phone, "My Mom says, 'Don't bother.'" Then, he slammed the receiver back into its cradle and rejoined them.

"What's up?" asked Claude mildly.

"Um, change of plans. Want some water or anything?"

"Billy," yelled Jonquil from the far end of the hall. Billy grunted, scooped up her leather purse that was lying on the desk, gave them an aggrieved sigh and trudged off.

"Do you play baseball, too?" inquired Claude.

"Bor-ing," Ramon replied with a face.

"So," said Claude, "want to bet on who's cooking dinner tonight?"

"Uh ... not Ms. Bloom, right?"

"Check."

"Then it must be where she ordered take-out from."

"You mean the place that just telephoned here to say that their stove blew up, so sorry, or their chef just quit, or the car they use for deliveries has a flat tire?"

Ramon was instantly onto the joke. "Or—or the chickens forgot to lay eggs today, *lo siento*, I mean, so sorry, in case Ms. Bloom ordered omelets."

Claude laughed. "Good one. You cook, Ramon?"

The boy swatted the air as if to dismiss the idea. "Only waffles, toast, tacos, rice, sandwiches, hotdogs, scrambled eggs, any eggs really, um, soup from a can—"

Billy reappeared at that moment. "Gotta go to the store. Mom'll be out soon. Her hair's still drying."

"Whoa," said Claude.

"Oh, man, I wasn't supposed to tell you guys that," groaned Billy.

"No, what I mean is, before you go to the store, let me and my man, Ramon, here check out the contents of your kitchen. If we can pull together a decent meal, you won't need to go."

Billy cast an uneasy glance down the hall. "She won't like it."

Claude clapped his hands. "You kidding me? She'll *love* it!"

CHAPTER 16

Ramon's Gift

She hated it. She couldn't believe her eyes when, mystified by the empty main room, she traced her guests and son to the kitchen.

"Guys, what's all this?" she uttered, wide-eyed. The doors to every cabinet were open while the contents of her refrigerator appeared to be spread out on the counter.

Claude straightened up and placed the mixing bowl he'd just located beside the carton of eggs on the counter, tapping Ramon on the shoulder to point it out to him. He then sauntered out to the dining area.

"You look bewitching," he began, reaching for her.

"Cut the charm, Claude," she replied, backing away. At her tone, he walked past her through the dining area to the main room and signaled for her to follow.

"I don't want the boys to hear us," he half-whispered. They were standing in front of Billy's portrait which had found its home on the wall above her rocking chair. "Now, what's the big

74

deal, Jonny? Oh, wait." He snatched up the planter and presented it to her.

She could no more hide her pleasure than she could avoid staring up into his devastating black eyes. What she saw in them made her voice falter.

"I-I ..."

"Me, too," he said and nodded. "So, let us make dinner for you. By the way, this drawing of Billy is incredible. It's new, isn't it? I want to hear all about it at dinner. If you want to help out, would you set the table, please?" He bent his head and kissed her and returned to the kitchen.

Jonquil decided to use her newest tablecloth and good silver. The tulips became the eye-catching centerpiece. She placed Claude at one end of the table with herself at the other.

The boys sat across from each other. Billy begged for Blackie to be allowed to join them. Since the puppy's plaintive whimpers could be heard through Billy's bedroom door all the way down the hall, she relented. When they sat down she was so rattled, she almost forgot to say grace. The food was scrumptious. She wanted seconds of everything—bacon and waffles, the "Eggs Ramon" as Claude called them, the cut fruit salad, topped with a tasty dressing Claude concocted out of mayonnaise, ketchup, and spices, plus toasted bagels with cream cheese. And for dessert? Peach yogurt still in the cartons.

Claude and Ramon had a running joke through dinner that Billy quickly grasped. Feeling excluded from their camaraderie, but loving the laughter, she kept quiet.

"'We had an earthquake, didn't you feel it? So, we can't deliver your dinner—so sorry,'" joked Ramon. She could not recall ever seeing him that lighthearted in the presence of a stranger who was also an adult.

"No, we were taken over by aliens and they ate our chef," replied Billy with a straight face. The two boys dissolved into giggles.

"Now, boys, those explanations are just plain silly," deadpanned Claude sternly. "Actually, the restaurant called up today and said, 'So very, very sorry, but we can't deliver your dinner because we were built on a sink hole and today ... we sank!'" Billy nearly fell off his chair laughing.

It was almost nine o'clock. Ramon needed a ride home. "I'll take him," offered Claude. "But first, boys, let's do the dishes."

"No, I'll do the dishes. You did the cooking. Fair is fair."

Billy put Blackie on his leash and walked Ramon out to the Jeep, which gave Claude and Jonquil their first moment of complete privacy that evening.

He searched her eyes. "Did you have fun tonight?"

"I wanted it to be special but I got tied up in stupid traffic and then the food I ordered didn't arrive because they lost the damn order—"

"Tonight was special. Ramon can cook. That kid's got a gift."

Jonquil paused, startled by his words. Things had a way of always taking her back to gifts. Was that true for all Ph.D. candidates? She relaxed, her face brightening. He drew her close and passionately kissed her. Not once. Not twice. Three times.

CHAPTER 17

Mrs. K Returns

The following week, Mrs. Kingston arrived punctually for her second appointment. She was dressed in the same plain gray cloth coat and hat. She did not remove her coat but took a seat and stared blankly at the blue feathered dream catcher displayed in one of the windows opposite Jonquil's desk. Jonquil took the seat across from her.

Sunlight streaming through the windows dappled the carpet surrounding them but could not dispel the woman's gloom.

"Mrs. Kingston, I'm glad to see you again. How are you today?" she began brightly.

The woman sighed heavily before meeting Jonquil's gaze.

"Oh, so-so." She crossed her ankles while keeping one hand on the purse in her lap.

"Did you have a chance to do the gift inventory?"

"I had trouble with some of the questions you asked," the woman whined.

"May I see it?"

"Oh."

She slowly opened her purse, removed the gift inventory, much wrinkled and smudged as though she'd split her attention between filling out the form and changing a flat tire, and handed it to Jonquil.

"Thank you. Please sit back and relax while I look it over. Would you care for coffee or water?"

"No thanks." The client's opinion that this was an ordeal to be politely endured was evident by her monotone.

Jonquil scanned the four-page document eagerly but her hopes quickly fell. Few questions had been answered, and few of those responses gave any details.

She looked up and said, "This is a good start." She thought to herself, *This is barely a start but perhaps it holds a clue.*

The woman's pleased look dissolved into a grimace. "I don't see what any of this has to do with honoring my daughter's memory."

Jonquil ignored the impatience in the woman's voice. "Tell me about your doll with long hair. Who gave it to you? What was the occasion?"

"My aunt gave her to me for my sixth birthday. I called her Suzy. She was a princess doll. She came with a brush and comb and I loved her. When I played with her I pretended we were both princesses. Best friends, too."

The woman's hands gestured with animation.

"What happened to Suzy?"

"Oh, I don't know. I guess I outgrew her."

The smile faded from Mrs. Kingston's face. Her hands flopped to her lap. Jonquil was disappointed to see that spark of life go out so quickly. She followed up with another question.

"Now, tell me about the vacuum cleaner from Harry. What was that occasion?"

The woman's expression turned sour. "It was our first Christmas after we were married. Harry was so romantic when we were dating, you know, surprising me with little foo-foos. But that first Christmas, when I saw that machine I broke down and cried."

"Why was that?"

"Because it meant more work for me. Like house cleaning, laundry, shopping, cooking, and washing the dishes. Work, work, work."

Jonquil's weekend reading on humanistic psychology came to mind, namely the works of famed psychologist Carl Rogers, who'd urged therapists to be empathic.

"I'm so sorry," she murmured.

She placed the gift inventory on her desk and said gently, "Have you given any more thought to how you wish to honor your daughter's memory?"

"I wish I could set up a scholarship at a nursing school in her name but I don't have enough money for that. I can only manage about a thousand dollars from my savings."

"Certainly that would be a generous donation in her name to any nursing school."

"Oh, sure, but then it would be over and done with and soon forgotten. I want her name on a plaque where people can see it." Jonquil perked up. Here, at last, was a tangible goal.

"You could have her portrait done or a statue made with a plaque put on it," she said, thinking of her talented friend Annie.

"I suppose." The idea clearly didn't appeal to her.

"Or …"

"Yes?"

"I'm considering how much you loved playing with your doll and how much that gift from your husband distressed you."

The woman snorted.

"I'm picturing how hard Carol worked and how much you wished she had relaxed more."

"That's right." The room grew still. Jonquil had learned that voicing her thoughts when she was unsure of how to proceed in a session often helped the process.

"I wonder if there's a link between those two separate scenarios." Mrs. Kingston looked dubious, so Jonquil changed course. "Tell me more about Carol. What was she like growing up?"

"Oh, Carol liked nothing better than to be outdoors. I'd have to track her down to get her to eat lunch." Jonquil reflected on how similar her own childhood had been. "We didn't have a park near us, still don't, but one of our neighbors back then had a swing set that Carol loved to play on. She was so happy flying through the air, higher and higher." The woman gazed at the dream catcher, remembering.

Jonquil realized that their time was almost up. It looked like they'd need a third session to get to the bottom of Mrs. Kingston's gift dilemma, when without warning the woman let out a shriek.

"I can *see* it!"

"What?" Jonquil jerked her head side to side trying to spot the item that had provoked her client's outburst.

"A playground on our corner lot. It's been vacant forever. A playground with swings and a sandbox. And monkey bars and ... and a big slide.

"A place where children can play all day. I'll ask Carol's husband to help and Rosemary, and all of their friends and Carol's co-workers and my neighbors and, oh! I've got calls to make." She stood up and then plopped down again, dislodging her eye glasses. She pushed them back into place and asked, "Where do I begin?"

"The city?"

"That's it, the city! Oh, and we'll name it for Carol and there'll be a sign, a *big* sign. Oh, Ms. Bloom, how can I ever thank you?" But rather than take time to do so, a fired-up Mrs. Kingston grabbed her belongings and scurried out of the office, almost colliding with Leigh.

Leigh stepped into the office, a frown on her face and a scarf in her hands. "What happened? Why is your client running away?"

Jonquil, her voice tinged with the thrill of success, explained how Mrs. Kingston had found a solution to her problem. Leigh listened without interrupting.

"I see," she said. "That's impressive even though it didn't lead to a store purchase. Look, Jonquil, I know my time in gift counseling is almost up. Have you decided on hiring anyone yet?

"Oh, by the way, I got this scarf in Paris, but I can't decide if I like how it looks on me. Would you mind putting it on so I can see how it looks?"

The request startled her, but since Leigh had stopped mangling her name, she didn't object. The minute her fingers touched the fabric, she wanted to know how it would feel on her neck. She stepped over to a mirror.

"I don't wear scarves much, Leigh. I'm not even sure how to wear them. Like this?"

Leigh walked over.

"May I?"

The idea she was giving Leigh Usher access to strangle her crossed her mind. But no, with a couple of quick movements, the taller woman deftly twisted and looped the scarf several times so that it fell appealingly around Jonquil's shoulders.

The color also happened to match her dress. A little too perfectly.

"Oh, darn," said Leigh. "That's not at all a good color for me. But it looks great on you."

"Really?" Jonquil asked, suspicious.

"Yes, keep it, why don't you? I have dozens of them."

"Oh, I couldn't." She started to remove it.

"Not even as a gift? Please do. I hate to see pretty things go to waste." She turned away.

"So, you haven't hired anyone, right?" Leigh repeated.

"No. I haven't found anyone as good as Vanessa Ford."

"Who's she?"

"Vanessa's the young woman who was a temp here right after Rita left. She fit in perfectly, like she was wired for the job. Wish Clyde's could have paid her enough to stay. Now she's up in Gowns because of the commissions.

"Of course, you're doing a fine job, Leigh," she added quickly, "but aren't you bored? Let's sit." They seated themselves opposite each other on the couches around the glass coffee table.

"Here's what I want to propose, Jonquil. I don't really need to work in the other departments. I already know how they operate. I'd like to stay here a while longer as your assistant and figure out how we can better market this service.

"I mean, what you did with that customer today was huge. I doubt it would have happened at a Bullock's or Robinson's-May. Or even on Rodeo Drive. No telling how many new customers that woman's word of mouth will draw to the store. Why, Clyde's can make a donation to the playground while publicizing the role gift counseling played. What do you say? Oh, and keep the scarf, I insist."

Later, when Jonquil strode through the Scentsations Department on her way to the elevator, she heard her name being called. She wheeled around to see Rita beckoning her over to the center counter.

"Sugar, what's cookin'? You're sure dolled up today."

"What? Oh, you mean the scarf? It's new. You like it?" Jonquil assessed her appearance in the cosmetics mirror on the counter.

"It suits you. With your nice long neck, you ought to wear scarves more often or dangly earrings. While you're here, want to try our new fragrance?"

She selected a sampler from the counter, and Jonquil dutifully extended her arm.

"Actually, the scarf's a gift from Leigh," Jonquil said while she sniffed her wrist.

Rita nearly dropped the perfume atomizer. "As in *Usher*? Well now, if that don't beat heck."

"Mm, Rita, that smells yummy, but Claude likes Gamine."

Rita proceeded to spray on both sides of Jonquil's head, then over her hair for good measure.

"Listen, if I were you, I'd watch out. Remember, Leigh only cares about Leigh. Don't let her shimmy shammy you. Time she moved on to another department."

"She says she wants to stay in gift counseling longer to help market it."

"My eye! She's up to something, you can bet on it. Sugar, there's no need to put up with her shenanigans one more day. Let Mr. Merrill know her time's up."

Jonquil fingered the scarf, sensing the uncomfortable possibility that this gift might have strings of treachery attached.

Meanwhile, one of Rita's regular customers appeared at Jonquil's elbow, so their conversation ended there.

CHAPTER 18

The Poppi Blair Show Revisited

Jonquil's return appearance on the Poppi Blair Show was scheduled for the end of February which necessitated a weekend trip to New York City, the show's regular site. Jonquil was grateful that, unlike her first experience, there would be no home audience call-ins during this taping. Air fare and hotel accommodations at the Waldorf were provided.

Little League was heavy into preseason practice. She wanted Billy to go with her but if he missed any practices, he risked not starting on opening day, so she decided to travel alone. Since Annie was out of town again, Billy and Blackie stayed with the Phillips, one of the car pool families. Joanie Phillips happened to be on Billy's team.

Suddenly, the spiky-haired production assistant cued Jonquil on set where she was warmly welcomed back by the jazzy talk show hostess to the sounds of boisterous applause, live music, and clicking cameras. Poppi, gowned in a swirl of blue minus her customary turban, grasped her hand and air-kissed her near both ears.

Jonquil, instantly recalling the noise, the hype, and her dry mouth as she became conscious of a vast invisible audience, licked her lips. The hostess invited her to sit on the love seat next to her chair. Then she took her seat and gestured to the studio audience to settle down.

After a brief chit chat, Poppi said, "So, now, Jonquil, tell the audience why your son's call into the show last Christmas Eve made you up and leave."

The audience leaned forward, many on the edge of their seats. They'd just been shown a video of Jonquil running off the show in Los Angeles and didn't want to miss a word.

"First, thank you for inviting me back," Jonquil began. "During my last appearance, I cut my visit short after my son telephoned the show because he needed me, and nothing at that moment was more important." Her quelling stare told Poppi clear as a cue card, "*Topic closed.*" The predominately female audience applauded with empathy.

Changing her tone and the topic, Jonquil continued, "Which means I never got to share with your viewers the exciting benefits of gift counseling. Now, everyone likes to receive a good gift, right? But don't we all want to be good gift givers, too?"

With her steady patter and encompassing gestures, she soon had the audience eating out of her hand, just as her faculty advisor had predicted would happen when she'd sought his advice earlier that week.

87

Jonquil proceeded to question the host about her own gift giving habits. Poppi netted scattered whistles when she described a trashy lingerie item she'd purchased as a Valentine's Day gift. Then, she smoothly turned the tables on her guest.

"So, Jonquil, what's your own heart's desire at this very moment?" she asked in such a seductive tone, that Jonquil fell headlong into her trap.

"Knowing if Daddy's alive or dead!" the gift counselor blurted. She immediately clamped a hand over her mouth. With just six words, the vigilant protection of her privacy had come undone. The talk show host's eyes bulged. A gasp went up from the studio audience.

Poppi announced with fervor, "We'll be right back with Jonquil Bloom and her *heartbreaking* dilemma after this word from our sponsors."

John Bloom, who now went by Jack, surprised his partner and came home early that same afternoon. He'd been out on the boat since early morning, giving tours in the marina. Business slowed down after lunchtime, so he decided to grab a nap before dinner.

The television set was on. Nora was watching one of her girly talk shows as she roamed the kitchen putting together his favorite pie. They had met in AA and had been together for eleven years. She was a member of the Coast Guard Reserve, divorced, with an adult daughter who lived in Tucson. Nora greeted him with floury kisses. "Jack, you're spoiling your surprise," she said with mock regret but quickly changed her tone. "Are you done for the day, babe?"

"Yep," he said, holding her close. As always, he felt utterly safe in her arms, the most peaceful place on earth to be.

A face on the television caught his attention. He stopped swaying her, and his arms slackened as he peered over her shoulder at the freckled young woman whom the lady in blue had just identified.

"Hold it," he said, his voice catching. "Did she just say Jonquil Bloom? *Is that my daughter?*"

CHAPTER 19

Father Tim's Gift

Sad news about Father Tim awaited Jonquil when she returned from New York. Her humble and dear friend's bad cold had quickly progressed to pneumonia, and he had died in his sleep. The news, delivered by the pastor, crushed both Blooms.

Jonquil wept and held broken hearted Billy tightly in her arms. Knowing their friend hadn't suffered a fall or long illness gave her scant solace. The absence of his beloved brogue, warm hugs, and simple holiness would be felt for the rest of her life.

The pastor's message asked her to stop by the rectory. There, he handed her two sealed envelopes addressed to her, explaining that he was carrying out Father Tim's wishes.

"We found these among Tim's few possessions. He often spoke highly of you and your son."

She thanked him and took them home to read. The larger envelope had a bright red "#1" circled on its front. She opened it but had to squint to read the cramped, familiar handwriting:

My dear Jonquil,

When you read this, know I am with God. Don't dwell on your sorrow, dearie. You and Billy have been good to me, and I will always watch over you. I have loved you as my family. My own family is mostly deceased. However, over time I tucked away funds for my dream to once more see Ireland. But the doctor says I'm going on a longer trip and soon. What can an old man do?

You go and take the boy with you. See your grandmother before it's too late. Jonquil, this is my dying wish. Go with all my love and blessings,

Tim

P.S. Call your travel agent. Go!

Her eyes brimmed with tears. Margo had been the one who took her in and raised her in Seattle after she was orphaned. She'd moved to Ireland ten years ago after Jonquil's wedding. Jonquil had often spoken of her wistfully to Father Tim. Now she opened the second envelope and found two round-trip Aer Lingus vouchers. She crumpled into the rocker, speechless. Blackie scampered over and jumped into her lap.

"But Father Tim," she whimpered, fingering the puppy's floppy ears, "this is too much." The kitchen phone rang. It was Claude. Quickly, over the dog's barking, she told him about Father Tim's generous gift.

"Something tells I should go soon."

"Can you get the time off?" he asked.

"Maybe. There's Billy's spring break. Down, Blackie, hush now. Yes, if we go in April at Easter. Billy will miss some practices that week, but that shouldn't be a problem. He'll need a passport, too. I can work it out with the store. Oh, but my dissertation—I'm so far behind."

"Work on the plane."

CHAPTER 20

Progress on a Ph.D.

D r. Mazziotti sank deeper into his high-backed chair, glasses propped halfway down his nose, silently reading through a copy of her gift inventory. One of his legs rested on his other knee, an Italian loafer occasionally swinging. Jonquil's gaze was drawn to the pattern on his exposed silk sock, her mind conscious of his proximity. The woman in her felt a powerful attraction to him while underneath, the child in her responded to his virile, authoritative style, wanting to please, yearning to be his favorite student. She associated those longings with the hole in her life her father's absence had created.

What would her father be like right now? She always pictured John Bloom as she'd last seen him. In these fantasies, he was not yet forty, with thick hair the color of tarnished pennies and shoulders that swung when he walked. Beyond his looks, when her rage at him permitted, she imagined a man like Dr. Mazziotti.

Jonquil worried that her layered, neurotic feelings toward the psychiatrist would harm her project. She had to remind herself that he was a skilled clinician who must have supervised other students with similar issues. Students who, despite their intellectual gifts, were emotionally needy.

She peered up at the framed diplomas on the wall behind his head. She could feel her face reddening; was it hot in here? Slowly she began reciting the Gettysburg Address. Her grandmother had taught her this trick to keep from wriggling when she had to sit still through haircuts. Another childhood memory evoked by her advisor's nearness. Unlike in childhood though, she did not say the words aloud.

But nothing she tried could block him out entirely. Not just because the inventory he was so openly scowling at was a key component of her research.

She couldn't ignore this man, period.

"So," he said, tossing the pages on his desk. He leveled an appraising glance at her and grinned. He knew the effect he had on her. The twinkle in his eye told her so.

"How'd you arrive at those criteria? By the way, Ms. Bloom, that's a ton of questions you've packed into this form. How many of your targeted shoppers will take the time to answer them?"

"I've collected thirty so far," she said, aware for the first time of his strong resemblance to Ricardo Montalban. Was it the courtly way he usually addressed students even though he himself preferred to be called Joe?

"Really? Since we last met? When was that, three weeks ago?"

"About that. More will be waiting for me when I get back from Ireland."

"Good. Problem is, you have too many variables. Age, gender, socio-economic strata, education, ethnicity. Cultural differences. Relationships. Also, there are phobias and compulsions to consider. Not to mention a myriad of gift occasions—holidays, birthdays, anniversaries, and so forth. How will you narrow down your scope? What's your plan, Ms. Bloom? You know how this works. You make a proposal at which point I either give it thumbs up or thumbs down, and we go from there."

She took a deep, fortifying breath. "Joe, my plan is to first collect three hundred of these questionnaires, using only completed ones in my project. At the rate I'm going, it may take the rest of the year to accumulate that many."

A discreet knock at the door made Jonquil's shoulders sag.

"Come in." The secretary handed him a pink message slip and quickly stepped out. "Sorry, I have to make a quick call. No, don't move. This will only take a sec."

Move? she thought. There was no place she'd rather be. His mere presence was a potent reminder that she was a woman possessed of her own charms. He picked up the phone receiver and in a lowered, terse tone had a conversation with someone about upping a dosage of medication. *What would it be like being his patient?* she mused, crossing her legs. *Better yet, what would it be like to be his co-therapist, co-anything?* But before her fantasy gelled, he was hanging up and gesturing for her to continue.

She bent forward again and resumed their discussion. "I don't want to exclude anyone yet. Age, gender, budget, background—all gift giving dynamics interest me, except the tit-for-tat kind."

He nodded. "I'm already seeing patterns in the process by which men choose gifts for women and women for men. So far, my findings corroborate other behaviors documented in the literature."

"Such as?"

"Drives and instincts … associated with object relations. I'm tackling sibling rivalry literature too as you suggested." She sounded vague and knew it. She tucked a lock of hair behind her ear. Being on hyper alert was exhausting.

"Is that so? Remind me, please, where does Freud say, 'True gifts are free'?"

He was trying to goad her, referring back to their first meeting, satirizing her pet hypothesis, but Jonquil was ready for him. "Freud admitted after some thirty years of practicing psychoanalysis that he had no clue what women wanted. But I'm a woman, and I think I may know what other women want."

"I see." He slowly stroked his mustache. The room was roasting like a desert tennis court, or so it seemed to her. He didn't appear the least bit uncomfortable. "But I'm a Freudian and your advisor and unapologetically male." He rapped his knuckles once on the desktop and sat back. "I want hard evidence that your research is based on terra firma, not wishful thinking."

She fought the urge to describe her feelings about him to him in graphic detail. Instead, she bought time by removing her water bottle from her purse and taking a swift swallow.

"Okay, so after I've accumulated three hundred completed inventories and scored them for demographics, and statistically analyzed them, and done the follow-up interviews, then I hope to

96

identify the gift giving behavior that supports my theory that true gifts have no strings attached. That contrary to Freud, altruism can be demonstrated. However, if the data points in another direction, I'll accept that. Maybe limit my focus to the ways in which men and women's gifts to each other differ and extrapolate the psychological application. I'll form my question, write my proposal, continue working on my bibliography, outline my chapters and then provide you with a preliminary time line." She set the bottle on the floor.

"Now, see? Was that so hard? You got your plan together in just under fifteen minutes. Here are my thoughts. Though your topic needs narrowing down, you've got me curious. You and I differ on the dynamics. Id-ego-superego, that's the construct that most interests me. But I think we can work together. This project's going to require substantive investigation. You're ambitious yet flexible and persevering so, proceed. Let's review your bibliography in progress at our next meeting." He grinned. "We still have time left on the clock."

She felt drained by the tension but her relief, that at age thirty-four she hadn't made an utter fool of herself in front of the professor she most admired, was greater.

So, she pressed on.

"I have a request, Joe."

"Shoot."

"I've been invited to be a guest speaker at the Santa Monica Women's Club luncheon in June."

"Ooh la la. Congratulations. Closer to home than that daytime talk show, hmm?"

His baiting her was to be expected. None of her classmates that she knew of were appearing on talk shows or speaking to prestigious women's groups. No, they were undoubtedly presenting papers at psychology conferences, or else living at the medical library and limiting all social contact to email. She wondered whether the extracurricular activities made her stand out favorably in his opinion, but this was neither the time nor place to ask.

"Would you, that is, could I use some of my time with you to prepare my talk for them?"

"You bet. As long as it forms the basis for a paper worthy of publication in a peer reviewed journal."

She agreed to his terms and realized that working with him on the speech would be fun. They consulted their calendars and scheduled the next appointment. As she was about to leave, he said, "Oh, Ms. Bloom?"

"Yes, Joe?"

"Enjoy your trip to Ireland. Be sure to hit a pub or two. By the way, how's your son doing?"

"Billy's fine, thanks. Long as his Little League team's winning." Opening Day from a week ago at Memorial Park flashed through her mind, the school bands playing, the waving banners and balloons, catching up with other parents. The sight of Billy ecstatically rounding the bases twice, with Claude cheering beside her in the stands. Then, she remembered where she was. "Why do you ask?"

"I recall when you were carrying him. You used to audit my auditorium lectures. That was smart. Nowadays, they tell pregnant women to listen to baby-fied Mozart but nothing beats a stimulating lecture on the Oedipal complex, you agree?"

He was mocking one minute, teasing the next. Now he was offering up a private memory. How could they work together when his effect on her made the simplest question sound baffling? "So far, he has his heart set on becoming a vet when he grows up. But if he switches to psychiatrist, you'll be the first to know." He shot her a killer smile. She fled out the door.

CHAPTER 21

What to Do About Claude?

I can't do this Thursday," said Jonquil to Claude over the phone. For the third time in a week, they were consulting their schedules. "Department meeting that night. Mandatory."

She swept aside the calico curtains on the window above the kitchen sink in hopes of catching a glimpse of his broad shoulders and hard hat as he walked the construction site across the street.

When she had last dated on a regular basis, back in college, how easy it had been to make plans. Now, three months into their relationship, she and Claude couldn't settle yet on a regular routine.

"How late will your meeting run? Maybe I could—"

She heard him flip a page. "Skip it. Golf game Friday morning before work. New client, also mandatory," he grunted. "What about Saturday night?"

"I'm free after four o'clock, and I'm free Sundays too, for now," she said, brightening.

"Jonny, that's great. Why don't you come down and see my place this weekend?"

"I'd like that. About time I saw where you live."

He chuckled. "You mean how I live, *mais non?*"

She laughed. "Hang on, let me check Billy's schedule." She tugged on the phone cord as she stepped over to the refrigerator. Her fingertip jabbed a box on the calendar taped to its door filled with scribbling. "Ugh! How did I forget? He's got a sleepover after his game on Saturday."

"*Bon.*"

"He's the host."

"Shoot." A loud sigh escaped him.

Neither spoke for several seconds. She leaned against the sink, her free arm wrapped around her waist, thoroughly enjoying the connection even though she felt disappointed with the outcome so far.

"When am I going to see you?" She kept her tone light.

"Before you go to Ireland, I hope. Are you home all day today?"

"Only this morning, I'm doing my taxes. Blackie needs brushing, too. Then I have a date with my laptop at the medical library this afternoon. Nothing but non-stop excitement for us grad students. So, where are you?"

She turned and peered out the window again. "I don't see you hammering any nails or yelling at your foreman."

"I'm inside the trailer waiting for an inspector to sign off on some plans. But I can break loose soon. Let's do an early lunch.

We can either go out or stay in. Your call. If we stay in, I'll bring the chow. Be there by 11:30."

She giggled. "You mean, drop everything just like that?" She snapped her fingers in wonder. Suddenly, the tension in her neck and shoulders evaporated, replaced by a flutter of excitement that she could feel all the way down to her toes.

"Why not? I miss you, too."

Her excitement billowed. "Count me in, you impetuous man."

After replacing the phone, she ran to the hallway mirror. "Eek!" she cried. Her hair looked frizzier than usual. Ink smudges dotted her face while her chipped nails were a sight not to behold. Nor had she factored a shower and manicure into the middle of her tight morning schedule. Well, if he was up for an impromptu rendezvous, she could also dodge her responsibilities for a couple of hours.

Couldn't she?

The phone rang. Jonquil nipped back to the kitchen and grabbed the receiver before it rang again.

"Good thing you called back. Turkey and Swiss on rye, please," she managed to say, sounding breathless. "I'll make iced tea."

There was a pause. Then, "JB?" It took her a moment to identify the speaker.

"Annie? Oh, Annie, I can't talk now. Claude's bringing me lunch in forty-five minutes."

"Aren't you the lucky girl. I trust he'll bring all the fixings, too," said Annie with undisguised innuendo. "And what about you, do you need anything?"

"Don't be silly."

"No worries. I'm at the Third Street Mall. I can get whatever you need and be there in ten minutes. Pink or lacey—"

"Damn it!" Jonquil surveyed the apartment with dismay. Dog hair or research files in every corner. "My place is a sty!"

"Hark, I'm coming over. I want to meet this guy. Got my key with me so I'll let myself in, sweep up for you, change the sheets, anything. Go get beautiful."

Tears of gratitude caught in Jonquil's throat. "This must be what it's like having a sister."

"Gal, hang up now."

She did. Then she spied the back of her late husband's framed photo in its usual place on her desk. She marched over to it without any hesitation and tucked it inside the top drawer before racing to the shower.

Claude arrived early. The two lovers were so eager to kiss, he set down the bags of food on the coffee table and didn't bother to shut the front door. Which is how moments later Annie stumbled in on their passionate embrace.

"Gal, I got stuck on the phone," she called out exchanging her sunglasses for her regular glasses. "Oops, a pox on me!" she said and giggled.

Immediately, Jonquil slithered out of Claude's reach.

"Annie, hi. Um, this is Claude. Claude this is my friend Annie."

Annie and Claude shook hands.

"I'm not staying. I only stopped by to pick up…" Annie's voice stalled as her eyes rapidly scanned the room for any plausible item. "That magazine," she said, pointing.

Caught off guard, Jonquil followed her eyes to the top of her pile of research reading material. "The International Journal of Cross-Cultural Psychology?"

"Huh?"

"*Voila*, you're the artist! You did this exceptional drawing of Billy, eh?" said Claude.

"Right. Well, gotta go. I'm bound for West Virginny and the Greenbrier later," Annie said, backing out of the door. When Claude wasn't looking, she signaled Jonquil to call her.

There followed a moment of silence.

"Nice lady. Oh, she forgot her—"

Jonquil, assuming the mood had changed, lifted up the bags of food. "No, she didn't forget anything. Let's eat."

Claude wanted another look at the drawing. Then his gaze drifted to the desk. The photograph of Jonquil's late husband was gone.

He clapped his hands and called out, "I've got a better idea."

He came up behind her, slipped his arms around her waist, and began kissing the nape of her neck. She squealed with pleasure. The knife she was holding clattered to the counter. She turned around to face him. He bent down and planted his mouth on hers, pressing with increasing urgency. She laced her fingers around his neck and pulled his body closer until everything else vanished.

Except Blackie, who wouldn't stop lunging himself at their legs and barking.

"Blackie," she cried after wrenching back from Claude. "Bathtub. Bathtub, now!"

Blackie whimpered, dallied briefly, then dashed out of the kitchen.

"It's a trick Billy taught him," she whispered. "'Hide and Seek' doesn't work, but 'bathtub' does. He'll stay hidden till he hears—"

Firmly he covered her lips with his fingers. "*J'aimerais faire l'amour avec toi.*" His voice sounded husky.

She knew enough French to quickly nod her head. They reached her bedroom just in time.

CHAPTER 22

The Talk

They hunched together afterward at a corner of the dining room table like co-conspirators. Blackie, freed of his hiding place, watched them covertly from an area on the rug bathed in sunlight.

"Awesome sandwich," Jonquil murmured, her voice still shimmery.

"Mmm, the iced tea is *très magnifique*," he replied, his eyes shining. Their knees were all but joined under the table. She wanted to sing, especially after he leaned in for another kiss.

"Rita assures me love can happen twice in a lifetime."

He scooped a generous second helping of potato salad onto his plate. "You've never told me about your marriage."

She set down her glass. "It was all my dreams come true. I didn't date much in high school, you see," she acknowledged with a tilt of her head. "Gerry changed that. We met in college. Actually, from the get-go, it looked like we hadn't a thing in common. He was a daredevil while I was a spoiled brat.

106

"But we were crazy for each other. And we wanted the same things, you know? He was passionate about his work, and I loved making us a happy home. I didn't come from a normal family, so when I became part of his, it fixed something inside me that had been broken most of my life. I grew up angry, but after we fell in love, the anger went away." Her voice grew faint. "When I lost him, the anger came back."

"I see." He took her hand and rubbed her fingers soothingly along his cheek. "Jonny, I can't compete with a memory."

"I don't expect you to."

A quiet few minutes followed as they quietly ate their lunch.

"I really should be mad at you," she said, raising one eyebrow. "As if my schedule wasn't already nuts, now I've got to get to confession before Sunday."

"Me too."

He didn't mock her beliefs, he shared them. That bubbly feeling inside her was about to burst. She freshened up their glasses with a trembling hand.

"We could avoid all the hassles by getting married." He reached for the chips.

"I'm not sure how I feel about you, or I should say, about us."

"Not yet?"

"Claude, there's a lot at stake. There's Billy, and my project, and ..." She couldn't continue with those fathomless, black eyes staring back at her that way.

It got very still.

He broke the silence. "I've got something to tell you."

Oh, boy, she thought, taking in the subtle change in his tone, *Here we go.*

"This may be for the best. A friend wants me to consult on a project of his in San Antone. Timing stinks, I know. But it's a huge financial opportunity for me. It could make certain plans of mine happen sooner."

"Oh?" His news startled her. "Texas? Huh. I've never been to San Antonio, though I hear it's nice." She tried to short-circuit her rising emotions by averting her eyes and picking up her sandwich.

"Can your crew manage without you?" She took a small bite.

"*Absolument*. Fred, my foreman, is quite up to running the show here. And I'll fly back on weekends when I can."

She tossed down her sandwich. "How long would you be gone?"

"It's a big job, Jonny, a commercial buildout. I'd say three to four months for starters."

She fell back as if she'd been poleaxed. Wave upon wave of disappointment bombarded her, causing her to ponder whether she had totally misjudged this man. "In the marketing world, Mr. Chappel, I believe that's called bait and switch," she commented archly. Several minutes passed before she could trust her voice again.

"When would you go?"

"Well, I figure you're headed to Ireland this weekend, eh? May as well go now. I'm taking my Jeep so I'll leave tonight, tomorrow morning at the latest."

"That soon."

It got quiet again. Blackie yawned loudly and resettled himself.

"Look, we're boring the dog." He cushioned his chin on his fists, while tracking Jonquil's every change of facial expression. "What are you thinking?"

"Does it really matter what I'm thinking?"

She pushed back from the table and stood. "Why don't you ask how I'm feeling? Just when I get to the point of ... you do this to me? Your timing more than stinks, mister. It hurts." Her voice caught in her throat. "What's really going on here? Are you punishing me for not marrying you right now?"

"I'm doing this for us, woman. For our future together. Sooner or later, you're going to have to trust me."

She fought the urge to act out, either by sobbing or raging. They gathered up the plates and left-overs in taut silence and deposited them on the kitchen counter. Then she reluctantly walked him to the door, Blackie in tow.

"I'll call you when I get to Texas." She felt his hand on her shoulder, a buzz on her cheek. Then he was gone.

But not *gone* gone, she sternly cautioned herself as she closed the screen door behind him. Not *good riddance* gone, she prayed as she went searching for Blackie's brush. Not *gone forever* gone. Her eyes shut tight at the ghastly possibility. Just plain, ordinary, everyday *now you see him, now you don't.*

Gone.

CHAPTER 23

Small World

Jonquil stepped out of her office at eleven o'clock on the following morning, loaded down with her tote bag, raincoat, and briefcase. She paused in the reception area to make sure she had all her gear.

"Leigh, I'm expecting a man named Fred to drop off a couple of baseball tickets sometime today. He works for my friend Claude."

"Right." Leigh sat examining the cuticles on her left hand as though she'd never seen them up close before.

"Just letting you know in case I'm not here when he shows up. Might be at lunch time and I'm on my way to UCLA now for a lecture. I won't be back till after two."

"I know. I keep your calendar, remember?"

Her unspoken "duh" hovered between them. Jonquil recognized that Leigh was in a bad mood and, rather than inquire about it, kept chatting to obliterate the gloom. "They're for tomorrow's game. Since Claude's away, he wants Billy and me to use them. The Dodgers are playing the Cubs. Luckily, Billy's game was cancelled."

Leigh suppressed a small yawn. "Uh-huh."

"Oh, and will you please give him a parking pass if he needs one? Although, he'll probably just run in and right back out again."

"Right."

"He's rather shy. So ..."

Leigh rolled her eyes and lifted her other hand to inspect the nails.

Jonquil suddenly wasn't comfortable with the prospect of one of Claude's men encountering Leigh in this mood. "Maybe I should just wait for him myself. You've probably made lunch plans."

Leigh smirked. "Fred what?"

"Fred is all I know. Does it matter?"

"Not really. I'll be here. I notice a few people always wander in at lunchtime. You know, it's not wise to leave the suite empty when working people can only get here on their lunch hour."

Jonquil nearly fused her lips together in order not to yell. She was sick to death of Leigh telling her how to behave or how to dress or what the company rules were or how to better perform her job. On the other hand, Leigh's astute observations, like the walks-in during the noon hour, were pure gold.

"Is there anything I can get you while I'm out?" She wished her advisor could hear her now, making a valiant effort to be altruistic toward this ungrateful nuisance.

111

"No thanks." Leigh's gaze dropped to the fashion magazine already open on her desk so she did not watch Jonquil go.

As soon as Jonquil was gone, however, she unlocked the bottom drawer of her desk and snatched up her purse. Yanking it open, she removed her make-up case. She flipped open the bronzer compact and gloatingly, from every angle, admired her flawless skin in the mirror.

At ten minutes of noon, a remarkably tall man entered the gift counseling suite's reception area. He was so large, he gave the illusion of having to duck his head under the transom.

Though she estimated him to be under forty, he tended toward stoutness, baldness, and jowls. But his boyish grin engaged his entire face, making him borderline handsome.

He didn't need to wear a hardhat to flaunt his membership in the construction industry. The flannel shirt with several button holes stretched to their limit, faded jeans, and leather belt pulled tight under his beer belly were dead giveaways.

Nor could he have looked more out of place if he'd tried.

Leigh opted to play dumb. "Can I help you?"

The man stood opposite her and gawked. His gray eyes bulged as though he'd been struck by flash lightning. "Leigh? Leigh Usher? Son of a gun, it *is* you, isn't it?"

She eyed him up and down in consternation.

"Have we met?"

"Met?! You were engaged for about a week to my baby brother in high school."

She froze.

"FR-FREDDIE?" she shrieked. "Freddie Devine?"

"Wow," he murmured. "Look at you. Look at this place."

He gracefully made a complete turn despite his girth. "You must have a mighty important job."

"I ... uh ..." Underneath fresh make-up, she blanched. "How's your brother? What's Bry doin' these days?"

Her whole demeanor changed in a way that was never witnessed before within Clyde's precincts.

"He's doin' just great. How's your sister? Julie, right?"

"She's okay."

Leigh's mouth crimped to one side. She had spent part of the previous evening with Julie and they'd had a fight.

An awkward silence followed.

"Hey, before I forget, I came by to drop off these tickets for Jonquil Bloom. Does she work for you?" He handed Leigh an envelope.

Her face broke out in a smile that rippled down slightly past her waist. "Sure does," she sang.

"Say, are you hungry? Can I buy you lunch? You know any place nearby where we can get us a decent roast beef sandwich?"

"Let me grab my jacket and purse," she replied. "Oh, say, Freddie, do you need a parking pass?"

"Nah, but thanks for asking. That's awful nice of you. I'm double parked out front."

"I'll meet you out there in two shakes. Gotta lock up first."

"Sure. Wow, this is something else. Leigh frickin' Usher."

He sauntered away, shaking his head.

She leaped up, glorying in her six-foot-plus frame and sexy three-inch heels. She tugged on her suit jacket, touched up her lipstick, and without any qualms, abandoned the suite.

CHAPTER 24

Easter in Ireland

On Easter Sunday, the Blooms flew to Philadelphia. Their neighbor down the block who was Blackie's original owner kindly took in the puppy while they were away, saving Jonquil the expense of boarding him.

Jonquil saw a chance to squeeze in a visit with Billy's paternal grandparents, the O'Keeffes. After her young husband's sudden death, Jonquil had reverted to her maiden name, in part because when she was a little girl, her grandmother had told her to "bloom" and she wanted Billy to bloom, too. The party of four shared a festive reunion at a steak house near the airport. They hadn't been together since Billy was a toddler, though they'd kept in touch. Jonquil saw how much the O'Keeffes had aged, observed how they searched hungrily for their son's likeness in Billy's every expression as he regaled them with stories about his puppy and school. Much the same way she sought traces of her side of the family in his features. An impassioned environmentalist, her late husband had impressed upon her the value nature placed on layering. Yes, even to likenesses. When it came time to say good bye, she embraced the O'Keeffes warmly, grateful for the memories the visit had sparked. It proved a most gracious sendoff before the late evening flight to Ireland.

Was it Claude who'd told her to work on the plane? She slept the whole way there.

They landed in Dublin Airport at dawn to a cool, overcast day. After a few minutes in customs, a waiting van sped them off to a hotel where they would stay the night to rest and recover from jet lag. But first they had a heaping Irish breakfast of eggs, bacon and sausage, grilled soda bread, potatoes and sliced tomatoes, a smidge of both puddings, fresh fruit, oatmeal, and beverages in the hotel's cavernous restaurant. There, Jonquil and Billy accepted an invitation from a newly arrived Canadian group to take a private city tour that morning that ended at Trinity College. Claude had given Billy a new camera and he was recording their trip in pictures including ones of Jonquil fast asleep on the bus in between tour stops. Later, after a plain supper of soup and bread, which they could barely stay awake long enough to swallow, they fell into bed.

The next morning, they rented a car and drove the four hours to Killarney. Jonquil's exhaustion slipped away and her pleasure soared as she took in Ireland's marvels for the first time. The island's lyrical beauty spread out over velvety green hills and dells in every direction, interspersed with rock hedges, ancient Celtic crosses, and castle remnants. Grottoes dotted the roadsides instead of ugly billboards. Billy laughed at the frequency of sheep crossing the roads. She rather liked the feeling that she was traveling inside of a Yeats poem.

A light drizzle began to fall. Her son kept count of rainbows and elatedly pointed to one shaped like a circle. She switched on the car radio. The number of stations, some Gaelic, devoted to impassioned political talk surprised her, but the gabfest bored her son. She let him search until he found a lively music station. Their Irish roots were immediately stirred. She kept time by beating the steering wheel with one hand while Billy hummed along. It took a while to get the hang of driving on the left side of the road, but Billy was a big help with shouts of "Get over, Mom. Mom! Other lane!"

"I've had sore eyes for a long time," she murmured aloud as she rounded a curve. "I bet you've never heard that expression before."

"Nope." He studied her profile. "You look okay to me."

She chuckled softly. "They aren't really sore, sweetie. It means that I missed seeing Margo so much that it hurt. So, I say I have sore eyes."

"Hmm." Billy peered into the distance, apparently mulling over his mother's words.

Margo Bloom was waiting outside her trim cottage when they arrived just before noon. Jonquil's face lit up with joy at the sight of her.

Her grandmother, now in her mid-eighties, was noticeably shorter and thinner than when they'd last been together. Wrinkles covered Margo's face like waves on the Irish Sea. Her once long braid had been shorn, and she now sported a pixie cut. Her wardrobe hadn't changed: she still favored loose sweat pants and a bulky knit pullover. Two collies ran around the front yard chasing squirrels. The air held a clean, bracing fragrance after the rain.

As they emerged from the car, Margo spread her arms wide and Jonquil eagerly ran to hug her. Behind them, Billy snapped pictures. The two women clung tightly and danced slow circles on the sidewalk, crying then giggling, before parting. Jonquil then reached behind her, put an arm around her son's shoulder, and drew him forward.

"Margo," she said, raising her voice, "this is your great-grandson, Billy. Billy, meet your great—"

"Now, then," cut in Margo, "there'll be no greatgran' spoken here. 'Tis a bugaboo mouthful! Call me Margo."

CHAPTER 25

The Bronze Star

Billy flicked his eyes uncertainly at his mom.

"It's okay, Billy. Margo told me the very same thing when I was a little girl." She edged him forward.

"Now where's the kiss I'm longin' fer?"

Billy almost disappeared into her waiting arms.

"'Tis John all over again," crowed Margo over his head to Jonquil. "A handsome lad. No need to shout—got me a hearing aid in honor of your coming over. Inside with the pair of you. I'll finish introductions, then wet the tea. Your bags can wait." Jonquil heard a soft lilt in her grandmother's voice that her written correspondence hadn't revealed. It reminded her of Father Tim. What a wise gift he'd given her.

Once inside, Jonquil immediately felt at home. Familiar odors wafted from the kitchen promising a hearty lunch of lamb stew. Margo's handicrafts decorated the rooms, her colorful watercolors of seascapes lined the white walls. A fire burned low in the small stone fireplace in the living room. Potted plants hung down from the ceiling's wood beams. As always with Margo, the furniture was spare but comfortable. A fiddle hung on one wall.

Turning to the genial man who was taking Jonquil's raincoat and Billy's jacket, Margo said, "Children, meet me husband, Tommy Toolan. Tommy, meet me granddaughter, Jonquil, and her darling boyo, Billy." Tommy had a full head of gray hair, bright red cheeks and an affable way about him. They tried to shake hands, laughed at the jumble of outstretched limbs, then hugged all around.

Jonquil and Billy were shown to a small guest room off the kitchen that featured twin beds and its own full bathroom, a welcomed surprise. They quickly cleaned up. When they joined Margo and Tommy in the living room for tea, they discovered a dozen Easter eggs waiting for them on the coffee table.

"Margo, you painted these!" exclaimed Jonquil, gingerly lifting the lilac one with the intricate Celtic markings, then turning it around carefully in her hand.

"Aye."

"She's been paintin' dem tings for tree weeks," added Tommy with pride.

"Wow," whispered Billy. Afraid he might break one, he dropped down on his haunches to study them at eye level.

"Ah, Billy boyo, Irish eggs are for eating. Chocolate inside, now aren't they?" said Margo.

That night Claude phoned. Jonquil withdrew to the bedroom to take the call in private. When she returned to the front parlor, it was clear that Billy had brought Margo and Tommy up to date on his mom's love life. Not a word was spoken about it then;

however, Jonquil could tell that Margo was itching to get her alone. The chance came on the following day when Tommy took Billy fishing along with the collies.

The women sat in the kitchen while breakfast progressed to brunch as Margo kept adding dishes to the meal. Jonquil told Margo all about having dinner with the O'Keeffes in Philadelphia. "I wish they lived closer. So does Billy."

Changing topics, Jonquil said, "I like your husband very much. It's grand meeting him finally." She couldn't resist sounding Irish.

"Oh, Tommy's a boon to me old age. Owned a pub, didn't he? I fell so fast, I didn't know if it were the Guinness he was serving up or a love spell he cast on me. He's a tad younger, you see."

It was an opportune time for Jonquil to broach the subject of her own love life. "Claude is nine years older," she volunteered.

"Tell me about your friend Claude."

Jonquil described him and then showed her pictures, which were eagerly admired.

Reaching for her hand, Margo said, "What about you, dear girl? Do you love him?"

"Honestly, my feelings are all over the place. I do love him, Margo, but it's not easy. He's great with Billy, and that's wonderful. He's working in another state for a few months—didn't tell me about it till the very last minute. At first, I was mad. Now, I think the separation is a good thing because it gives me time to think things over."

"He's staying in touch with you, so he cares. You've been alone for a long time now, haven't you? Used to having tings your own way. Remember, no man's perfect. We women must make do."

They shared a light giggle.

"Dearie, I've been keeping something for you." Margo rose and walked over to a cabinet, pulled open the middle drawer, and removed a manila envelope. She placed it in her granddaughter's hands. Jonquil turned over the envelope and saw that it was from the United States Army. Her eyes widened. She stared up at Margo.

"What's this?"

"'Tis the Bronze Star your *feyther* earned in Korea."

Jonquil reached into the envelope and shakily withdrew the contents. She put aside the paperwork to flip open the oblong black box. The beribboned medal she discovered sat on a cushion of velvet. The medal felt cold to her touch.

Silently, the women reflected on their individual searches for John Bloom. Margo, still a Seattle resident back then, had badgered the Veteran's Administration since 1972, the year her son disappeared. By then, so much energy and attention was focused on the Vietnam War veterans, that Margo had trouble getting anyone's ear. She had contacted every bureau and agency even remotely connected to finding missing persons. Jonquil had joined the search during college, even traveling to Chicago on two occasions to hire a private detective. Nothing new was discovered beyond the information that a John Doe matching his description was admitted to a county hospital on the same day John Bloom vanished. Whether John was alive or dead remained a mystery to this day.

When Tommy and Billy came back with a string of fresh trout, the women had just returned from taking a walk. Jonquil showed her son the medal his grandfather had earned in Korea, then read the citation aloud:

> Corporal John Bloom, a member of Company F, distinguished himself by conspicuous daring and indomitable courage in a combat zone. On the afternoon of June 7, 1951, while pointman on patrol, his unit was ambushed. His commanding officer, gravely wounded by enemy fire, could not be moved. Corp. Bloom, Army Ranger, with no regard for his own safety, volunteered to stay with him when the unit returned to camp. He fought off and killed or wounded enemy combatants during numerous assaults in the next thirty-six hours, and sustained painful injuries in hand to hand combat with his bayonet when ammunition ran out. His bravery and commendable care for his fellow soldier kept the commander alive until they were duly rescued. His selfless actions and consummate devotion to duty are in keeping with the highest traditions of military service.

"My grampa's a hero!" cried Billy, eyes shining.

"Aye," Tommy affirmed. "You can be very proud o' him."

"Very proud indeed," echoed Margo pointedly to her granddaughter. "What he did that day should have earned him ten medals, for it went agin his deepest nature to stick and not run."

Jonquil felt resentment scalding her throat. How could her father stay by the side of a soldier but later abandon his own daughter when she was just a little girl, or not come back for her after her mother died?

That evening, over baked fish, green beans, and scalloped potatoes, Billy asked, "Where's my grampa now? Do you think he's still alive, Margo?"

"Billy, now, ain't me poor *mither's* heart aching to know?" she said.

"We should find him."

"We've tried," replied Jonquil, wearily.

"We should try harder," said Billy.

Chapter 26

Irish Songs

The rest of the week sped by with day trips to Adare for glitzy high tea at the hotel, the Blarney Stone—Billy's favorite stop, Ballynahinch for a tour of the famed castle, foggy Donegal, and Sligo for its sheer Irishness, shopping, and dining. Jonquil found a warm cable knit to add to Claude's sweater collection, while Billy bought a tartan dog collar for Blackie. Everywhere they went, they encountered warm Irish hospitality, inspired no doubt by the Agreement with Northern Ireland signed just that Good Friday, which hopefully would end the Troubles for good. Hope filled the air. The weather reflected optimism, too, giving way to sunshine by midweek.

While the touristy trips were too strenuous for Margo, she and Tommy did join them twice for dinner in Killarney pubs that featured local singers, dancers and ribald raconteurs. Peace was the common topic on everyone's lips.

More than once Jonquil felt the eyes of men on her. Some favored her with a bold wink. She grinned back at them, wondering at the same time what cute little cowgirl might be giving Claude the same frank overture.

Jonquil attended morning Mass at Saint Mary's Cathedral daily with her grandmother. They took daily walks along the river, chatting with neighbors they encountered along the way. During those times, she felt young and carefree.

On the last night, Margo invited over some of their friends for a sing. Each one brought a dish or bottle or extra folding chairs. Among their guests were other fiddlers, an accordion player, two drummers, a piper, and a tin whistler accompanied by their families. The cottage soon rang with music, stories and gales of laughter. Tommy lit a fire. Then he took the fiddle down from the wall.

The musicians favored The Chieftains' songbook but also performed traditional airs more familiar to the young American visitors. After the supper break, Margo said, "Give us a song, Jonquil, dear. Give us the lullaby, child."

"Sure, Margo." Jonquil could not refuse her grandmother anything, though her face flushed as red as Tommy's cheeks at the thought of singing solo. "Only if you'll do it with me."

They circled their arms around each other's waist as the bulging room became hushed. After the piper cued them, they began to sing in harmony:

God's blessing be with you, achora machree.

In sadness, in gladness, in grief or in glee.

From dusk until dawning, no matter where ye be,

God's blessing be with you, achora machree.

126

The last note rose an octave, hung, then faded into silence. Shouts for an encore were duly honored, during which the others played their instruments or hummed along in soft harmony. Afterward, Jonquil and Margo curtsied, beamed at each other, and hugged. True to such gatherings, Tommy hit the downbeat and the room clamored again with a raucous jig.

She could see that Margo was tiring, so Jonquil announced apologetically to those assembled that she and Billy needed to get an early start in the morning. The neighbors soon left, but not before showering the Americans with affectionate embraces and urgings to return soon.

Farewells early Saturday morning came too fast. Though Shannon Airport was under an hour's drive away, Jonquil still had the rental car to return, so she and Billy needed to get going. Tommy gave the boy a final hug and then retreated with the collies into the cottage to allow the women privacy. Margo pressed Jonquil tightly to her bosom one last time and then presented her with a bag of sandwiches, fruit, and sweets for the flight home.

"Tommy's tucked in a surprise, too," whispered Margo through her tears. "Keep singing, dear girl. Your *dah* would want you to. Now, off with the pair of ye!"

While settling in before takeoff, Billy said, "I'm thinking of changing Blackie's name. Would that be okay, Mom?"

Jonquil mumbled, "Um-hmm." She was only half listening as she opened her large purse and removed the bag of ham sandwiches.

"What's this?" She removed a small box.

"I haven't made up my mind yet what I want to call him," her son added through a yawn.

"Billy, look. Tommy recorded last night's music session for us." She held up the cassette.

"Cool." He twisted open his bottle of water and took a gulp. "Mom, I never knew you could sing like that."

"Like what?" She handed him a sandwich.

"I don't know, like somebody famous."

"Ah, go on with ye." She reached over to tickle him.

Smugly smiling to himself as he dodged her fingers, he unwrapped his sandwich while a memory claimed her full attention.

She was clad in her best dress and party shoes that her fussy mother, Pauline, had finally approved of that morning. Now she clung to the cold microphone stand, trying to block out the childish ribbons in her hair that made her freckles more prominent. She stood on the stage at school facing a full auditorium. It was her first (and last) appearance in the annual student talent show. She was singing a ditty with many choruses which her father had taught her about a long suffering Irish farmer and his three "high maintenance" chickens. The song made the audience, teachers and students alike, roar. But it also showcased her voice which her father deemed a gift. He had promised to attend the performance so, even though her mother was seated in the front row, she glared at the double-doors in the back of the room that never opened. Her angry demeanor only made her performance funnier. The song ended with calls for an encore. She curtsied low to hide her tears, then ran blindly off stage and straight into her father's arms. Overjoyed, she shrieked, "Did you hear me, Daddy?"

"Every word, Gumdrop!" He held her tightly.

"Ladies and gentlemen, please fasten your seat belts. We're cleared for takeoff," she heard the captain intone. Tears escaped down her cheeks.

"Mom! We're moving." Billy turned to her. "Are you crying?"

Smiling through her tears, Jonquil adjusted the seat belt before she bestowed on Ireland a loving last look.

CHAPTER 27

Name Change

I'm changing Blackie's name to Ranger," Billy informed
Ramon as the boys removed their bike chains. They had just
finished eating lunch at Ramon's house—chicken tortillas, beans
and rice, tamales and fresh fruit—followed by a noisy session of
video games.

"Ranger?" Ramon reared back his head as if to avoid a punch
in the nose. "How come, dude? I never heard of a dog called
Ranger in my whole life!"

"I'm naming him after my grandfather. I learned in Ireland
that he was a Ranger in the Army in Korea. He got a medal for
bravery."

"That's cool. But how do you change a dog's name? I mean,
you can't just say 'Blackie, you're not Blackie anymore, now
you're Ranger.' That won't work."

They stowed their bike chains.

"Nah. I'd ask Claude, but he's gone away."

"For good?" Ramon's voice rose in alarm.

"I don't think so. Him and Mom talk on the phone every night." Billy wrapped his arms around his torso and made smooching noises that started Ramon giggling.

"Ask your mom for help, why don't you. She used to have a dog."

"See, I want to surprise her."

Ramon studied Billy. "Yeah, right. Surprising your mom doesn't always turn out so good."

"Well, he's my dog." The boys mounted their bikes and pushed off.

Ramon pedaled ahead of Billy and called over his shoulder, "We could go to the library and ask."

"Hey, yeah. Let's go!" The boys turned at the corner onto Abbott Kinney Way and headed toward the Venice library branch.

CHAPTER 28

Who's Jack from Minneapolis?

Jonquil pulled into Clyde's parking garage early the first Monday after the trip, happy it wasn't her week to do her son's carpool. She wanted to get a jump on the day before Leigh showed up.

Gathering her purse, she smiled down at her stylish new suit purchased in Sligo, Ireland. Oatmeal in color, with a nubby texture, it hugged her body. Jonquil couldn't wait to show it off. She also felt a thrill of anticipation about what might await her after a week's absence. Hopefully, no complaints.

She guessed that mid-April would have netted a barrage of Mother's Day and wedding gift inquiries—with their array of psychological conflicts—besides the routine birthday and anniversary related calls.

Surprises awaited her. First, the reception area had been redecorated. The walls had been repainted from light blue to a lemony yellow. Behind the receptionist's desk facing the entrance, a montage of assorted gift box tops had been mounted on the wall similar to what one might see in the gift wrapping department. A letter was affixed to each box gleefully announcing the "Gift Counseling Department." The change in wall color focused attention on the relief's design. Jonquil had to admit the alteration was a clever improvement.

But when she reached the office, she was alarmed to find her desktop bare except for two pink message slips. One was from Leigh saying she would be late to work. The other contained a name Jonquil didn't recognize and no phone number.

Where, she wondered, were the stacks of product endorsement requests, phone inquiries, or speaking engagement invites needing her attention? Mystified, she turned at the sound of a familiar rap at the door.

"Rita! You're here early today. You brought me coffee? Awesome." At the sight of her former assistant, Jonquil's features relaxed into a grateful smile.

Rita looked vivacious, her henna red tresses brushed up into a becoming knot, with tiny curls framing her face. She wore a lime green cashmere sweater accessorized by a butterfly print neck scarf, soft and feminine. As she came closer, her scent for the day became evident. Chanel No.5. *Romantic choice,* thought Jonquil with a smile. Rita set a mug of fresh coffee carefully down on Jonquil's desk blotter.

"Sugar, welcome back. New suit?"

"Yes, you like?" said Jonquil, pivoting.

"It's very chic. Did you and Billy have a good time?" They both sat down.

"Oh, my, did we ever. I'm still a bit jetlagged," she added. "We landed at LAX late on Saturday." She palmed her mouth and yawned.

"Ireland was a treasure, and being with me darling grandmither again, simply divine." Jonquil sat back contentedly. "Margo's married to the sweetest man who took a fierce liking to Billy boyo." She blew on her coffee a couple of times before taking a sip. "Mmm, grand."

"You sound jetlagged and real Irish," said Rita.

"Still? Ah, the brogue. It comes and goes. Oh, I have a souvenir for you, a piece of the old sod, literally." Jonquil reached into her purse, locating a round green marble pin the size of a fifty-cent piece, which she placed on the desk within the redhead's reach. Rita eagerly snatched it up.

"Thank you. It matches my outfit today. I'm going to put it on right now." She fiddled with removing the souvenir from the card it was mounted on and pinned it to her sweater.

"So, what's up with you, pretty lady?" Jonquil leaned back and swiveled in her chair.

"Ha! Big Al and I get along like a pair of old slippers."

"Not old," Jonquil protested, gently setting down the mug.

"Not new either. Oh, but it feels so good to be in love again. I get my kicks cooking for two." Her smile widened. "And we dance after doing the dishes almost every night.

"So, how's Claude?" Rita asked, changing the subject.

"Far away in Texas." As she spoke, Jonquil opened the top drawer of her desk, frowned, and slammed it shut. She set the coffee mug aside, lifted the phone and frowned again.

"Did you lose something?"

"'Scuse my bad manners, Rita, but this is odd."

Slowly, she lowered the telephone. "After being gone a whole week, wouldn't you think there'd be a pile of messages waiting for me? All I have are these two, this one from Leigh saying she'll be in late, and this one about someone named 'Jack' from Minneapolis. No phone number, no message."

Rita opened her mouth to reply. Just then, they heard a noise in the reception area.

Both their heads turned in time to see the cleaning woman emptying out the trash, which gave Jonquil the idea to lean over and check her own waste basket. In so doing, she tipped over her coffee mug, spilling coffee on her lap and her desk.

"Arrrgh!" she exclaimed.

Rita sprang to her feet and called out to the cleaning woman to bring a rag.

"Now, sugar," Rita said, fingering one of her curls while crossing her knees, "there's a reason I wanted to see you first thing today." They were seated again, having sent the stained skirt up, at Rita's suggestion, to Women's Business Attire on Two for a quick steam cleaning.

Jonquil's eyes narrowed.

"What's she done now? Rita, if that woman so much as messed with one client, I'll never forgive—"

"Leigh said she was only trying to help you."

Jonquil grunted. "How?"

135

"She made copies of your questionnaire and handed them out to everyone who came in the store and to all the employees, too. Even Mr. Merrill."

Jonquil lunged forward. "No."

"She refused to give people gift advice over the phone. She told them they'd have to meet with you first and to call back for an appointment this week."

"Wh-what?"

"She turned back all brand endorsements explaining that gift counseling is about the process not the end result. I heard that from Al."

"You're scaring me!"

"Sugar, she ran her butt off just to keep up."

Jonquil's perplexity deepened.

"Why, Rita? She didn't have to do all that."

"I really couldn't say. But it's the strangest thing. She's different. Not nicer, mind you, nor meaner. Just diff—"

"Well, isn't this cozy?" Leigh called out from the doorway.

Jonquil stood up without thinking, and Leigh burst into laughter.

"Is that an Irish custom, coming to work in your slip?"

Jonquil sent Rita a perplexed look and quickly sat down again. Rita gestured with her hand, "Wait."

Jonquil's cheeks flamed. "I spilled coffee on my new suit."

"How awful! Rita, can we get it cleaned in house?"

"I already sent it up to Biz Wear, Leigh," replied Rita, staring straight ahead while giving Jonquil a quick wink.

Jonquil now grasped what Rita had meant. The words coming out of Leigh's mouth weren't at all smart-alecky and the tone was scarcely unrecognizable. Almost sincere.

Rita stood and collected her mug. "I need to go. Doors open in five minutes."

Jonquil thanked her again for the coffee. She snatched up the mysterious pink phone message before walking her friend out to the reception area.

After Rita left, she glanced around admiringly at the fresh new decor of the reception area and smiled. Lemon was a smarter choice for the walls than pale blue. The box tops added a touch of gaiety, too.

"I really like what you did here, Leigh."

"Really? I had it done as a surprise for when you got back. It's a gift I have, know what I mean? If I hadn't chosen retail, I might have gone into interior decorating. And guess what? You can change the wrappings to match seasons and holidays whenever you like."

Jonquil nodded. To hear Leigh speaking like a normal person felt disorienting. "By the way, who's this Jack who called? He left no message?"

"No. He said he saw you on television, that you reminded him of someone he knew in Minneapolis. But when I asked if he wanted to make an appointment with you, he hung up."

"Did he now? I left there when I was very young."

"This guy sounded older, I'd guess late fifties or sixties."

"I see."

Jonquil pursed her lips, wondering whether "Jack" was an old friend of her parents'.

She felt a flutter in her chest, almost like hope, rise and fade. Startled, she nonetheless tore up the pink form and let the pieces scatter in Leigh's waste basket.

"Well, he'll either call again or not." Then, remembering she was still in her slip, she said, "When you're settled, let's get caught up."

"I'll be right in," said Leigh eagerly. "I've got lots to tell you."

CHAPTER 29

Let's Fix Up Fred

S omething strange is going on at the store," Jonquil confided to Claude late that night when he telephoned. She was sitting in bed surrounded, as usual, by academic journals and her laptop.

"Tell me."

When she heard him moving things around at the other end of the phone, she wanted to fling everything around her to the floor and magically transport him to her side. The intimate tones in his voice made her tingle, sending pleasurable sensations racing through her body. She forced herself to stay on topic.

"It has to do with Leigh Usher."

"Uh-oh."

"She's been acting odd, even for Leigh. Rita thinks there's a new man in her life."

"Well, from the way you've described her to me, that wouldn't be unusual, or would it?"

She smirked at his insinuation. "Rita doesn't believe Leigh's ever been married but the lady does have a reputation. Her nickname in the store is Lady Lay. Rita says the way Leigh's behaving, all warm and fuzzy, is a sure sign she's in love. When she caught me up on how she handled things while I was out— even getting the office painted—it sounded too good to be true.

"Well, I know better," Jonquil muttered. "She's using me to get her old job back."

"Come on, sweetheart. Why not be happy she's in a friendlier mood? You don't want to get bogged down in store gossip, now do you?"

"Heck, no. I have enough on my plate, thank you very much." She adored hearing him call her "sweetheart" and pressed the phone closer to her mouth. "Miss you," she whispered.

But later that week when she found herself in a supervision session with Clyde's president, store gossip took center stage on their agenda. They sat in Mr. Merrill's fifth floor office drinking cappuccinos. Glorious afternoon sunshine poured in from the bank of windows facing the ocean. One window was slightly ajar, admitting soft, ocean breezes into the business meeting, as if taunting her to come out and play.

Mr. Merrill, nearly six feet tall, with steely blue eyes, gray hair and a direct style, was a kid at heart. A shrewd business man, his favorite occupation was testing out new merchandise before it reached the toy department. Miss Egnar, his smart secretary, had learned to give him ample warning so the telltale firetruck or game or baby doll could be stowed away before she showed a visitor into his office.

Now, however, Mr. Merrill firmly set down his cup. "Jonquil, how are you and Leigh getting along? She's already requested two extensions in the gift counseling department. I didn't see that coming, did you?"

"Mr. Merrill, I think she's up to something," said Jonquil.

"Yes, but what?" He gave her an encouraging smile. His openness appealed to her.

"She wants her old job back. Now. She said so yesterday, and she expects me to persuade you to give it to her. It's that simple."

"Well, say, I'd like to give it back to her. Two reasons. My wife is away from home too much doing the head buyer's job. And that particular position requires a young attitude. Has she been absent from work much?"

"Not really, except for the occasional long lunch."

"Just between you and me, her steady attendance usually means her sister is staying out of trouble. I hope that's true." He paused in thought. "Al tells me Leigh's made excellent suggestions in every department she's been in so far. Has your department benefitted from her presence and if so, how?"

Jonquil tucked a stray curl behind her ear before replying. "It's true, she has made some good observations and improvements." She gave examples and refrained from telling him about Leigh's annoying, personal criticisms.

"But you have difficulty complimenting her."

"I don't trust her."

"Then it would be foolish to reinstate her just yet. Let's drop the subject for now, shall we? Bring me up to date on how your work is progressing."

Jonquil proudly handed him a spreadsheet that detailed her department's activity, including number of visitors, their demographics, length of appointments, and outcomes. He listened attentively and expressed enthusiasm with her work in general that was drawing new customers to the store. He hadn't yet reviewed the gift inventory Leigh had given him but it was on his to-do list. They agreed upon her hours for the rest of spring. He assured her that after June, she could discontinue working weekends until October.

"How's your son?"

Jonquil reacted to the question with surprise. *Funny how everyone asks about Billy*, she thought. *Even people like Mr. Merrill and Dr. Mazziotti, who've never met him.*

"He's doing fine. He's invited me to Career Day at his school next week. I have to give a short talk about gift counseling."

"Maybe you'll recruit a youngster or two to follow in your footsteps. Be sure to ask Leigh about taking a selection of Clyde's cookies with you."

"I will," she said, hiding her frustration at being saddled with Leigh indefinitely. *When pigs fly.*

CHAPTER 30

The Choir

After Sunday Mass on Mother's Day, Ed and Katie Ryan stepped over to where Jonquil stood at the hospitality table, her nose in the church bulletin. Billy had departed with a couple of his teammates to have breakfast before the game. First, Katie inquired about her Mother's Day plans. Jonquil managed to answer the question while masking her fatigue. "An afternoon baseball game that will probably go into extra innings, and then a barbeque dinner with the team and families in the coach's backyard. Coach's divorced, so we all lend a hand. Oh, and Billy gave me this lovely corsage." Katie admired it, then pointed proudly to her own.

Ed said, "You're just the person I hoped to run into today, Jonquil. I'm starting up a new parish choir. It will be just for special liturgies. Our first 'gig' if you will, is the Mass on Thanksgiving Day." Seeing a neighbor out of the corner of her eye, Jonquil waved. She had a glimmer of where the conversation was headed and wanted to scream.

"Would you like to be in the new choir?"

"Oh, gee, Ed. Nice of you to ask me, but I don't see how I can."

The thought of taking on another responsibility seemed overwhelming, yet this invitation was hard to turn down since it was Claude's brother-in-law asking. It was even an activity she enjoyed. Her mind scrambled to find a polite way of telling him no. "My time's stretched to the limit. In fact, I have to rush off right now to work. Maybe I could join next year after I finish my project?"

"Only an hour and a half a week. Rosemary and her husband are in it—you met them at our house. Rehearsals will be in the parish hall, so parking won't be a problem. Music is good for the soul. It relieves stress. It's a healthy workout for the diaphragm and—"

Katie chimed in with, "Ed, honey, you're forgetting the most important thing."

Turning to Jonquil, she said, "You have a beautiful voice. The choir would be lucky to have you."

"Thanks, Katie. To tell you the truth, I've missed music." *What're you saying—nip this in the bud!* her inner voice scolded.

"Think about it," urged Ed. "Tryouts are this month, and rehearsals begin in August. But you won't have to tryout. If you're interested, you're in."

Say no, she ordered herself. Yet, she heard herself say, "I'll think about it."

"Great!" Ed beamed.

"What do you hear from my brother?" asked Katie.

Glad the subject had changed, Jonquil grinned. "Only good things. The work seems to be going well, but unfortunately he doesn't know when he'll be back again."

"He's a smart guy. He won't stay away too long." Katie winked at her, patted her arm and smiled. Hand in hand, the Ryans drifted away.

Chapter 31

Alarm in the Library

Jonquil sat at a desk on the first floor of the Darling Medical Library surrounded by her notebooks and textbooks. It was nearing noon on her day off from work. The various commentaries on Freud's interpretations of altruism had occupied her all morning. She gently massaged her eyes. Through a window, she spied the person responsible for making her do this exhaustive search, Dr. Mazziotti, approaching the library entrance in the breezy May sunshine, a female student in tow. He was looking particularly juicy in a dark brown suit, and laughing, his bright teeth a contrast to his olive skin.

She felt a fierce pang of jealousy well up inside of her toward the unknown student.

How could anyone dare speak to the Mazz so familiarly? Every time Jonquil met with him, she suffered acute dry mouth throughout the session and had to keep a water bottle within reach. Probably that other woman was a medical student and therefore favored. Medical students trumped graduate students every time, especially at a teaching hospital as large as UCLA. Then too, the other woman was probably more fun to talk to than Jonquil, younger, and not weighed down by the ordinary cares of raising a son alone, bills overdue, and getting a quirky dissertation on track. She watched them disappear out of sight and exhaled a long, frustrated sigh. And then gasped.

Was she falling for the man? Mistake, mistake, *big* mistake! In the first place, he was her faculty advisor and in the second place, he was a happily married man about whom there was no hint of scandal.

In the third place, almost an afterthought, there was Claude.

This revelation was quite unsettling.

Just then, the fire alarm went off. Students eyed each other skeptically across the wide, open room. No matter how inconvenient the timing, Jonquil never questioned the authenticity of a fire alarm. She shoved her notebooks into a book bag, grabbed her laptop and purse, and hurried to the nearest exit which happened to be the front door. On the way there, she overheard a librarian say, "Keep moving. There's been a bomb threat." Sure, right before exams.

She left the building and stood at its entrance, beneath the library's huge, iconic overhang as more students and staff streamed out. Among them was Dr. Mazziotti who walked straight over to her.

"What's going on?" he asked.

"There's been a bomb threat," she explained, feeling both grateful and exhilarated that he was there.

"Then, why are you standing here directly under this two-ton steel overhang?" She glanced upward with a shudder at the library's looming adornment. "Go home, Ms. Bloom." Not waiting for her to reply, he ducked his head and scuttled down the stairs, through the crowd, and away.

She thought about the work she had yet to do. Then she gazed at everyone else milling about, laughing, smoking, and slowly nodded her head with comprehension. *When, if ever, will my grasp of reality be as clear as his?* she wondered. She left, work unfinished, warmed by the knowledge that he had spoken only to her.

On the drive home, however, Jonquil mulled over how her crush bordering on devotion for the Mazz meshed with her truly romantic feelings for Claude. Not that she missed the closed off years when no one had excited her. But what did she have now? One of them was over a thousand miles away, while the other was beyond reach.

She felt excruciatingly lonesome.

CHAPTER 32

The Old Ball Game

Claude's news that evening that he would be spending the long Memorial Day weekend in California set her flagging spirits soaring. Friday evening after work he'd fly into LAX, rent a car, spend the night in Orange County, then see her Saturday.

"Billy has a makeup game. Want to go? It starts at eleven."

"I'd love to."

"Annie will be there."

She made her voice sound suggestive.

"Um-hum."

"Why not invite Fred to the game?"

There was a distinct pause.

"Your foreman," she added, hastily reverting back to her normal voice.

"Jonny, you do realize how risky it is to interfere in other people's business, don't you?"

"Sure. I also remember you telling me he's shy, so...." Jonquil eyed the water marks on her bedroom's ceiling and waited.

He let go of an exasperated sigh. "Guess it won't hurt to ask him. Give me the directions."

She rattled off the park's location in Santa Monica with aplomb. "If they both show up, we'll play it cool, hon. It's not like we're setting them up."

"Oh, no? What would you call it?"

"Uh … um—oh! Synchronicity. The eminent Carl Jung wrote heaps of papers about it."

Claude roared with laughter. "Good old Carl. Let's invite him, too."

Saturday, Jonquil awoke, feeling bubbly with anticipation. She hummed her way through her morning walk with Ranger (formerly known as Blackie), and she hummed her way through making breakfast and doing a load of laundry. She burst into song in the shower.

Annie, home from her cruise jobs until autumn, arrived just as Jonquil finished dressing. She looked her friend over and applauded. Jonquil wore a sleeveless white blouse, pale blue capris pants and blue espadrilles, Billy's Little League team colors. She fastened on mini baseball shaped earrings, tied a red bandana around her neck and spritzed on a smidge of Gamine.

Annie volunteered to take Billy home with her after the game once she learned that Claude was in town. Ranger, too. Jonquil felt a rush of gratitude for her friend and almost spilled the beans about the other invited guest. Fortunately, Billy interrupted their conversation with impatient pleas for help assembling snacks.

At the first sight of Claude in two months, Jonquil's pulse started racing. Dressed in a blue polo shirt, leather belt, tan slacks, no socks, and loafers, he dazzled her with his smile. It felt so good to be in his strong arms again, she momentarily forgot time.

But they had to keep moving. After bending down to give Ranger the two-handed scratching his aerial leaps begged for, Claude stowed the snacks and ice chest in his rental car. Jonquil added her overnight bag in secret.

Meanwhile, Annie put Billy and Ranger with their respective gear in the back seat of her convertible. "See you guys there," she sang out before pulling away from the curb.

On the drive to the park, Claude said, "What are we doing after the game?"

Jonquil smiled. "Going to your place? Where, among other things, you will serve me broiled lamb chops with all the trimmings as good as last time?"

Claude grinned broadly. "I've gotta start coming back every weekend. And Billy?"

"Annie's taking him and Ranger for a fun sleepover in Westwood."

"A win-win. And if his team wins today, a win-win-win!" he added, giving her left knee an affectionate squeeze.

"I'm feeling lucky already," she replied sweetly. They nudged shoulders simultaneously.

It did seem like luck filled the air as they parked the car, and opened a thermos of coffee at a picnic table before the game. Annie and the dog soon joined them. Claude kept an eye out for

Fred. They were sharing a rollicking laugh when Fred appeared, though not alone.

Jonquil's jaw dropped. Claude blinked rapidly. Annie turned to see what her table mates were gawking at.

Behind her, a very tall man was holding hands with a statuesque woman wearing Jackie O sunglasses.

Claude waved the new arrivals over while whispering in Jonquil's ear, "Looks like we should have invited Carl after all."

She snorted in reply.

"Here you are," said Fred, relief in his voice. "We parked way over on the other side."

"Surprise, Jonquil," sang out Leigh, clearly enjoying the moment.

Apparently clueless as to why the vibes around the friendly table had suddenly gone sour, Annie jumped up and introduced herself. Claude rose, too.

Jonquil remained seated. She could not decide what shocked her most: the marked change in Fred's appearance—for the better, she conceded—the sight of her nemesis by his side, or the fact that these two even knew each other.

Fred had lost weight since the day he'd fixed up her car. A ball cap concealed his baldness, and his shirttail was tucked into a pair of cargo shorts. Above all, the oafish look had diminished, no doubt the victim of a fierce fitness regimen.

Leigh wore plaid Bermuda shorts and a figure-pleasing halter top. A floppy straw hat, matching bag, and three-inch sandals rounded out her outfit.

What a mess, Jonquil griped to herself later as the group took seats on the tiers facing the field. All, that is, except Annie, who stood on the sidelines keeping Ranger company.

Claude pointed out Billy warming up to the others. "Yo, Billy!" he yelled with a wave. Billy apparently couldn't hear him. Claude reached for his camera and began snapping pictures. Jonquil excused herself and went to find Annie.

"Put Ranger in the car and come sit with us," pleaded Jonquil.

"Methinks five's a crowd. I'm fine where I am. But why are you in a snit, JB?"

"I'll explain later, my exceptional friend." Jonquil bent down and hugged Ranger before hurrying back to her seat.

Claude smelled so good, manly and fresh, sitting next to him, her anger quickly ebbed. Still, she remained perplexed. How did it happen that Fred and Leigh were here? Together!

"Have you learned anything?" she whispered in Claude's ear.

"Yeah, they met in high school."

She stared at him and shook her head, incredulous.

He added, "Leigh was engaged to—"

Just then, Fred on her other side leaned over and said, "I brought binoculars if anyone wants to use them."

Behind sunglasses, Jonquil arched an eyebrow. "No thanks." *Has Fred never been to a Little League game before?* she wondered, before chiding herself. *Leave him alone, he'll catch on.*

Billy's first time at bat began with a swing and a miss, strike one. "He's too tense," murmured Claude.

153

"It's just a make-up game, no worries. He's swinging a bat again and showing off because you're here." Claude smiled, caressed the back of her neck, and they kissed. Then they heard the crack of bat on ball and jumped up to cheer.

"Don't slide!" she cried out, leaning far over and gripping Fred's arm for support so she could follow Billy's progress down the first base line. But the ball was ruled foul, so he jogged back to home plate, waving exuberantly in their direction.

"He's as happy as Ranger is at suppertime," she crowed.

Leigh leaned past Fred and shouted to her, "Jonquil, Billy's absolutely the cutest little boy *ever!*"

"Thanks, Leigh." She turned her attention back to the game, flicking her eyes at Claude, before the sound of bat and ball contact again propelled them to their feet.

Jonquil kicked herself for not having paid closer attention to Fred when he mentioned where he'd parked. After all, it was his first time at Memorial Park, he lived in El Segundo, so he had no experience with the terrain. Nor of the rise in complaints about long balls converging with windshields on Olympic Boulevard that put a damper on home run glee.

However, Leigh Usher's unexpected arrival had thrown her for a loop. Now, after joyfully watching the ball disappear over the far fence, she didn't hear the impact. The deafening car alarm, however, was undeniable. Other parents in the stand exchanged "Uh-oh" looks but the members of her party remained oblivious.

Meanwhile, Billy tore around the bases, his ecstatic teammates screaming him home.

"Fred, where did you say you parked your truck?" she asked.

"On Olympic."

She patted his arm consolingly, then joined in the yells and applause. *No sense upsetting everyone until after the game*, she reasoned. Chances are, that ball could have hit someone else's windshield. She put the matter out of her mind until the game's end.

CHAPTER 33

Extra Innings

The very last thing Jonquil wanted to do after the game that day was to spend any more time with Leigh Usher. She mulled over her choices—whether to whisk Claude away or face the inevitable by accompanying Fred and Leigh back to his truck—and couldn't decide.

They were milling around and chatting pleasantly, she and Claude, Fred and Leigh, Annie with the dog, when Coach Hillman and Billy joined them. Billy couldn't stop wriggling he was so keyed up. Ranger jumped up on him and adoringly licked his face. Billy giggled and took over the leash Annie handed to him. From behind, Jonquil put her arms around her son, drew him close and bestowed a motherly smooch on his baseball cap. Claude slapped him a high five while enthusing about how well he'd played.

Everyone congratulated Billy on his home run and the coach on an exciting game. The Comets had won easily which helped ease the pain of a less than triumphal season. Jonquil quickly made introductions. The women greeted the good looking coach with pleasure. Coach Hillman firmly shook hands with everyone before moving on to other families.

Annie watched him saunter away, then emerged from her trance and said that she and Billy had to go, too, if they were going to eat before their swim. Jonquil kissed her son good bye and bent down to give Ranger an affectionate pat. "Have fun, you guys!" she cried, standing up again.

"So," said Leigh, anticipation evident in her tone, "now what?"

No one spoke. Then everyone jabbered at once.

Jonquil reluctantly prevailed. "Claude and I have plans, but we'll walk you back to Fred's truck first."

"My truck's at Leigh's place. I drove her car here."

Jonquil palmed her mouth and covered up a groan just barely by tagging on a fake cough. She also chose to evade Claude's inquiring glance.

"Well, a Lexus is just easier to park, right, honey cakes?" Leigh asked Fred in a flirty voice.

Fred beamed. "Sure is, sweetie pie." He grabbed her around the waist, and they lurched side by side out of the park. Jonquil reached for Claude's hand and followed the tall couple a few paces behind.

Claude squeezed her hand. "What's up?"

"Oh, nothing but a possible cracked Lexus windshield," she said airily.

Claude whistled.

They could hear Leigh's shriek from half a block away. Claude and Jonquil exchanged looks, then jogged to the scene. The windshield wasn't cracked after all. It was the car's rear window that the ball had smashed to smithereens.

Leigh bit down hard on her trembling lower lip, misery etched in her eyes, as Fred gingerly unlocked a rear door.

Then Claude made his move and lunged forward to carefully retrieve the baseball. Holding it high for all to see, he said, "Well now, that's some trophy!"

Jonquil watched him with wonder. Had he, during their short jog, prepared a one liner to amuse and distract her nemesis and save the day?

"Why, yes," chirped Leigh with a sudden uptick in her mood. "Maybe it's even the actual ball little Billy hit."

"Oh, in that case," added Fred, "he should have it."

At first, Leigh appeared unsure whether she agreed, but after a lengthy moment, she snatched the ball from Claude and handed it to Jonquil, and that was the end of it.

"You, Mr. Chappel, are a magician," remarked Jonquil a short time later when they'd folded themselves into the front seats of his rental car. "How on earth did you think up that line about the trophy?"

"I'm a big fan of Neil Armstrong." He put the key in the ignition.

"Ha-ha. Come on now, I'm serious. You saved the day."

"Jonny," he said, shooting her a roguish smile before heading into traffic, "do you think Billy's the first boy who ever broke a window with a long ball?' He chuckled. "I can assure you, my pop used that line more than once when I was a kid. *Mais non*, I wasn't about to let a measly baseball, even a home run ball, eh, come between you and me this weekend."

She leaned in and kissed his cheek. "Well-played, *mon ami, well-played.*"

CHAPTER 34

Work on a Paper

Jonquil squared her shoulders in front of her bedroom's full length mirror. She wet her lips, gripped her notecards, and nodded right and left, acknowledging an imaginary audience comprised of the Santa Monica Women's Club. Panting, Ranger sat on his haunches and gave the dress rehearsal his undivided attention until he felt the urge to stretch out, his eventual snores nearly drowning out her voice.

"Thank you for inviting me to speak today.

"The *bugaboos* as my Irish grandmother would say, are the gifts men give to women and women give to men. Please insert any relational context you prefer. For the purposes of this talk I will focus on male and female gift giving behaviors.

"Etiquette experts agree: the more intimate the relationship, the bigger the chance for success or disappointment. Bad gifts can be a sign that the relationship is already in trouble. Bad gifts can also do harm to a new relationship. Whereas, good gifts move the relationship forward to deeper trust and greater pleasure.

"A huge stumbling block is the reluctance by one party or both to communicate their wants." She took a swig of water and continued.

"This is where psychology comes in. My gift counseling sessions reveal that withholding wants is done more often by women. One possible explanation proffered by research is their wish not to have to be explicit about their desires.

"'Surprise me,' she says, but on a deeper level, her withholding behavior may really be challenging him to show her how well he knows her. Right, ladies?"

She anticipated subtle nods of agreement and paused.

"Like all of us, she acts out learned patterns of giving and receiving, often unconsciously. She hopes he will divine her desire since she imagines he studies her as thoroughly as she studies him. She consciously wants him to be as romantic ten years into a marriage as he was when he courted her with little foo-foos, and not turn practical. Hence the famous maxim: 'Don't give women anything with a plug.' She wants romantic sex not mechanical sex. She wants to be wooed again and again over her lifetime. For her, any gift is on a continuum of interactions that never ends."

Jonquil paused, hearing the telephone ring. She let it go to the machine. She reached for a pencil and inserted "from her beloved" after the word "gift" and continued.

"That said, a man will not necessarily welcome her input when deciding what to give her. He may dismiss cues from her, too.

This behavior is similar to him not asking for directions when he gets lost. His gift may not be so much for *her* but more a demonstration of *his* problem-solving skills, his resourcefulness, his clever ego. These behaviors may not be entirely unconscious. Women are mysterious. Yet, the obvious solution—ask this exotic creature what she wants or doesn't want, don't guess— goes against his boyish thinking, 'I can do this myself.'"

She imagined a knowing titter ripple through the audience.

"Her input, if it's sought, may be put aside as he goes on to choose a gift that best serves *his* agenda. It's not to say that gift giving means less to men. It's that men see gifts as a means to an end. What is the end? Is it sex? Fine. Done. Until the next birthday, holiday or anniversary. The process begins again with a definite goal." She let a moment pass to allow for anticipated laughter.

"What if he asks her but she won't tell him what she wants? He's thrust into an awkward position. She is turning the task of gifting into a guessing game. Men like games but not games that demean them. What if he asks her and she *does* tell him what she wants? The choice is his. Let's hope he can overcome his stubborn nature.

"She may yearn for something but feel she doesn't deserve it. That's a double-edged sword because, should she receive a gift of lesser value *emotionally* than what she desires, her resentment goes sky high. Getting to the bottom of why she feels this way is not a job for the man in her life. It's the job for a gift counselor." She smiled, recalling how Dr. Mazziotti had applauded her unabashed plugs for gift counseling.

"But he likes to be surprised, too, surprised by what he wants." She scanned the imaginary audience before continuing. "Does he tell her what he wants? Perhaps. Unless he too is into playing cat and mouse.

"What gets in a man's way of enjoyment is any gift that's a put down. He may enjoy a fun gift, such as a miniature basketball hoop for office use, but there's a line that must not be crossed. A gift that makes him feel stupid, confused or unmanly won't do. Also, he doesn't want any negativity associated with his gift. The prior experiences he had with embarrassing or inappropriate gifts may be an issue he can laugh off with the guys. But woe to the woman who doesn't take him seriously on this point. He is being direct—none of this intuition stuff for him. To sort this out, he may benefit from talking to a gift counselor." A glimpse of the wall clock told her to hurry up, she had to get dinner started. So, she flipped through the remaining cards to the end.

"Is it the thought that counts? Much preparation has gone into many an inappropriate gift. Your thought may be way off the mark. The so-called gag gift is a prime example. The emphasis is on 'gag,' not 'gift.'

It can backfire.

"Whereas, good gifts have less to do with thought and much more to do with feelings. Good gifts are solely for the recipient's benefit. The man who presents his wife with a new ironing board so she can press his shirts is gifting himself. The woman who gives her man two season tickets to the ballet he hates is gifting herself.

"These stereotypic examples are merely my shorthand. You may be the wife of a ballet fanatic or you may be a grownup tomboy who'd empty an expensive bottle of perfume down the drain." She smiled broadly and paused until she imagined every eye on her.

"Most of us are familiar with O. Henry's classic tale, '*The Gift of the Magi*', often cited as the gold standard of altruistic gift giving between lovers. A couple of economically distressed newlyweds put so much care into their Christmas gifts that they each sacrifice their dearest possession in order to please the other. And though the outcome makes us wince, we readers can imagine how favorably it will affect the relationship for the entirety of the marriage. We may not be able or be inclined to sacrifice as much as Della and Jim each time we give a gift, but we can emulate their motivation if we make the effort.

"It's the message of *I care* that transforms an item into a gift. Care involves thought, observation, and more. Care involves putting aside your agenda, your desires, your preferences and placing the emphasis on the gift-ee.

"Finally, gifts are linked to fantasies of who we want to be. We all, male and female, want to be loved passionately. The smart man says with his gift: 'I want to win your heart now and always.' The smitten woman, like young Mary Hatch in the film *It's a Wonderful Life*, says with her gift: 'George Bailey, I'll love you til the day I die.'

"Thank you."

CHAPTER 35

The Slow Onset

The presentation to the women's group was warmly received. Visits to the store and to gift counseling in particular soared, reinforcing both Jonquil's value to Clyde's and her own job security. Leigh continued as her assistant, grudgingly impressed by the increased activity.

Amidst the wedding season, Father's Day loomed. Jonquil steeled herself through the forty or so appointments pertaining to it. Some client situations which involved separations, divorces, and associated, unresolved feelings were trickier to deal with than others. A few clients were guilt ridden as expected. Nonetheless, she strove to bring each session to a satisfactory conclusion.

The conflicted clients were easily offset by the vast majority whose more practical, less emotional issue ran along the lines of "What can I get my pop for under twenty bucks?"

Personally, she hated the annual reminder—Billy too—but they didn't confide their feelings to each other about a celebration neither of them could enjoy. This year, not even their good friend

Father Tim was around to choose or make a gift for, or invite out for pancakes. Billy at least could appreciate that summer recess had begun so he didn't have to listen to his friends gab about their family plans.

As it turned out, on the morning of Father's Day, Billy woke up not feeling well. Jonquil skipped Mass and also cancelled dinner plans with Claude. *Just as well,* she thought since she hadn't the energy to be entertaining.

Claude was home from Texas for good and glad to be back. Though he'd enjoyed the time in San Antonio, especially the meaty paycheck, he had told his friend there to find someone else to finish the work. He couldn't stand any more separations from his fledgling company or from his *chérie amour.* Jonquil heaved a sigh of relief. They could pick up where they'd left off and move forward.

Clyde's company picnic took place on July 4th which fell on a Saturday. The store was closed so that everyone from administration to housekeeping staff could attend. The catered affair was held on the rolling back lawn of Mr. Merrill's spacious mansion overlooking the ocean. Besides food and a full bar, games, rides, and face painting were featured. Families and significant others were welcomed, so Jonquil invited Claude. Fred and Leigh attended but kept to themselves. Fortunately, there didn't seem to be any lingering grudge about the smashed car window.

Rita and Al couldn't be there because that was also the day of their wedding in Hawaii. The bride's two sons and their families lived on Maui so the nuptials took the form of a private ceremony on the beach. Jonquil's wedding gift to the couple was membership to Salsa City, a hot new studio for moderate to advanced level dancers in West L.A.

When Billy complained again of not feeling well after lunch, Jonquil made excuses and asked Claude to take them home. She called the pediatrician and described his symptoms—periodic morning headaches, an intermittent fever, the occasional stiff neck. He said to bring the boy over to his office where Billy received an overall physical exam. Blood and urine samples were taken to rule out infections, meningitis, allergies and so forth. The doctor checked Billy's tonsils, too. Finding no identifiable cause other than a low-grade fever, he prescribed antibiotics. They seemed to work for several weeks. When the headaches started up again, the doctor recommended Tylenol, less television, no video games, and rest.

CHAPTER 36

Billy's Eyes

Jonquil and Billy had big plans that Sunday in mid-August. The Atlanta Braves were in town and Claude had given them his tickets before flying to Oakland for a golf tournament. Only a recurrence of Billy's sporadic headaches would prevent them from going, but for the last three days, he'd been symptom free. So, as a sign of good faith, she'd consigned the thermometer and Tylenol to the bathroom medicine cabinet where she hoped they'd gather dust!

Jonquil lay in bed watching the morning breeze make the curtains on her three windows gently billow and recede. Like waves, airy and peaceful, now in—whoosh, now back—thwack— suctioned against the screened windows by airy currents that soon sent them flying again. Half in a trance, she observed their motion, the converging shadows the curtains cast on the ceiling and walls, sure that two of the windows signified Claude and her—the pulsations of love.

And the third window? Who was that? Certainly not Joe Mazziotti.

It dawned on her that she almost never thought about her advisor off campus. Her feelings for him amounted to nothing more than transference, a neurotic ache similar to the unconscious feelings patients frequently experienced in therapy. She was not now nor had she ever been in love with Joe Mazziotti! She heaved a loud, exultant sigh of relief.

There was no longer any reason to delay. Jonquil would let Claude know that very day that she was ready to marry him. Elatedly, she pumped her arms and pounded her heels on the mattress. She looked up again. Could the third window be Gerry? Nah, that didn't fit either. Then a single word popped into her mind: daughter. Meaning what? Her rapid associations grew incomprehensible until one dazzling possibility emerged.

Claude and her ... having a daughter?

Brilliant!

Outside chatty birds exchanged greetings, then flew off perhaps to a breakfast nook in a nearby tree. She yawned contentedly and stretched down to her toes. Then curled up for ten more blissful minutes.

A strange shout from the direction of Billy's room instantly woke her. Her heart contracted in reply. That timbre of his voice meant trouble. She leaped out of bed and clutched at her robe.

Again, Billy yelled, "Mom! Help!" so urgently this time that his voice cracked.

"I'm coming!"

She flew down the hall past the guest bathroom and linen closets on alert for clues. Did she need a weapon? Had someone broken in—was Billy in danger—was someone else there?

Why hadn't Ranger barked?

Just as she reached his room, she heard a heavy thud. Then Billy began to wail in earnest. She pushed the door to his room wide open. It was dark inside, the drawn curtains drawn to block the rising sun. She pressed the light switch.

"Mom?" he cried. "Mom, are you there?" He lay on his back in the small space between his bed and the wall, his legs tangled up in the sheets, his arms flailing wildly.

"I'm right here, sweetie. What happened? Did you fall out of bed?" He didn't answer. Mystified, she bent over him and saw the terror on his face. "Honey, what's wrong?" As she loosened the sheets around his legs and felt his forehead, hot with fever again, he said a most extraordinary thing.

"Mom! I can't see!"

Lifting all seventy-five pounds of him up off the floor in one ungainly motion, Jonquil propped him on the side of his bed. She knelt down in front of him and brushed the tears off his cheeks. Only then did she hear the dog bark from some distant corner of the apartment.

"Shush now, let me look."

He was flushed with fever again and shaking. From what she could ascertain, there didn't seem to be any swelling or bruises.

"Did you hit your head on the wall?" she asked and carefully patted the back of his head.

"Uh-uh, I woke up and … and I couldn't see anything so I thought it must still be nighttime but … but then the alarm clock went off, and … and my neck wouldn't turn … so I leaned over and then I … fell. My head hurts bad."

170

She yanked the coverlet off his bed and pulled it tightly around his shoulders. Placing her hand first over his right eye, and then his left, she checked whether he could see out of either one. He shook his head impatiently, mumbled "blurry" and grasped her hand tightly.

Ranger darted into the room and jumped up on the bed. "Ranger, get down!" she yelled, exasperated.

Billy flung his arms toward the excited puppy. "Let him stay, Mom. Don't make him go. Please don't make him go...." Billy's voice broke off in ragged sobs and his hands seemed unsure of Ranger's proximity. She forced down the fear rising from the pit of her stomach.

"All right, sweetheart, you hold him while I get the thermometer."

Maybe by the time she returned from the bathroom, Billy's vision would clear. But when she placed the instrument under his tongue and stared directly into his eyes, she saw how unfocused they looked.

This is not happening! she wanted to scream.

His temperature was one hundred two degrees. After phoning his pediatrician, who said he would meet them at the emergency room of UCLA's main hospital in Westwood, he cautioned her not to give him anything to eat or drink beforehand.

What to do with the dog? She coaxed Ranger into his crate. Later, she'd phone Annie from the road to come feed him.

She then drove Billy, still in his pajamas and wrapped in the coverlet, to the hospital, too anxious to wait for an ambulance.

UCLA, home of the renowned Jules Stein Eye Clinic, she thought, maneuvering swiftly through light early morning traffic. *Sure, they'll fix him up in a jiffy—how fortunate to have stellar help so close by.*

But two ghastly hours later, after numerous tests and eye exams, the doctors had no answer, and so Billy was admitted.

Chapter 37

A Trip to the Ocean

Jonquil had fought down panic all day but now, well into evening, it was lodged in her throat. Sweat trickled down her spine, her head throbbed, her legs felt weak while her pulse hammered in her ears. She felt cornered, queasy. Now, she couldn't breathe. Would she pass out? If she didn't leave immediately, she thought she'd die!

Unbidden, her hands jerked up and flattened in front of her face like two concrete barriers. "No more. I need a break," she blurted and seized her purse. The attending physician, neuro-surgical resident and ophthalmologist peered at her, startled.

"I'll go with you," volunteered Claude who had arrived late that same afternoon.

Unable to answer him, she gestured "no" vigorously with her hands.

Jonquil swung her purse over her shoulder, though he tried to stall her, and raced out of Billy's room, making it obvious she didn't want to be followed.

SHEILA M CRONIN

"Jonny, don't drive anywhere," he called after her.

But she didn't hear him.

To wait for an elevator wasn't possible. She raced to the nearest exit sign and tore down the brightly lit stairwell in a fury. The speed felt good, her mouth took in greedy gulps of air.

Run! her body thundered. *Hurry, faster, go-go-go!* Her haphazard descent landed her near the hospital's vacant lobby. Momentarily, she was stymied. *Where's the car?* A century ago, she'd pulled up to the emergency entrance with Billy. She had no clear recollection of what had transpired after attendants had placed him on a gurney, right up to that latest numbing consult with the doctors minutes ago.

Her car keys were in her hand! Someone must have given them back to her after Billy was admitted. Quickly she located the all but forgotten parking stub in her shirt pocket.

Soon she was seated at the wheel of her VW Beetle racing down Wilshire Boulevard, to the ocean.

And release.

You must be in shock, she told herself. *You shouldn't be driving.*

Twenty minutes later, she reached the ocean. At that hour—it was after ten—the Santa Monica pier still bustled but the beach was mostly deserted. A drizzle earlier had cleared it. She parked in the lot near the pier, removed her shoes and trekked across the cold sand. Familiar ocean-scented breezes greeted her like old friends but failed to comfort.

Instead, medical terms whirled in her mind like gnats. Intracranial pressure, swelled optic nerve. Toxicity. Bi-lateral. His

174

condition was bi-lateral meaning both eyes were affected. A CT scan in the emergency department and an MRI performed that afternoon in the hospital had revealed swelling but thankfully no lesions. More tests were scheduled.

Migraine was ruled out early. Great. One diagnosis down, how many more to go?

The doctors' questions were relentless. When did the headaches begin? Was the fever new? She answered as best she could. His pediatrician covered the symptoms and medications he'd prescribed thoroughly but admitted with a doctor-to-doctor scowl that he couldn't say what had initiated Billy's symptoms.

Repeatedly she assured the UCLA doctors that they hadn't been to Mexico in over two years. Philadelphia and Ireland in April—but the headaches hadn't shown up until late July. The medical team shook their collective heads—all twelve, at one point, including medical students. If some exotic bug had bitten Billy, it had left no mark.

They drilled her about his medical history, allergies, diet, sports, play habits, hygiene, toys, computer use, what tooth paste and laundry soap she used. Meanwhile, his temperature spiked to one hundred four degrees. He'd never been so sick.

They didn't want to give him any medication that might confuse test results. Instead they applied cold packs and started an IV. Billy cried, then vomited. Right in the middle of getting his blood drawn a third time, he fell asleep.

She and Claude ate some soup.

That was two hours ago.

She stumbled forward on the beach until the noise on the pier faded. After thirty or more paces, she halted and lifted up her head to the starlit heavens.

The immense black sky seemed artificial. A movie backdrop. Rather than soft or romantic, the stars looked impossibly far away and cold. Uncaring. Glitter out of a tube. Farther from the pier, it became harder to see, a cruel reminder of what had brought her there. Ten yards from the ocean she heard but couldn't see the bold boom and flush of waves.

She felt puny and forsaken.

"How could You?" she shrieked. This was the question she'd choked back since Billy's admission to the hospital that morning.

"I'm talking to You!" She threw down her purse and shoes and glared up at the stupid sky.

"First Daddy. You took him away from us. Don't deny it. You took him. Or *lost* him—huh? Then, Mommy got sick, yeah, they had to cart her away. And *she* died. I never got to say good-bye to either one. Then, my husband, my love. You took Gerry, too. You made me an orphan and a widow. Why?"

Tears dammed up since morning gushed down her face.

"But that's not why I'm here screaming at You in the middle of the night like a maniac. You know why I'm here. You've taken my son's sight. Why? He's just a sweet little boy. What did my precious son ever do to You? Ya big bully!"

She fell to her knees on the wet sand. "How could you *do* this? Do Ya think I'm made-a steel? I'm not! MAKE HIM WELL, GODDAMMIT!" She pounded sand till her fists throbbed. She screeched and hollered till she gagged.

176

But no peace filled the long silence that followed.

Soon exhausted, her fury reduced to sporadic shudders, she became aware of other voices in the distance laughing and swearing drunkenly. Abruptly, her mood shifted from towering anger to shrinking fear. She climbed to her feet and quickly wiped her nose and eyes with the back of her hands. The voices already seemed closer.

She bent down and groped around for her purse and shoes and started to sprint toward the car. After a dozen paces she slowed down. It wasn't wise to run across the beach barefoot in the dark. One could easily fall into a hole, twist an ankle, or trip over some discarded toy. It was dangerous. Like the drunken strangers. Scary. And she was already scared.

All at once, she realized that the raging anger that had sent her to the ocean had masked fear, her true reaction to Billy's condition.

Would his eyes be permanently damaged? The B word was unspeakable. Could he die? All those whispered confabs between the various specialists, the concern on the nurses' faces. Were they being frank with her or were they holding back?

Then it hit her—Billy's lumbar puncture was scheduled for six A.M. What was she doing at the beach? She must get back to him. Shield him! No wonder the doctors and Claude gawked at her abrupt departure. What had she been thinking? That a trip to the ocean would give her a cathartic release? Was she nuts? Billy might be awake now. He needed her. She must get back to her son and never leave his side again.

CHAPTER 38

High Anxiety

As soon as she got settled in the car, Jonquil removed the mobile phone from her purse. There were two missed calls from Claude. Heart pounding, she punched in his number.

When he answered, she blurted, "Claude."

"Where are you?" His tone sounded distant.

"I'm in Santa Monica. What's happened?"

"Nothing. Billy's still asleep. I got worried when you didn't call me back. I searched everywhere for you. What the heck are you doing, Jonny?"

"I'm sorry. I...."

She tried again. "I panicked."

He cleared his throat but made no comment.

Her eyes welled up. "I couldn't breathe."

"We'll talk about this another time, eh? Just come back now. Drive safely."

Jonquil couldn't begin to fathom her own behavior. With Billy so sick and vulnerable, how could she have done a bolt like that?

Not even telling Claude where she was going. But she hadn't known herself what she was going to do, she reflected, until spotting the Beetle sitting docilely in the hospital garage. Like it had been waiting for her.

Driving back, she tried to dredge up a similar situation. She'd never run away from home in childhood, even when her mother became incapacitated. She'd never run away from Margo. Nor her brief marriage. And when she relocated to Southern California, it was a planned move.

She'd run off the Poppi Blair Show last Christmas Eve for the whole world to see. But that was toward her son, not away from him.

Recollection of another recent incident made her hands clench the steering wheel. She'd run out of the restaurant on her first date with Claude in reaction to an argument they were having about Billy wanting a dog.

What was this startling new behavior about?

Her thoughts turned to Billy, his many scrapes and skinned knees. Fortunately, last year's arm fracture had been the most serious misadventure until now.

Of course she'd been there every time to dry his tears, apply Band-Aids, and offer consoling kisses and hugs.

Her consternation deepened.

"I went AWOL!" she hollered at the windshield. The passenger in the convertible zooming by on her right stuck out her tongue. Jonquil shouted curses and flipped her the bird.

Turning off Wilshire, she navigated the winding streets of Westwood, recalling how on the way to this same hospital's emergency room the night Billy was born, her driver had gotten lost twice. How was it possible she could have abandoned her son?

Those words had a familiar ring. Turning into the hospital garage entrance, a groan escaped her. "Oh my God. I went AWOL just like Daddy!"

The stark realization rendered her speechless.

A grim-faced Claude met Jonquil in the emergency room. She'd been gone over an hour and the main entrance was now closed for the night. She fell into his arms. "Honey, I'm so sorry."

She drew back. "Any change?"

He shook his head no while he examined every corner of her face. "Jonny, you look pale. You sure you're okay?"

"Yeah, just hold me a bit longer." His arms tightened around her, then relaxed.

"I'm bushed," he said and yawned. "Gotta get some sleep. I'll stay at Katie's tonight so I'll be close by."

She stroked his cheek where whiskers were beginning to show. "Yes, go. I'll be all right. We'll talk in the morning. Thanks, love, for staying till I got back." His perfunctory tone and kiss confirmed her suspicions that he was upset with her. Small wonder; she was angry at herself. They'd have to thrash things out, but later she thought, as she rushed to Bill's bedside.

The lumbar puncture procedure had relieved Billy's headache and stiff neck instantly. However, the overall eye exams and blood test results were inconclusive. Tuesday morning the decision was made to transfer him by ambulance to Children's Hospital in Hollywood. A neuro-ophthalmologist on staff there specialized in rare diseases of the optic nerve. Time was of the essence.

Jonquil went home once to pack up clothes and contact people only after Claude swore he would not leave Billy's side. They were polite to each to each other but their conversations were perfunctory.

Annie volunteered to keep Ranger as long as necessary. Jonquil called Mr. Merrill next and explained the situation. Kind and supportive as usual, he assured her that matters at the store would be taken care of, she should concentrate on her son. Was there anything he could do? The simplest questions baffled her, even those offering help, so she mumbled a hollow request for prayers and hung up.

Children's Hospital featured a special unit for the families and young victims of sight disorders. They were given a private suite overlooking Sunset Boulevard. Sensitive to her brand of hovering, the staff let her stay at Billy's side through eye examinations, CT scans, and more technical procedures, let her feed him, a thing she rarely did except for the infrequent bouts of flu, let her bathe him with sponges—when had she last done that?

Her fear was so consuming those first few days that she couldn't properly catch her breath, couldn't eat, couldn't sleep. Each day was one long emotional workout. Billy's room had to be kept dark day and night. The goal, a chunky Filipino nurse named Gayle explained, with one part gravity and three parts reassurance, was to eliminate stimulation. This meant lowered voices, no television, and limited activities with one of the Child Life specialists.

Infection seemed to be the culprit initially, hampering vision in both eyes, while playing havoc with his temperature, now up, now down, sometimes in the space of an hour. The clinical language—so heartless—boiled down, after forty-eight hours and nearly as many tests, to this: fever, cause unknown, sudden vision loss, cause unknown. The uncommon diagnosis of pseudotumor cerebri had been raised, but it would stick only when all other possibilities were excluded.

Billy had been admitted to rule out a tumor elsewhere in his body, meningitis, and other diagnoses. A day later, the medical team explained to her that they now believed hypertension, which had caused swelling in the brain, may be impinging on the optic nerve, the same way a tumor would, hence, pseudotumor. His eyes were not damaged. They now believed pressure on the nerve was the cause of his blurry vision. Though his headache had not returned since the lumbar puncture, the fever hung on.

The doctors proceeded with caution, hoping, they explained, to avoid surgery by medication that would reduce the production of cerebrospinal fluid. If they waited too long, however, Billy's vision loss could become permanent.

CHAPTER 39

Not Seeing Eye to Eye

W/*here's the gift in all of this?* pondered the gift counselor, who wanted to believe that everything in life was a gift.

How could something so cruel happen for a good reason?

Billy lay calm in his bed for hours on end, accepting the minute to minute turn of events with an equanimity far surpassing anything in the staff's considerable experience of ten year olds with sudden vision loss. Only when his temperature spurted did he moan and fret but even then, just drowsily. There were no hook ups to machines to impede him, only an IV drip, but the fever kept him in bed. His sole request was to hear baseball games.

The second day, a compact, portable radio turned up on his tray table in a brown paper bag. The anonymous gift suited his needs perfectly. That, rest, and the illicit hotdogs Claude snuck in. By the second or third inning, Billy would drift off to sleep, playing out the remainder of the game to his vivid dreams' content.

Not so his mom, oh, so not so. No doubt the staff expected more of her. Jonquil was, after all, a therapist too. Presumably versed in sickness, differential diagnoses, and uncertain prognoses. In reality, she was a mess. Lack of sleep, loss of bearings, fear, and love unable to produce a cure had turned her into a harridan.

She'd immediately grasped the meaning of rich language that staff entering Billy's room were expected to employ. "Rich language" meant describing to him in fine detail the contents of his tray, including guiding his hand to items, so he might avoid a spill, or the clear explanation for a staff member's visit, i.e., a vital signs check, or the announcement of a stranger, name, title, and so forth. She was vigilant about this necessary courtesy and took those who forgot out into the hall for a terse dressing down. She hassled the medical staff and blasted the cleaning people for making too much noise but worst of all, she brought her fears to his bedside.

Though he couldn't see her face clearly, he could guess its contents.

"Mom, am I gonna die?"

This was Thursday afternoon.

"Mom, take care of Ranger for me."

"Sweetie...." Her whisper became cascades of uncontrollable tears. Gayle, there to change his bed sheets, pressed her shoulder indicating the need for a private chat beyond his hearing.

That little cautioning talk hardly compared with the one she received from Billy's treatment team in the unit's conference room Friday morning.

184

"There's no easy way to say this, Ms. Bloom," prefaced the attending physician, Dr. Marshall, a tall Howard Hughes clone.

Bracing for the worst, Jonquil fought off numbing fatigue.

"He's got real guts for a kid his age. The tests and frequent eye examinations aren't easy. Some are downright painful, we know. It's complicated. On one hand, there's the affected vision and headaches, on the other, the fever. We believe they may be two separate and unrelated phenomena. Our differential diagnosis of pseudotumor cerebri never presents with the same symptoms in any two patients. Fever can be part of that disease, too. So, to be absolutely certain, the tests must continue and we shall need to enable Billy to stay as calm as he can be for accurate results."

Her hackles were up and rising. She rudely consulted her wristwatch. Billy's lunch tray was due in twenty minutes.

"What Dr. Marshall means, I believe," amended neurologist Dr. Whaley, a striking, petite black woman with a South African accent, "is that we all want what is best for your son." That told Jonquil nothing. She almost shouted, *Get to the point!*

Nell Weiss, the Child Life specialist looking smug in her "I'm Real Important" dark silk suit, eyed Jonquil covertly and nodded. So did Gayle, Billy's primary care nurse, her thick hair squashed into French braids, showcasing artful dabs of TGIF eye make-up.

A second and third year resident were also present. Rounding out the crew was Dr. Marty, the silver maned neuro-ophthalmologist, East Indian by birth. She'd gone on the web and checked each clinician's credentials and it was clear that Dr. Marty was the star of this show: a Baylor Medical School graduate with two Mayo Clinic fellowships, who had ten years at

Perkins School for the Blind in Boston and countless scholarly papers under his belt before transitioning west to Children's Hospital in Los Angeles. He favored wide Toy Story character ties under his immaculate white coat.

The meeting turned to a review of the case. Results from the morning's CT scan, latest blood analyses and other data were presented. The third year resident neatly summed up the findings, and focused primarily on Billy's response to the new medication.

"Which brings us now to you, Ms. Bloom," intoned Dr. Marty. "We need your help."

Chapter 40

Blind Faith

Jonquil glanced around the table at each of them. She recalled that just yesterday Dr. Marshall, in contrast to his formidable manner, had talked baseball with her son for a full hour. Nell's suit now seemed attractive, not intimidating. She discovered Dr. Whaley was a thumb-twiddler, as well as a focused listener. Even Gayle's Pollyanna face was puckered with concern. Jonquil needed to believe these people knew what they were doing, that they'd find the cause and administer the cure.

Almost a week had passed.

Granted, the headaches had ceased but Billy's vision remained blurred in both eyes while the fever continued unabated. She pinched the top of her nose.

One solid night of unbroken sleep would have helped her handle this confrontation. But last night, the nurses had been in their suite again to monitor Billy's vitals, or replace the IV bag, or adjust his blanket. And she'd gotten up each time to hold his hand.

"I won't leave his side if that's what you're suggesting," Jonquil said in a dull voice. "He's weak now. I must fight for him. He needs me more, not less."

She bit down on her trembling lip as one by one the others spoke up. A discussion of Billy's poor appetite, speech content, and listless attitude during games and activities geared to his condition ensued, balanced gently with praise for his overall cooperation with the hospital routine. He missed his dog. He wanted to go home.

Someone, Nell perhaps, suggested that a tutor twice a day might break up the monotony. Archly, Jonquil assured them that she could tutor her son. She'd made her living doing so when Billy was a toddler, but her remarks were politely ignored.

She lowered her head and listened. Murmurs back and forth argued Nell's point—too soon, too much—but eventually they agreed to start that morning. Dr. Marty did not join in the discussion. She felt his eyes on her and looked up.

"Your concern is understandable, Ms. Bloom."

His words pierced her to the bone. How had he guessed what lay beneath her frantic behavior? He stared at her intently and said, "He is not yet out of danger."

"So—"

"It is wearing on the nerves." He paused. "The many doctors, the repeated eye exams and other tests, the different medications. You son's condition is very rare. I cannot even promise you if or when he will fully regain his sight but for now … to help stabilize him, we need for you to be patient." A prickle of hope started up her spine and stalled.

"Jonquil," intoned Nell more familiarly. Days ago—or was it yesterday—Nell had remarked to her that sickness brought out the Jewish mama in all mothers. "We're monitoring Billy for depression. Although he's understandably sad and anxious about what's happening to him, we want to avoid it if possible."

The room became still.

At the mention of a term from her own discipline, Jonquil's defenses kicked in. "What do you want from me?" Her shaky tone demanded an end to the meeting so she could get back to him. Dr. Marty gestured that the other clinicians could leave. Jonquil watched them quickly exit the room, sorely regretful that she hadn't asked Claude to be there. Soon, just she and Dr. Marty sat facing each other across the table.

"I have some data here, Ms. Bloom, that I'd like to review with you." He addressed her differently than the attending doctor, as if they were equals. He opened a thick file and turned it around on the conference table so it faced her, then leaned toward her, his large brown eyes darting from the pages to her face. Whipping a ballpoint point from his front coat pocket, he pointed to the printed reports and circled numbers on them. "These are printouts of Billy's pulse, blood pressure, and temperature readings taken over the last week. See these spikes here and here? And again," he added flipping to the next page, "here and here? These were taken while you were in the room with Billy. These escalations are signs of agitation not associated with his illness." Her jaw muscles tensed.

"Are you saying I'm making Billy worse?"

He squinted his eyes as though trying to communicate with her telepathically.

Mutely, she stared down at the reports for several second. "And there's no other explanation?" she asked.

Dr. Marty said, "You're devoted to each other. It's obvious this emergency puts you both under tremendous strain." He continued to stare at her. "So now, if *I* were Billy's parent and *you* were his doctor, in light of this information I've shown you, what would you recommend that I do?"

Slowly, her glare softened to a nod of comprehension. "You want me to … go back to work?"

He patted her hand and said, "A break during the day will do you both good."

Chapter 41

Damage Control

When Jonquil eventually agreed to return to work, but only part-time, some of the tension stored in her neck and shoulders eased. She'd been worried because her gift counseling job paid the rent. Now, she could do her job and let the doctors do theirs.

She set up a schedule, with the staff's approval, of people to visit Billy daily. A neighbor, his regular babysitter, and Annie. Over the weekend, she would coach them about rich language. They could read to him, keep him company and be present at mealtime if he needed assistance, doing the things she'd done for him.

Next, she telephoned Dr. Mazziotti's office to cancel their upcoming appointment and asked to be put through to him. After a short delay, she heard him say, "Ms. Bloom? Is there a problem?" The familiarity of his voice utterly comforted her, less like a crush now, more so a trusted and close friend. "Joe, it's my son. He's very sick."

"What's going on?"

"He's at Children's with sudden vision loss. It started with headaches. They say it's due to hypertension. He has a fever, too. They're still doing tests." She struggled to keep her voice even.

"Sorry to hear that." His tone was grave. "Good docs over there. Have faith. Anything I can do?"

"I don't know when I'll get back to my project."

"Understood. How are you coping?"

"Thank you for asking." Her voice caught in her throat. "I'm scared."

"Sure you are. Ms. Bloom, a word if I may. You're a good mother from what I can see. Hang tough. Remember who it was who stood at the foot of the cross. She didn't cut and run like the rest."

Jonquil bowed her head. Cutting and running was exactly what she'd done. But she'd come right back, she wearily reminded herself. Sighing, she murmured, "Thanks, Joe. Bye now."

She phoned Claude. He asked about the morning team meeting and after supplying him with the pertinent details, she told him that she'd be going back to work part-time.

"Really?" His voice sounded doubtful.

"We should talk," she added quickly. "I need to explain something to you."

"I'm stuck in Orange County this weekend."

"Okay." She waited for him to offer an alternate plan. Silence.

"Claude, are you avoiding me? Because of my behavior the night Billy got sick?"

He cleared his throat. "Let's not get into it over the phone." She took some measure of hope from his use of the word "let's" and the fact that he did want to talk. But he sounded distressingly curt. They agreed to meet for breakfast Monday at a diner on the Third Street Mall around the corner from Clyde's.

Jonquil went home, did a load of laundry, paid bills, rescheduled their dental appointments, got gas and slept through dinner. That night she returned to the hospital. The usually bustling floor had shifted into weekend mode by the time she arrived.

"Mom, did you buy me this neat talking watch?" Billy greeted her. "Thanks!" He was sitting up, visible in a table lamp's soft light, and smiling. A dramatic improvement.

"No, sweetie, I didn't. How are you feeling tonight?" Jonquil bent over to kiss him, and felt his forehead. Normal. She then sat down on the side of the bed. "Let me clean your face." She wetted a tissue and gently wiped away a smudge on his cheek.

"Listen, it tells me the time." He sounded animated and more like his usual self than he had since admission. He couldn't yet focus properly so he used his thumb to locate a button on the watch which he squeezed. A male voice announced the date and time.

While he prattled on, she thought back on the other gifts that had arrived in the same fashion, in paper bags left anonymously on his food tray. The portable radio with the cassette player. That gift had proved a godsend when Billy couldn't sleep. She'd brought from home the tape Tommy Toolan had made of Margo and her singing the Irish lullaby. Playing it over and over had calmed him down. Next was the cunning, oversized Rubik's Cube with the raised bumps on the exterior. When he was too listless to do anything else, his fingertips memorized the bumps so he could twist the sections into harmony. Now this watch that was "cool" instead of a reminder of his visual problem. Where were these thoughtful, age appropriate gifts coming from? She intended to find out.

The nurse came to settle in Billy for the night. Dr. Marshall and the residents stopped by and updated her on Billy's progress but would not yet give a discharge date. Disappointed, Jonquil prepared for bed, but, like every other night since his admission, sleep never came.

CHAPTER 42

Soul Search

The daily drive back and forth to the hospital from Clyde's increased Jonquil's fatigue. She had spotted a small chapel near the hospital on one of her commutes and asked Annie to sit with Billy while she ducked out to Sunday Mass. A walk, if nothing else, would be good exercise.

She barely heard a word of the homily. In queue for communion, Jonquil felt a dull ache, part angst, part exhaustion, from head to toe. Her body was functioning on automatic pilot. She followed the person in front of her up the main aisle and found herself kneeling down at a communion rail, a thing she had rarely done. A few parishes, like this one, clung to the old ways at certain Masses for the sake of older parishioners. She leaned forward, her forearms touching the cold marble railing, fingers interlaced in front of her, knees pressing into the velvet cushion, head bowed, gaze falling on the polished sacristy floor below. For a moment, her soul quieted until she remembered why she was there and not at her parish church.

Billy's vision remained blurred. Her powers of insight had darkened, too. She couldn't focus, so prevalent was her fear that Billy might still go blind. How would they cope?

One day while downing a cup of minestrone soup in the hospital cafeteria, through the wide doorway she spotted a woman near her age and a boy near Billy's age in the gift shop across the lobby atrium. The mother, she assumed, was calmly describing T-shirts to her blind son, no doubt with the aid of rich language. He laughed, then wrinkled his brow at her next remark. *Had he been blind from birth?* wondered Jonquil. *Or had his vision loss occurred later and he was straining to recall a shape, a color? Would she ever be as brave as that mother?* Something in Jonquil had recoiled. Fear fused with anger, the same feeling she had that night a week ago when she'd bolted to the ocean. She would not run away again but she needed to talk out her anger toward God with someone. To pierce her own darkness, she needed the rich language of a spiritual guide.

"Body of Christ," a voice above her murmured, holding the host.

"Amen," she murmured. She put the host in her mouth and stood.

Instantly she was caught in the pre- and post-communion traffic jam that cut short any pretense of piety but rather demanded fast decisions—*duck behind this person—follow that person who'd knelt beside her—why were they blocking the obvious lane? Take initiative, oops, merging traffic—slow down behind the woman with the cane, watch out for stragglers coming in the opposite direction, now, down the side aisle—yikes, is that woman actually wearing hair curlers in church? Pay attention!*

"Phew," she grunted to herself when she finally knelt down again in her pew. Not once in the journey back to her seat did she have the presence of mind to pray "I love You, Lord," or anything loving. She barely remembered to swallow the host.

The Mass concluded with a series of actions by rote. Stand, kneel for the final blessing, and then stand in place until the priest had left the altar. Jonquil knelt down one last time trying to recapture the peace she'd felt briefly at the communion rail. But it had vanished somewhere during her disjointed trek down the side aisle.

Help me, Lord, she implored silently, *I'm in the dark.*

She stared at the tabernacle, then exited the pew, genuflected, and quietly left the church.

CHAPTER 43

Breakfast with Claude

Monday morning when Jonquil spotted Claude at the diner through a front window, relief flooded her body like a cresting river. He buzzed her cheek and took her by the elbow, saying, "Let's find a quiet place in back."

The diner was huge. Mouthwatering smells of bacon, eggs, toast, and roasted potatoes permeated the air.

While many of the red Formica tables were already occupied by the before- work crowd, a booth steps away from the kitchen afforded them privacy. A waitress brought them coffee and menus.

"Do you know what you want?" asked the waitress.

"Give us a few minutes, please," said Claude glancing up.

"Sure thing," she said and hustled off.

Claude leaned back in his seat. "How was Billy when you left him this morning?"

"He's getting better. The doctors are amazed," she said while unfolding her napkin. "A neighbor is with him now. Oh, and someone keeps leaving him gifts in brown paper bags. It isn't you, right?" she asked, placing the napkin on her lap.

"Right. Now, Jonny, what is it you want to tell me?"

Jonquil licked her lips and bit her lower lip. A busboy brought water.

She gazed into Claude mesmerizing eyes and cracked a smile. "I blew it."

He scoffed and settled more comfortably in his chair. "I know. You really blew it. Why?"

The waitress returned. "Ready yet?"

Jonquil glanced at the menu while Claude spoke up. "I'll have the special with rye toast and sausage."

"I'll have the same," Jonquil murmured, her eyes never leaving his face. "Except, with cinnamon toast and Canadian bacon." The waitress took their menus and scooted away.

Their coffee and then their breakfasts got cold as Jonquil revisited the day Billy became ill. How she'd woken up so blissfully happy that morning, ready to tell Claude that they could become engaged. Claude inclined his head, the only sign he gave that this was significant news. But her joy died the instant Billy had cried out. She described how the excruciatingly long day at UCLA had taken its toll. How she'd fought down the panic, for Billy's sake, until she no longer could breathe. How she'd fled, after finding her keys and her car. How she'd needed to be alone.

"You couldn't tell me?"

"No, not while it was happening."

He rubbed the back of his neck. "I don't know what to say. You've done this to me twice. It's not right, Jonny."

The noise of the diner seemed to magnify, increasing her discomfort.

"Can we leave? I don't like having this talk with other people around." He signaled to the waitress for the check.

Back on the street, they slid on their sunglasses and by mutual agreement walked west three blocks to the park. It was a perfect day by Santa Monica standards: mild and radiant. People hurried in the opposite direction toward their jobs. An ambulance, lights flashing and siren screaming, roared past them and turned onto Ocean Boulevard. Her thoughts instantly went to Billy. As if he read her mind, Claude reached for her hand and squeezed it.

They found an empty bench and sat down. Below them, rush hour traffic hurtled along Pacific Coast Highway but did not distract from the breathtaking sprawl of the sand and ocean. Sailboats could be seen in the distance. Meanwhile, around them sea gulls and pigeons vied for their attention. She was grateful she felt no lingering angst about seeing the ocean again. Squaring her shoulders, she turned to him.

"Claude, have you ever had a panic attack?"

He spread his arms wide on the back of the bench, filled his lungs with sea air and exhaled slowly through his mouth.

"*Mais non.*"

"Then, you can't understand. At first I couldn't breathe so I ran. Next thing I knew, it felt like I was being grabbed by giant hands and forcibly expelled from the hospital."

She touched on the drive to the beach, her anger at God that night, the voices in the dark, and the ride home during which she faced the awful realization that she had run away like her father.

"Like you did in the restaurant on our first date? Or like your son did on Christmas Eve?"

Her throat immediately tightened. "Please leave Billy out of this. This is between you and me."

"True. Yet, it was me you left your son with in the hospital, *oui?*"

"I don't need your goading this morning, mister." She stood, arms folded across her chest and began to pace. After a few steps, she wheeled around and glared at him. "My God, can't you see the pressure I'm under? Talk about being blind." At the word, she covered her mouth, horrified.

He glanced away from her toward the pier, his lips a tight line.

Tears threatened but she willed herself to not cry. "I'm feeling a bit overwhelmed, Claude."

"Is that why the doctors asked you to go back to work?"

She nodded. He interrupted her train of thought. "Come, sit."

Jonquil sat down beside him, removed her sunglasses and turned to him. "You know, you aren't exactly perfect either. You get real passive aggressive when you don't get your way. That's almost as bad as—"

"What are you talking about?" He scowled and folded his arms tightly across his chest.

"The first time I noticed it was when we'd begun dating and you wanted to spend the weekend with me and Billy and I said no. You couldn't tell me you were mad at me for not letting you join us, so you just stayed away. Admit it."

"Ancient history, woman."

"And Texas. You—"

"Don't even go there," he broke in. "I went to Texas to make money to fast track our future together."

"Maybe so, but then how about this weekend? You hid down in Orange County rather than face me and clear the air, didn't you?"

A few seconds passed in silence. "*Oui.*"

She glanced at her watch and then at the horizon. "Thanks for not denying it. At least I'm not completely paranoid."

He grunted. "I feel like you don't want to be a couple. You try to handle everything by yourself and leave me out in the cold. It frustrates me."

His words brought back her grandmother Margo's wise observation that Jonquil, after years being a single mother, was used to having her own way. Could she change?

Claude took off his sunglasses and leveled his gaze at her. "Look, I'm in love with you, Jonquil Bloom, freckles, freak-outs and all. But when you ditched me that night and I couldn't find you and you wouldn't pick up your phone, it was obvious you still don't trust me. What's it going to take?"

"Ah, Claude, with Billy so sick now, I can't focus on anything else."

He huffed and studied the pavement. "You don't have to do it all alone." He blinked and his eyelashes glanced off his cheeks.

"I know that. I've asked you for tons of help."

He grunted. "When Billy first got sick, I told myself this was no time to expect you to make a commitment. How could you? How could I with the way you reacted?

"Now you say that right before it happened you were on the verge of us getting engaged? That's big news to me. You like to psychoanalyze me, don't you—well, two can play that game. All this running away is because you don't have an anchor. Let me be your anchor *no matter what* the future holds so we can become a family. I'm so damn ready." His voice sounded husky.

She scooted over, drew him to her and sweetly kissed his cheek, his chin, the tip of his nose, then urgently kissed his mouth until he willingly returned her embrace. Behind them, a lusty wolf whistle from someone tooling along on a bike made her pull away. They eyed each other like sheepish teenagers.

They held each other's gaze for a long moment. He murmured, "Let's get married. Let's do whatever it takes to make that happen."

She clung to him tightly and whispered in his ear, "I'm getting there.

CHAPTER 44

Back to Work

After Claude and Jonquil parted that morning, she walked to her office but then didn't know where to start. She stood over her desk lost in thought until discreet knocks made her aware of someone observing her in the doorway.

Rita.

"Sugar, oh, sugar!" The two women ran to the middle of her office and hugged. Jonquil was treated to the additional embrace of Rita's spicy Monday fragrance and relished its familiarity.

"I'm so sorry about Billy. What're you doing here?" Tears glistened on Rita's cheeks.

"The doctors said I was making him anxious. They asked me to go back to work part-time."

Rita twittered, dabbing her eyes with a tissue. "Ha! Bet it was you making those high and mighty doctors nervous, you being so smart and all." She noisily blew her nose.

Jonquil hung her head. "Not this time."

"I gotta get back on the floor. Pre-Labor Day sale begins today. Can't do lunch but maybe a coffee break later? Your department's been closed—Al can tell you what's going on." Rita lowered her voice. "FYI, Lady Leigh's out in the reception area waiting to see you."

"What does she want?" mouthed Jonquil. Her issues with Leigh Usher seemed like so much nonsense now.

Rita's hands fluttered. "Search me. She let me go first. Want me to get rid of her?"

But before Jonquil could answer, Leigh came barging in. "My turn now."

The perfume sales associate mumbled words along the lines of catch you later and scurried away. Leigh pointedly shut the door behind her and locked it. She arched one eyebrow in Jonquil's direction, then wasted no time hastening over to her desk.

"How's your son? Is he better now? Are you just visiting or are you back here for good?"

Her rapid-fire questions and strange demeanor put Jonquil on guard. *What now?* she wondered, *Is this about her job or mine?*

"Leigh, please have a seat. Billy's still in the hospital but he's much better. Thanks for asking." She narrowed her eyes at the former head buyer. "You weren't by chance at the hospital this week, were you? Did you drop off anonymous gifts to Billy in brown paper bags?"

"Brown paper bags?" Leigh gave her shoulders a saucy twitch like she was fending off noxious fumes. "Not hardly. Sit down, will you? You're the only person I can turn to."

That remark struck Jonquil as highly improbable but she dutifully lowered herself into her chair. "What's wrong?"

"This is all your fault."

"What's wrong, Leigh?" she repeated testily

"It's Fred—my sister—me. It's a disaster."

Jonquil scratched an imaginary itch on her forehead in an effort to slow things down. Then, barely suppressing a groan, she folded her hands on her desktop. "I'm listening."

Leigh shot to her feet. She was noticeably agitated, pacing while fingering a heavy silver pendant dangling between her breasts. Jonquil was reminded of a stethoscope which made her wonder what Billy was doing at that moment. Catching her mind wandering, she forced herself to concentrate on the conversation at hand.

"I know you have a big problem right now, but so do I. I can't believe what's happening. I think the jerk's always been in love with my sister. He was only dating me to get to her. He was using me. And you know how I loathe that feeling."

Jonquil lightly strummed her fingertips on the desk to cloak her unease. Leigh's last statement seemed to harbor a threat. She longed to throw open the door at the far end of the room and put as much distance between the two of them as possible. On the other hand, the former head buyer seemed to be showing— between quirky accusations—a well-hidden vulnerable side that piqued her curiosity.

She'd have to set ground rules first.

"Leigh, sit down. We can't have a serious discussion with you roaming around like a nomad." Leigh complied.

"Now, begin at the beginning. You have my undivided attention for—"

She had the presence of mind to consult her watch. "Fifteen minutes. Then I have to call the hospital."

Leigh plunged into a description of how she and Bryan, Fred's younger brother, were once high school sweethearts. They'd become engaged secretly when she thought she was pregnant. A week later when it turned out she wasn't, they'd broken off their engagement with vast relief on both sides. Besides Leigh and Bryan, only Leigh's older sister and Fred, who were both seniors at the same school, ever knew.

Jonquil's mind warp speeded ahead to a ridiculous scenario: Was Fred, Claude's genial foreman, threatening to blackmail Leigh?

But Leigh cut short her musings. "So, see? It's your fault. If you hadn't needed those baseball tickets to be dropped off, Fred would never have come to Clyde's and found me here that day and gotten the impression that I was your boss."

At which point Leigh burst into tears!

Reflexively, Jonquil picked up a flower-print box of tissues on her desk. She propped it within Leigh's reach, mystified that the woman was confiding in her but feeling more empathy than she might have before her son's illness.

"Leigh, I'd like to help but really, this is so personal, wouldn't you be better off talking to a girlfriend?"

"I don't have girlfriends," snarled Leigh. "The store's my whole life."

"Then—wait." Jonquil mentally rewound their conversation back to the moment before Leigh's tears began and frowned. "Fred thought you were my boss?"

"Yeah," Leigh barked, eyes ablaze. "He did, and he was damn proud of me. I completely fell for the guy when I saw that look of adoration on his face. An old friend who knew everything about me, you know? He even knew that Julie had turned to drugs in college.

"I'm so sick of travel, sick of airports and hotels, sick of customs snafus, sick of trying to keep up with an industry *that changes every damn season!* I can't tell you how good it felt to be with someone from home.

"Oh, we started dating that same day. Remember, when we showed up at Billy's baseball game together? I'll never forget the look on your face. Ha!"

I remember, thought Jonquil, *since you spoiled my plans to get Fred together with Annie.* But she'd had to let go of that agenda. Now, hearing Leigh's perspective on Fred, maybe it was for the best.

"Everything was going fine till he ran into my sister at my apartment. Julie told him the truth about my job status. She turned him away from me. Since then he hasn't called. They're dating now, I'm sure of it, and I—I'm mis-er-a-ble." Her story ended in a wail.

"I'm so sorry, Leigh."

She felt detached watching Leigh shed tears in her office. It was similar to having spied a driver in the car next to her on Abbott Kinney Way balling her eyes out one day. Jonquil told

208

herself that that driver had been weeping for joy and then had changed lanes.

"The only thing I know for sure about love is, if it's meant to be, it will be."

"What?" squeaked Leigh. "Is that all you can say?"

"There are no guarantees," Jonquil went on, stuck in a list of platitudes. "Let Fred go. If he loves you, he'll come back to you. If not, then, better to face it and get on with your life. Now, pull yourself together," she said firmly. "Get busy. Find things to do. Take a trip or—"

"Jonquil," Leigh shouted, "you don't get it. This time I really am pregnant!"

CHAPTER 45

Baby, Baby, Baby

The insistent sound of knuckles hitting the other side of the door spared Jonquil from having to voice her reaction. A muffled voice could be heard over the din, followed by the doorknob being rattled back and forth. "Ms. Bloom, are you in there?"

"It's Al Yates," hissed Leigh. "You can't tell a soul what I told you."

"I won't, Leigh."

Leigh crossed the carpet, unlocked the door and tugged it open. She gushed at her colleague effusively as though his noisy intrusion was the high point of her day.

"Hello, Al. Say, I really like that tie." With her left arm, she made a sweeping gesture sideways saying, "She's all yours." Leigh cast a searing look over her other shoulder at Jonquil, before she flounced out of the suite.

Al hung near the door way, baffled.

"Is this a good time?" he asked.

210

Jonquil checked her watch. She had a few minutes left before she had to make her call. "Sure, Al, have a seat."

He sauntered over to the desk. "Rita told me you were here. How's Billy?"

"Better, thanks."

He plunked down in the chair Leigh had just vacated, then leaned forward, hands clasped between his knees, rocking slightly, ever the gung-ho administrator who needs more than wants to know the score. Marriage to Rita evidently agreed with him; his belt looked tight around his waist. Jonquil filled him in on Billy's condition, managing to blank out her alarming conversation with Leigh until Al himself brought it up.

"And Ms. Usher? What'd she want?"

"Oh, you know, girl talk."

He sat back and scratched the front of his nose. "Between you two? You're putting me on."

Jonquil coyly smiled back at him in silence.

"Well, as it happens, she's the reason I want to talk to you. She worked for you for several months. Did you notice any, shall we say, change in her attitude?" he asked.

"Can you be more specific?"

"I mean showing a more cooperative spirit than we have seen in her heretofore," he replied.

Jonquil sank farther back in her seat and idly speculated on when Leigh might begin showing. Then, "Why do you ask?"

"Leigh's very concerned with the time you've needed off from work."

She nearly swore. So! Leigh was up to her old tricks, looking for ways to criticize and belittle Jonquil and make her tenure at Clyde's unbearable. And who better to conspire with than Big Al, suddenly behaving like a gullible man, but with a long-standing compulsive streak, whose idea of a day well spent amounted to crossing innumerable t's and dotting uncountable i's.

"Al, I have every intention of making up the time. I won't do any overtime while Billy's still in the hospital, of course, but—"

"No need to worry. The family leave policy covers that. No, that's not why she came to me."

He sat back and crossed his legs. "Leigh's concern was that the Gift Counseling service stay active during this time. She's really come around about the work you do."

"And?" Jonquil tried to remain calm.

"So, there's this salesclerk in Evening Gowns upstairs who wants to work for you, apparently did work for you briefly, and who now needs a transfer."

"Is her name Vanessa?"

Al nodded. "Yep, that's the one. Leigh came to me about it. She wanted to make sure this transfer got done as soon as possible so gift counseling would be covered, whether you're in the office or not. Let me tell you, I was stunned. A significant salary adjustment had to be made first. Mr. Merrill said to do it."

Minutes later, Al left. Jonquil planted her elbows on her desk and lowered her forehead onto her balled fists, straining to remember every word she'd said to Leigh that morning. Had she been snippy? Had she been judgmental or made light of Leigh's broken heart?

Certain, ultimately, that she had nothing to regret, she picked up the telephone receiver and dialed the hospital nursing station for a report on Billy. He'd complained of a slight headache during his meeting with the tutor, was given Tylenol, and was now resting.

Dr. Marshall was paged while she waited. He picked up quickly and apprised her of the situation.

"If I leave work now I can be there in less than an hour," she told him, fending off waves of anxiety.

"There's no cause for alarm yet. If he isn't better after lunch, the nurse will contact you, Ms. Bloom."

"I prefer to come now, just as soon as I handle one thing." She cradled the receiver. Billy!

Why, oh, why did everything have to happen at once? Caught between tears, anger and the inexplicable gift that Leigh Usher had made possible, she pushed back from the desk and went to find the woman.

Jonquil's first stop was the Scentsations Department where Rita, who was capably juggling customers, informed her that Leigh could be found in linens on Four. Jonquil thanked her and hurried to the elevator.

She paused when she reached her destination to survey the area nestled between home furnishings and bedding. Counters were spread apart allowing ample room for displays of table cloths, matching napkins, china and cutlery. Even though the lighting was bright, and the tableaus were artfully enhanced with candles, crystal, and flake flowers, the muzak that morning sounded especially grating. The few customers who loitered in the area did little to break up the monotony. She soon spotted Leigh at a counter tagging new merchandise. Her blank expression clued in Jonquil that Leigh was seriously bored.

"There you are," she said, borrowing a favorite greeting of Claude's.

Raising her chin, Leigh crimped her mouth to one side.

"We didn't finish our conversation. Is there somewhere we can talk privately for two minutes?"

Leigh put aside her pile of table cloths, caught the eye of her current supervisor, and pointed to a corner office before leading Jonquil there. It held a small desk, lamp and enough room for two chairs.

"Well? Look, if you have more clichés to preach at me, you can save your breath."

"How did you get Vanessa Ford transferred?"

"Who?"

"Vanessa Ford, the young woman who started as a temp in Gift Counseling after Rita left me but then took a job in Gowns because she needed the commissions."

"Oh, her. Is that why Al wanted to see you? Ford, right. She came looking for you last week. She needed a transfer and wondered if the receptionist position was still open. You'd mentioned her name to me once, said she was a good worker but there was a problem with pay. Humph, having done the job myself now for many months, I knew the hourly rate needed to be upgraded." She added, "Substantially. Well, you know, I'm still on the payroll. I still have clout."

Jonquil could hardly believe her ears. Was she going to be beholden to this woman, her nemesis? What could be more awkward?

"But, Leigh, how'd you arrange it so quickly?"

"That was easy. She had a doctor's letter that said she had to stay off her feet, because of her medical history and because she's expecting twins. Not till spring, but she can get you through the holidays, so...."

"That's awesome. How can I ever thank—"

Leigh cut in. "Let's be crystal clear about this. I didn't do it for you. I did it for her and for Clyde's. It just makes good sense to put people where they will work the hardest." She glared out at the linen department.

"Agreed. When can she start?"

"Whenever."

Leigh appeared to have already lost interest. Jonquil sensed there was more to the story but it would have to wait. She explained that she was leaving for the hospital but would contact Personnel about getting Vanessa back as soon as possible.

"Now, about your situation, Leigh."

Leigh snorted. "What about it?" She started to get up.

"I didn't mean to sound uncaring. Please wait."

Leigh stopped moving and nodded. "You want to know what I'm thinking. Or no, you of all people want to know how I'm feeling, am I right?"

Jonquil watched her expression turn sour, heard her tone harden, and waited.

"I can't say because I have no clue. But here's what I want, Jonquil Bloom."

Jonquil braced herself for an ultimatum or attack, but Leigh surprised her again. She spoke with checked emotion. "I want everything you have. A job I can be proud of again. A man, a real man in my life, not just for kicks but for the long haul. I want a precious child to care for, maybe two and a home where we all live happily ever after. And I don't want some of it, I want it all!"

She jumped up, fists clenched, and stalked away.

CHAPTER 46

Round Two

By the time Jonquil reached the hospital in Hollywood, Billy's headache had developed into a full blown episode with neck stiffness. A second lumbar puncture had been ordered. The sound of Billy moaning was offset by the staff's crisp preparations and reassuring directions to him. She signed off on the required permission forms, thankful that she'd followed her instinct and come ahead instead of waiting for them to call.

Jonquil hoped the procedure would go as smoothly and painlessly as had the first one at UCLA. She was prepared to insist on being present, but it was taken for granted. Children's mission to avoid unnecessary pain was uppermost in her thoughts. Nonetheless, she gritted her teeth as though her own spine was being prepped with iodine by the doctor's assistant.

Images of Billy in his baseball uniform and cap flooded her imagination. Every time he suited up he looked older to her, confident, eager to get in the game. So darn handsome. Would he ever play again?

She halted that train of thought, afraid it might make her sick to her stomach. Billy's eyes clotted with tears, but whether it was due to the agony of the headache or anticipation of the needle thrust, he didn't say. The assistant positioned him on the table in the small procedure room and held him down while Jonquil stood nearby, keeping her focus on her son's face rather than the actions of the medical team.

The entire procedure took thirty minutes. Specimen tubes were rushed to the lab and the sheets draping him were removed. He was told to rest afterward but within minutes of the doctor cleaning the site, applying a Band-Aid, then adjusting his hospital gown, Billy's blue gray eyes popped open for a split second with joy.

"Headache's gone!"

The same result had happened before. The lumbar puncture entailed removing spinal fluid which instantly reduced pressure in the brain.

After he was transferred back to his bed, Jonquil sat with her son, gently tracing circles in his hair and softly humming until he fell into a deep sleep.

The resident stuck his head back in the doorway to report that Dr. Marshall was handling an emergency but that the procedure had gone well. Billy could eat whenever he woke up from his nap and they would be reviewing his medications again.

She wanted to stretch her legs so she left the room and walked down the hall to use the unit restroom. Smells of milk, soiled diapers and clinical paraphernalia accompanied her on the way there.

218

She splashed handfuls of reviving cold water on her face, then patted it dry with paper towels. A glance in the mirror told her she was overdue for a haircut and a ten day vacation in Tahiti.

Avec Claude. She phoned her love and left a brief message.

On her way back, among the children and families, IV poles and toys dotting the hallway, she noticed a man about her age striding toward her. He was approximately her height, stocky, with short, sandy hair. Visible under his white lab jacket were a black shirt and Roman collar.

"Father?" she said on impulse and reached out to touch his arm.

He stopped mid-step. "Yes? May I help you?"

"My son's here. Would you have time to give him your blessing?"

He nodded and followed her to Billy's room. Billy lay on his side, having not moved an inch.

"What's your son's name?" he whispered.

She told him.

He touched Billy's forehead lightly with his left fingers tips and raised his right hand in blessing. Immediately, she felt calmer.

It was as if Father Tim himself had come back to bless her child. Then she remembered that Tim had also been a hospital chaplain and smiled at the coincidence.

After another bit of silent prayer, the priest motioned to her to join him in the hall.

"I'm Frank Williams, a chaplain here," he said, extending his hand.

They shook hands. "I'm Jonquil Bloom."

He tilted his head as if to say, did I hear you right? Then, "So, Jonquil, how are you holding up?"

"Father, I haven't been able to pray... since...." Her voice faded away.

"It's Frank. I'm free now. Wanna talk?"

CHAPTER 47

Smooth Sailing

The conversation with Frank preoccupied Jonquil the next morning as she made her way from the parking garage to her office. He'd been a chaplain at Children's Memorial for ten years and had witnessed all kinds of illogical behavior, not as a judge he was quick to assure her, but as a source of spiritual help. Her mad dash to the ocean hadn't shocked the priest; rather, he'd listened intently, his compassion obvious.

"I *had* to drive to the beach," she said as they huddled over coffee in the cafeteria. "There was no place else big enough for me to vent my gigantic fear and anger. Can you possibly understand that?"

"Yes, I can. This is not a matter needing God's forgiveness, Jonquil. Look at it this way: God got you safely down to the beach and safely back to Billy's bedside. Thank him and move on."

"I'm so distracted, Frank, I can't even pray. Why, oh, why did this happen to my son?" She stared at him balefully. "Such a stupid question, I know. It's Basic Faith 101, right? Life is full of woe? I must sound like—"

"You sound to me like a loving and careworn mother."

She sighed and her clenched shoulders eased. "Thank you for saying that."

Frank patted her hand and after a little more talk, they agreed to meet again soon.

Jonquil, reaching the end of her recollection, gratefully turned her full attention to her new assistant. Vanessa Ford joined the Gift Counseling department officially that Wednesday as an administrative assistant.

Though her hair was cut shorter, and the pink streaks in front had disappeared, six months in Gowns hadn't altered her style one iota. She still favored the least clothing allowed, now in larger sizes, and conspicuous hoop earrings, and filled in the blanks with the sweetest smile in the store. Excitement about incipient motherhood made her smile constant.

Jonquil felt renewed purpose with Vanessa on board. Rita initially had brought maturity and common sense to the position. Leigh, when not finding fault with Jonquil, had applied her business acumen to enhance the suite's appearance and marketing opportunities. Vanessa brought the incomparable gift of her cheerful disposition.

"Ms. Bloom—"

"Please call me Jonquil."

They were seated across from each other in Jonquil's office, sipping Perrier from bottles while putting together a to-do list.

"Okay," she said with her soft giggle. "Upstairs, it's all Ms. this and Ms. that."

"Down here formality, like crystal glassware, is reserved for customers," said Jonquil wryly. "Oh, and also for administrators when they drop by. You know about the BBs, right?"

"The what?"

"The 'who,' actually. The store's accountants, BB1 and BB2. They're the Burney brothers. No one calls them by their first names except Mr. Merrill."

"Okay." Vanessa batted her big brown eyes and giggled again, like the joke was on her.

Her boss couldn't resist chuckling, too. It was not that she wasn't curious, thought Jonquil, it was that gossip had no place in Vanessa's world. She radiated an inner joy that Jonquil would have given her eye teeth to possess. The rare quality fit the Gift Counseling unit to a T.

"Vanessa, I'm so glad you're here. Did you and your husband buy the house you wanted?"

"Oh, yes. The Good Lord provided. It's so adorable! We have a backyard, too, for when the babies come. I can sit out there with my iced tea and read my book while they take their naps."

Mention of a backyard made Jonquil think of Claude. He'd broached the idea of them buying a house and then completely blew her mind when he proposed that they design and build their own house.

He wanted Billy to have a backyard. He wanted her to have as many closets as her apartment-weary heart desired and an office. For himself he wanted a work shop in the garage. He'd hung a rough floor plan on the Bloom refrigerator for anyone to add ideas.

Billy promptly scribbled in a doghouse for Ranger.

The phone on her desk purred nudging her back to the present. It was her private line.

Vanessa bounced up, grabbed the pile of correspondence that awaited replies, and withdrew to the reception area.

"There you are," said Claude warmly. Immediately, Jonquil recalled using the same greeting with Leigh.

"I've been meaning to ask you," she said. "How's Fred these days?"

"My Fred? Fine, far as I know. Why do you ask?"

"Um, I haven't heard you mention him in a while."

A pause followed. Then, "Told you not to meddle."

"I didn't meddle. If you recall, I was going to introduce Fred to my friend Annie. Was it my fault Fred and Leigh knew each other back in high school?"

He grunted. "What's up?"

"I can't tell you."

He huffed into the phone. "Fine. Now you made me forget why I called."

But he soon remembered and their conversation resumed. Before saying good bye, however, Claude admitted, "Fred's been off lately."

"'Off,'" she repeated.

"I mean, he's at work, eh, but his mind's elsewhere."

"Like in a good way, a happy way? Like he's mooning about his next hot date?"

"Nah, more like— No, just off. Sorry, got to go."

He disconnected before she could ask more questions.

CHAPTER 48

Gift of Mercy

Billy made friends easily. He had ever since his birth when the first nurse to cuddle him glimpsed something in his face that made her croon. The nurses at Children's Memorial were no less enthralled with the boy who loved baseball. But they had been put on high alert for signs of depression, anxiety, and withdrawal. This was not because Billy had displayed any troubling behavior. Quite the contrary, he'd been almost too cooperative. But Dr. Marty, the specialist whose practice included patients like Billy, regularly warned the staff to pay close attention to the quiet ones.

Ten days had crawled by since Billy's admission. The erratic fever that had kept him isolated, weak and mostly in bed was ebbing. The second lumbar puncture had removed his headache and it had not returned. He was tolerating the new medication well.

His vision however had not yet returned to normal. It had improved. He no longer saw people as dim, shadowy shapes. Yet at different times of the day, the blurriness increased without warning.

His doctors brought in students and consultants to witness or administer frequent neurological evaluations or eye exams. Blood was drawn, vitals were checked, and his temperature was taken while he listened to baseball games on the radio with his daily visitors. He could go to the toilet on his own but was monitored when he took showers.

The nurses, the orderlies who escorted him to scans, even the old dude who worked nights, as well as the cleaning staff were, with rare exception, engaging and friendly. It helped his nerves not having his mother constantly there. Nonetheless, his fear had developed into a major issue, confronting him first thing in the morning, then after naps, then at night. He didn't trust his eyes anymore, nor had he much hope they'd go back to how they were before the headaches began. Mornings were the scariest for his hopes were highest then that he'd awake completely cured.

He kept these feelings a secret. He missed Ramon and ached to be with his dog again. School would be starting after Labor Day, and he loved school. But how could he leave the hospital if his eyes didn't work? So, the longer he kept them closed, the longer he could pretend he was well.

That morning his breakfast had grown cold but he still had not opened his eyes. Nurse Charlotte, Lottie for short, entered his room. Billy knew who it was from her shoes. He knew everyone on staff by sound or smell or by the charge they gave off when they drew near.

Lottie wore cherry-colored crocs that made a squeaky noise on the tile floor. She had dark skin, gold-colored tresses, a saucy accent, a prominent chest and she favored jackets with deep pockets full of treasures. Even with fuzzy vision he could tell she was the prettiest of them all.

Now, she leaned in close. Her make-up's citrus fragrance wafted over him.

"Billy Bloom, are you awake?" she asked in a low monotone.

Instantly, under the blanket his body tensed and he held his breath.

"Billy, I'm Detective Smart Stuff of the L.A.P.D. I got a call from Nurse Charlotte this morning." She stood up and turned away from him to adjust a window blind which let him sneak some breaths. Over her shoulder, she explained, "Nurse Charlotte said you were still asleep though it's already nine o'clock. She's worried about you, that's why I'm here. Are you asleep? If you are, nod once."

He nodded. Then, his lips puckered and his whole upper body caved in. *Imagine falling for that old trick,* he thought. It was the sound of her voice, so solemn. And staying in bed all day bored silly was making him act at times like a little kid.

She sat down by his side. "Will you open your eyes for me? It's really me, Lottie."

He shook his head no.

"Can you tell me why not?"

Again, he shook his head, this time more vigorously.

"Can I guess? How many guesses will you give me?"

228

His brow wrinkled, then he sighed resignedly. There was no avoiding her, plus he wanted to tell someone. He wanted to tell her.

He raised three fingers.

"Three? Oh." He heard her move on the bed like she had turned away from him and was staring down at the floor deep in thought. Now her body shifted back and she was facing him again. "Okay, my first guess is: You hate the color of this room."

A puff of air escaped his mouth, a show of boyish disdain.

"Ah," she said. "I see. Your reason is more serious. Hmm." She waited a moment and then snapped her fingers theatrically. "You think I'm ugly. Ay-ay-ay, I'm so ugly! You don't want to look at me."

He had difficulty changing a smile into a frown so he raised a single finger.

"Ah," she said. "One more chance. Hmm." She dropped all pretenses. "Please tell me." She stroked his cheek and added, "Maybe, you feel afraid, no? Every day you are getting much better. Your headaches are gone, your stiff neck—all gone. And Gayle told us nurses that the chief is pleased with your progress. So, what is it?"

"I'm afraid," he said slowly with his eyes still shut, "that when I open my eyes I will be blind and I will never get to go home." His voice broke off in a shudder.

"Can I give you a hug?"

He opened his eyes. He sat up and she put her arms around him and rocked him. He liked that she didn't do what most adults

229

SHEILA M CRONIN

did, make silly promises or lie. He could be scared with her and not feel bad.

Tears chased each other down his cheeks until she murmured, "You are a very brave boy."

He leaned back, wiped his eyes, and studied her face. "How come you say that?"

"I meet sick kids every day. You know what? They are all brave. Even the criers, the complainers, even the ones that make me cuckoo. They don't want to be sick either so they fight and fight and don't give up. They are fighters. They fight fear and pain every hour, day and night. Like you. But they don't do it alone. They let us help them fight.

"Don't keep secrets, Billy. You can tell me or Gayle, anyone, about what's on your mind. That's why we're here. Ah, but first...." She reached into her left pocket and found a carton of orange juice with a straw attached. From another pocket, she extracted a snack box of oatmeal cookies and handed both items to him. "You need energy to fight."

She gave him a final squeeze and stood up.

"I will heat up your eggs. After you eat, we will take a walk and meet some of the other fighters here, okay?"

Fighter. The image fired up powerful associations. Of his team, the Comets, of the Dodgers, too, fighting to win. Of Grampa, his unmet hero.

He would fight hard to get well.

Chapter 49

Discovery

The night before Billy's discharge, Jonquil felt collected if not entirely calm. After forty-eight hours of no fever symptoms, and continued stable test results, the doctors decided he was ready to go home. Follow-up doctor appointments were scheduled conveniently at a Venice Beach outpatient clinic. The disease might recur, she was told, though in rare cases involving children, one episode could possibly be the end of it. Eye glasses weren't prescribed since it was the swelling that had caused his vision to blur, not a problem with his eyes. Billy must in fact use his eyes, strengthen their muscles, and return to school as soon as possible.

His belongings were neatly packed and stacked, there was nothing more to do. Jonquil took a shower in the hospital suite's bathroom and lay down in the narrow alcove bed. She had intended to stay awake for a while in case the anonymous gift giver showed up. However, she quickly succumbed to slumber.

But a noise woke her shortly before midnight.

She rolled over just as the door opened and someone stealthily entered the room. The shadowy light from the hall did not identify who it was yet instinctively she knew it was a man. He softly placed something on the tray at the foot of her son's bed and then stood and faced Billy. Then, he stepped back, the door closed behind him and all went quiet.

Swiftly, Jonquil rose, slipped on her robe and clogs and darted after him. He'd already gotten halfway down the hall, clad in the maroon colored scrubs the orderlies wore. A surgical cap hid his hair. His shoulders were broad but he limped which made him walk like an old man. Yet, there was an eerie familiarity about the swing of his shoulders.

She picked up her pace. Farther down the corridor, a woman was rolling a cleaning cart out of a closet. Otherwise, the floor was vacant. The man looked over his shoulder once before he vanished through a fire escape stairway exit.

"Stop!" she hollered.

He didn't.

She ran faster, until she too darted out the exit, calling louder. Two doctors running up the stairs from below brushed past him and blocked his path. They rushed past her but she ignored them because in his effort to avoid a collision with the doctors the man had been forced to flatten himself against the stairwell wall, facing in her direction. For a split second, she saw his face. She recognized him! She gasped, and her frustration reached a crescendo.

"For God's sake, stop!"

232

Her shrill voice bounced off the walls, broken by the sound of a door slamming shut somewhere below.

She slumped over the banister, staring fixedly down the stairwell, as her thundering heartbeat subsided and the truth took hold of her.

Her father was alive!

CHAPTER 50

One Mystery Solved

Billy couldn't wait to go home. His eleventh birthday was fast approaching and he wanted to leave quickly before the doctors changed their minds. A wheelchair was brought to take him down to the car. He'd acquired many new belongings during his two week stay, including the mystery gift the night before that turned out to be a baseball signed by Ted Williams! Billy had never heard of him but the vintage baseball thrilled him.

Claude peered at the left fielder's flowing scrawl and murmured, "If this is real, it's valuable, son. Don't lose it."

A cart was furnished to transport the pile of booty he'd acquired—toys, get well cards, and balloons—to the elevator. The flowers and untouched treats were left for staff and patients, except for the largest arrangement from Clyde's own florist. Jonquil chose to take that one home.

Claude went ahead and transferred the items to his Jeep. Jonquil asked Nurse Gayle for the telephone number for human resources, explaining as she scribbled it down that she wanted to get the treatment team's names and correct titles for personalized thank you notes. That much was true but her ulterior purpose was to obtain more information about a certain orderly on the night shift.

On the way to the elevator, she tensely scanned the faces of the many staff and patients who'd lined up to say good bye and wish Billy good luck. The walk took time as the doctors, nurses and families each wanted a farewell hug. She was relieved her father wasn't among them.

They made a stop at In-N-Out Burger at Billy's request for a take-out lunch before arriving at the apartment. Annie was waiting there with Ranger. The year-old cocker spaniel could barely contain his joy at being reunited with Billy, barking, yelping, chasing his tail, racing in all directions and causing general canine commotion. Tears welled up in Jonquil's eyes as her son threw his arms around the dog.

The kitchen bulged with dishes neighbors had dropped off. Even Coach Bobby Hillman showed up which struck Jonquil as particularly thoughtful. She introduced him to Annie, then was reminded by Annie that they'd met at Billy's Little League game. She got the impression from the way they smiled at each other that they were more than acquaintances.

Well, well, well.

Billy's friend Ramon stopped by with a quart of Moose Tracks ice cream. The boys quickly tore into it.

Claude left by mid-afternoon. Jonquil held him close and asked him whether she could call him later. He searched her face. "Anytime," he said.

Annie departed after the dinner dishes were done. Billy and Jonquil finally were alone. It was time for her to tell him the news about his grandfather. Waiting was not an option. The unpredictable man could show up unannounced when she was at work. He might telephone the apartment when she wasn't there.

His actions up till now seemed benign, but since he'd been secretive, Billy needed to know. She had learned her lesson about keeping secrets from her son. Ranger's presence would not let her forget.

"Billy, we need to talk." She resisted staring into his eyes because he'd become self-conscious about people giving him that searching look.

"Okay. What about?"

He was tossing Ranger a squeaky ball. The dog had ripped out the noise maker, so it was a quiet game.

"About the presents that came in the brown paper bags at the hospital."

"You mean my mystery gifts?" He tossed the ball again, barely missing a lamp.

"Yes." She would have to rein in his behavior which had gotten somewhat out of hand in the hospital, his attitude too, but not on his first night home.

"They're all from Jack," he replied matter-of-factly. "Here, boy, here you go."

"What did you call him?"

"Jack. He's the old dude that works there at night." Ranger started barking when Billy stopped tossing the ball.

Jack.

"How do you know his name? Ranger, quiet! Why were you talking to him?"

"Are you mad?" Ranger barked again. Billy told him to hush and dropped the ball on the floor.

"I—you've known all along who they were from? Why didn't you tell me?"

He pursed his lips and shrugged. "I forgot." Then, he gathered up Ranger in his arms and snuggled with him.

"Let's backtrack. When did you first talk to this Jack?"

"I don't know. He came in one night to see how I was doing. Told me he was Jack. Asked me if I liked the radio. Said he'd surprise me again. Told me he was pulling for me to get well. That's all." Ranger squirmed out of his arms, caught the ball in his teeth and raced out of sight.

She shook her head slowly from side to side, getting angrier by the minute.

"What, Mom?"

"Billy, that's what I want to tell you. That man? Jack? He's my father. And your grandfather."

Billy lunged forward, eyes wide open. He clutched her arm with both of his hands. "For real, Mom? It's really him?"

"Yes."

He sprang to his feet. "Well, uh, uh, where's he right now? Where does he live? Let's go see him."

"I don't know where he lives." She couldn't mask her irritable tone.

He appeared confused. "But you want to see him, don't you?"

"Yes." Hesitation cramped her tone.

"Mo-om."

"Billy, this has all happened so suddenly. I need more time. I need to get us organized. Everything's been put on hold since you started getting sick, sweetheart, and I—"

"Mom! You don't need any more time. You've had years and years. You and Margo."

Margo.

"Let's call Margo and tell her we found him." He was bursting with energy for the first time in many weeks. Ranger darted back into the vicinity, his frantic barks echoing Billy's excitement.

"Slow down, buster," she said thumping the cushion next to her. "Come, sit down here."

He plopped down beside her. "Why? What's the matter?" Ranger came and put his paws on Billy's knees, begging to be scratched.

"Billy, I know you think he's a hero."

Instantly, he shot to his feet. "He is so a hero!"

"Yes, all right. I said that wrong. Please don't interrupt me. He's also my father," she added. "He deserted us, Mom and me. And he never came back for me after she died. Never wrote me a letter or called or anything."

"So? He's back now. I gotta pee."

Later, after he was already under the covers, she sat on the edge of his bed and resumed the conversation.

"I can't just forgive him like nothing ever happened."

"Why not?" Ranger lay beside him, panting contentedly. Billy reached out to pet him.

"Billy, I don't expect you to understand. He hurt me. You can't possibly know how much."

"Huh! My pop died before I was even born. I never even got to meet him. At least you can see yours again." His eyes blazed with intensity. "Stop staring at me." Hearing his stern tone, Ranger growled at her.

Jonquil knew when she was outnumbered. She stood up. "We'll talk more tomorrow." She arranged his blankets and kissed his forehead before reaching for the overhead light. The last time she'd made the same motion was after his frantic shout, two weeks ago, that had brought her running. Her body trembled involuntarily at the flashback.

"I'm so happy you're home."

"Me too."

She bent and kissed him again. "I'll leave the desk light on." She paused in the doorway.

"Mom?"

"Yes, Billy?"

"He's my grampa."

"I know, sweetie. Pleasant dreams."

She lifted up the phone receiver by her bed and dialed Claude's number. He answered before the second ring.

"There you are," he greeted her.

"Sorry, it took a while to get Billy settled down. I'm on alert for nightmares and the return of headaches." She sighed. "Ah, but it feels good to be home. Billy should sleep tonight after his long day, don't you think? Without any nurses barging in to check his vital signs? I bet if one suddenly showed up, Ranger might tear her to pieces."

"And you, Jonny? What's going to keep you up tonight?"

"Claude." Her voice broke and she began to weep softly. "Oh, Claude, he was at the hospital. I saw him with my own eyes." Before she could stop herself, she was sobbing.

"Hey, hey, easy, now. You saw who?"

"Wait. I have to put the phone down for a minute." She hurried over to her door and pulled it nearly shut so Billy couldn't hear her. She quickly blew her nose and vigorously wiped her cheeks before resuming the conversation.

"John Bloom, my father. He was at the hospital. He either works there or was posing as an orderly. He was the person who left Billy those anonymous presents in brown paper bags."

"No kidding. When did you figure this out?"

"Last night. He came into the room. He dropped off one last gift—that signed baseball."

"Wow, that's got to be worth real dough. Wait a sec. You said he was dressed like an orderly. You sure it was your father?"

"Yeah, because I chased after him. He went down a stairwell. I saw his face just for a blip. And he saw mine. It was him all right." Her grim tone gave way to scalding tears. "I called out to him, but he disappeared. Huh, I should say he disappeared *again*."

240

"I wish you'd told me this earlier."

"I'm sorry but I wanted to get Billy home first. He's beginning to get well, Claude. It's so unfair. I had to let him know, so I told him after dinner. I mean, who knows what this old man will do next or what he's really after.

"Billy can't understand why I'm not overjoyed," she continued. "He sure is. It was rather brutal, him saying he'd never met his father, couldn't I be glad mine was back in town, so to speak? Get this, they talked a few times. My father called himself Jack but he never told Billy who he really is."

Her fury heated up again.

"The bum. After all this time, he picks now. How did he know Billy was sick? Has he been stalking us? What does he want?"

"It must have been a big shock to finally see him again. How'd he look?"

She pictured her father flattened against the stairwell wall. "Old."

"What are you going to do?"

"I don't know. Call the hospital Monday and see what they can tell me. Why is he suddenly here? Has he been living here all along? Or was it some god-awful coincidence that Billy ended up in the same hospital where he works?"

"I doubt that."

They were quiet. Her breathing gradually slowed.

"You need to go to bed. You're exhausted. There's nothing more you can do tonight. Bed, woman, or do I have to drive back and put you there myself?"

She smiled through her tears.

"Love that idea," she whispered.

"Me, too. Why don't I head up in the morning and take you guys to brunch?"

"Oh, that would be...."

"See you after eleven. Go. To. Bed."

She replaced the receiver and took a long, indulgent shower to wash away any traces of the hospital. She had just gotten into bed, when she heard her bedroom door creak open. Then, energetic panting. Followed by, "Mom, can we sleep with you tonight?"

Rolling over, she flung aside her blankets. "Sure. You, here. Ranger, on the floor." But the puppy's aggrieved noises made her stop, then chuckle in the dark, then scoot over farther.

CHAPTER 51

Sunday Brunch

So, are you excited about your birthday tomorrow?" Claude asked Billy while handing his menu to the waitress. They were seated at a table on the patio of Figtree Café alongside the Venice Beach boardwalk. He noted that each of them needed to wear sunglasses to block out the honey-bright sunshine. He profusely thanked *le bon Dieu* that Billy's eyesight had improved to the point that dark shades were necessary. A busboy deposited their beverages. Around them the bustling sounds of a popular eatery at brunch time filled the air.

"Did my Mom tell you we found my grampa?" Billy said. "I mean, he found us." Billy dropped his little bomb before taking a generous gulp of milk.

Claude's and Jonquil locked eyes. Then she gazed off toward the ocean, lips compressed, hands clenched. A light breeze blew her hair in her face. She fished a scrunchie out of her pocket and pulled her hair into a ponytail in silence.

"Yes," said Claude cautiously. "I did hear about that."

"We're going to find him and bring him home to live with us."

"Billy," chided Jonquil.

Her son glared at her defiantly. "We are. And he's never going to be alone again."

In the silence that ensued, a group of young people wearing bikinis raced by them on roller skates, followed by a bearded, bald man hauling two toddlers in a squeaky red wagon.

"That's sounds mighty generous of you, Billy," said Claude as he reached over and cupped Jonquil's fist. "Now, where's he going to sleep?"

"My room. He can have my bed. I can sleep on the couch. I did it before when I was in second grade. We got my room painted after the earthquake. It's fun."

The waitress broke into their conversation and with flair deposited their plates on the table. "For you, miss, the California omelet, and you, sir, the eggs Bandolier, and you, young man, the puffed pancakes with a side of roasted potatoes. Good choices all. Enjoy."

"This looks delish," said Jonquil in a tone that brooked no comeback. She lowered her chin and peered over her glasses at Claude. "Eat up now. Don't let your food get cold."

He cleared his throat in irritation. Communication between this particular mother and this particular son was trickier to decipher than a wrinkled, old blueprint.

Confound it!

He was tired of the bounds imposed by his not fully committed relationship with Jonquil. He wanted to speak to Billy like a father and to her like a husband. The situation so frustrated him that he pushed his plate aside.

"Right now, I'm more interested in your plan, Billy, than I am in breakfast."

"Claude—"

"No, Jonny. We're sitting all together for the first time in months in one of the most heavenly spots on earth, and I just can't play the game today. Sorry." He kept his voice low. "Please tell your son what it is you want, or don't want, to happen."

"I just want to enjoy my breakfast in peace."

"She's mad at him. Mom's real mad. But I'm not. He's my grampa and I already love him. And I never want him to leave us."

Jonquil burst into tears. She quickly removed her sunglasses to wipe her eyes. Claude withdrew his hand and patted his pocket for a handkerchief.

She waved it away. "I have tissues."

"Cripes, you're both so damn stubborn," snapped Claude as he fell against the back of his chair. "Is that an Irish thing?"

Jonquil blew her nose and replaced her sunglasses unbeknownst to their waitress who came over holding a pot of coffee aloft. "How're we doing?" she crooned. "More coffee?" She noticed that the two adults weren't eating. "Is anything wrong?"

"No," said Claude evenly. "We're just taking our time."

"Hokeydokes. No rush. I'll check back with you later." She moved on to the next table.

"We don't know if he is lonely," said Jonquil. "We don't know where he is. We don't know anything." She sipped her juice with a shaky hand.

"Agreed. Billy, do you agree?" asked Claude.

"We don't know if he's lonesome yet. We don't know where he is yet. We don't know everything ... yet." He was scarfing down his food with gusto. "He could be right here in·the restaurant watching us."

Jonquil sprang to her feet.

Claude dropped his knife and fork on his plate. "No way! Come on, woman, sit back down so we can hash this out. Please, Jonny."

She stalked away.

"She'll be back," said Billy confidently, wiping his mouth with the back of his hand. "She left her purse and sweater." He burped.

"So she did." Claude hungrily dug into his eggs and motioned to the waitress to now bring fresh coffee. They ate in companionable silence for a few minutes. Then said Claude, "You spoke to—"

"Jack? Yeah. Two times, maybe three. He's got a limp."

"Oh?"

"He got it cleaning a boat," added Billy.

"Interesting. Did he tell you anything else? Anything that would help us find him?"

"Well, sort of. He gave me his card." Billy produced a business card and was on the verge of handing it to Claude when Jonquil, having suddenly reappeared, snatched it out of his hands.

246

"Mo-om."

"What's this?" she asked, taking her seat again. "When did he give you this?" Billy pinched his lips together. She read aloud: "Jack Bloom, Harbour Tours, Sanibel, Florida." She looked at Claude. "Florida, huh? So, what's he doing in California?"

Billy shrugged. "I forgot he gave it to me."

"Only one way to find out, eh," said Claude in answer to her other question.

"You're right. He's got a boatload of explaining to do. Years of it," she added, punching the numbers on the card into her mobile phone.

Billy and Claude stared at her, slack-jawed.

"Ringing," she mouthed.

"Still ringing ... ah, a message." She held up her index finger. After an interval, she stuck her chin in the air, shut her eyes tight, took a deep breath, exhaled, then spoke into the phone. "This message is to say that Billy Bloom will be hosting a delayed eleventh birthday party with his friends at our apartment next Saturday from noon until 3 P.M. No more gifts, just bring yourself if you dare. I'm sure with your diligent reconnaissance, you know our address." Jonquil disconnected and dropped the phone into her purse.

She eyed Claude with apparent defiance. "There, it's done. Let's finish our breakfast."

CHAPTER 52

Next Steps

I'm calling Margo when we get home," announced Jonquil as they approached the Jeep. Her mood had improved in response to ample nourishment and eventual, hearty laughter during brunch. "It'll be evening in Ireland, well past her bedtime. But she'll want to know."

"What will you tell her?" asked Billy.

She thought for a moment. "I'll say you were sick but you're getting well and that he just happened to work at the hospital you were at, how amazing is that? She'll be overjoyed just to know he's alive. A trillion prayers answered."

They climbed inside the Jeep. "*Bon, ma chérie.* But your voice sounds funny," observed Claude inserting the key in the ignition.

"Margo will understand."

"Naturally Margo can't wait to see Jack," Jonquil told Claude afterward when she brought him a mug of fresh coffee. She had telephoned Killarney from the kitchen while Claude burrowed through the *L.A. Times* in the main room. "It's a long trip for her. I suggested they could meet halfway, maybe in Florida where he lives."

She set the mug on a coaster. Claude rose and used the remote to mute the Dodger game on television. Billy was in his room asleep.

"Why not take it one step at a time?" He took her in his arms and she leaned against him.

"It's just … we've talked about this possibility ever since I was a little girl. Is he alive? Where is he, what's he doing? How is he? And the killer question, why'd he leave in the first place? So, it feels odd going through this without her."

"Can't Margo and your father talk directly to each other by phone?"

"She wants him to call. Should I leave him another message with her phone number? What do you think?" She stepped back. Her eyes searched his anxiously.

"I think you need to slow down. Wait and see if he even shows up Saturday. You're taking a huge chance, eh, Billy's party and all. You can't control this thing, babe. Right now, Jack Bloom's a stranger. You don't know yet why he's come back into your life or whether he's here to stay."

Claude had spoken the truth.

She couldn't control the situation now any more than she could back when her father left. However, this time she didn't have to go through it alone. "You'll be here on Saturday, won't you?"

"You know I will." They stood facing each other in the middle of the main room. The intimate tenderness in his voice encircled her like gift wrapping. She laced her fingers in his.

She swallowed deeply. "I'm ready to marry you."

"What did you say?" The abrupt change of topic, not to mention the choice of topic, made his eyes bulge.

"I'm ready, Mr. Chappel. Anytime, anywhere." Tears made her eyes glisten. "If you'll still have me."

"*Mais oui, mais oui!*" he shouted loud enough for the tenant using the building's laundry facilities on the first floor to hear. Claude placed both hands at her waist, lifted her up, and effortlessly swung her around.

Ranger and Billy came tearing down the hall. "What happened?"

"We're getting married!" cried Jonquil. Claude set her down and they kissed.

"Ya-ay! When?" demanded Billy, hopping about and clapping his hands with excitement while Ranger made loop-de-loops in the air.

"Thanksgiving weekend?" blurted out Jonquil. Turning to Claude, she added, "How does that sound to you? Can your family—?"

"They'll be here, whoever can make it. Katie can put up our folks and the rest are welcome to stay at my place."

She smacked her forehead with the heel of her hand. "Wait, what am I thinking? We won't find a church that weekend, or a restaurant, either. They'll all be booked solid by now. It's impossible." Her face fell. Billy's shoulders slumped. Ranger growled.

"Did I ever tell you that my sister Katie won't take no for an answer? The minute and I mean *the minute* I tell her we need a church, she'll move heaven and earth. Restaurant? No prob. She'll open her own house, her kitchen, her backyard, and garage to us. Find us a caterer. Order the flowers. You watch."

Jonquil scooped up her car keys and purse, elation fully restored. "Please let her know right away. I'll call her later, too. Okay, gentlemen, I hate to get engaged and run," she said gaily, "but I'm late for choir practice. The roast is defrosted. You *will* have a totally scrumptious, celebratory dinner on the table, vino decanted, by the time I return, right?"

"*Oui, oui,*" said Claude as Billy turned to rev up the game.

Still chortling, she threw the door wide open, blinked at the shadowy figure backlit by sunlight and stepped backward unsteadily. There, on the other side of the screen door, dressed in slacks, a wide striped gold and navy polo shirt and boat shoes, clutching a bouquet of daisies to his chest, stood John—Jack—Bloom. "Daddy?" she whispered. The room tilted and her knees gave way. Ranger's urgent barks had alerted Claude who caught her just before her head hit the rug. He hustled her over to the stuffed armchair.

Billy cried, "What happened?"

"Get a glass of water, quick," said Claude. He crouched down in front of her and told her to put her head down.

Billy sped to the kitchen, Ranger at his heels.

251

CHAPTER 53

Face Time

I'm all right," protested Jonquil. "I didn't pass out, I sort of … stumbled." Handing her the half-spilled glass of water Billy had raced back with, Claude insisted she drink all of it. Billy lingered nearby.

"Give us a minute, okay, pal?" asked Claude. After she drained the glass, she lowered her voice and told him the cause of her shock. Billy and Ranger meantime slipped outside.

"Can you see? Is my dad still out there?"

Claude straightened up, stuffed his hands in his back pockets and peered through the screen door. "Yep. He's downstairs sitting by the pool talking to Billy."

"Billy, Billy, Billy." She shook her head with wonderment.

"What do you want to do?" asked Claude.

"Sneak out the back door, but my car's parked in the garage so I have to walk past them to get to it." Resolutely, she stood up and retrieved her purse. "I'm not kidding. I'm going to choir practice as planned. Please don't scold."

"Here." He handed her keys to the Jeep. "I'm parked two houses down on the left."

"I love you." She pulled him close and kissed him, then hurried to the kitchen. "As for my dad, you guys are welcome to have him come in out of the sun. I may call later to see if he's still here." She ducked out the back door.

Driving in bright afternoon sunshine the few miles to the parish hall in Santa Monica, Jonquil took stock of her feelings. She had to admit that her father's sudden appearance following the terse message she'd left on his voice mail was a good omen. He'd taken matters into his own hands. He hadn't let a whole week go by.

Were they each fighting for control of the situation? Maybe that was a trait they had in common. He had shown up early but she'd eluded him, sending him a deliberate message: not so fast, buster. What was her ambivalence about? Or else why had she avoided facing him? Well, for the next ninety minutes she'd put the situation on hold and sing her heart out.

Thank God for Claude, asking her what she wanted to do, then not objecting when she told him. She heart filled with love for him.

The daisies greeted her from a glass jar on the coffee table. Her father, however, was not there when she let herself back into the apartment. Jonquil felt rather disappointed, her adrenaline had been pumping conspicuously on the drive home from choir practice.

Claude explained, "He had a meeting to go to—AA."

"Oh?" She pondered that information while she followed him out to the kitchen. "I don't remember him being a drinker. Mmm, something smells incredible. Is that gravy?" she asked, inclining her head over a pot on the stove. "Did you talk to your sister?"

"Oh, man, Katie's jumping for joy. I think getting me married was the top item on her wish list."

She laughed as she stirred the gravy.

"I told her you'd be calling later. Dinner's about ready."

He drew her into his arms. "Sure you want to get hitched to an old dude like me who's set in his ways and likes to be the driver when he's in a car, and prefers Gordon Lightfoot to today's rock, and never sleeps on the left side of the bed and a million other quirky things you can't even guess?"

"I know enough. The rest will work itself out." She framed his face in her hands and kissed him. "I'll call Billy."

Billy was bursting with news at dinner. He couldn't wait to tell her all about Jack, starting with his name change. She listened and marveled at how grown up he sounded. "He used to be called John, see, but he changed to Jack when he moved to Florida. He said it was like starting over again, like, how some women get face lifts and some men grow beards? He changed his name."

Jonquil didn't like the sound of that. "Why'd he have to start over?"

"Please pass the rolls," interrupted Claude.

She handed the basket to him and decided to change direction. "What else?"

254

"He has a girlfriend. Her name's Nora. They live near a marina where he gives tours. He likes working outdoors."

Girlfriend? That gave her pause. It felt vaguely uncomfortable, like listening to the intimate details of a stranger's life. She realized then that Billy was only speaking about Jack Bloom's current life, not about the deeper things she wanted to know, so she didn't probe any further.

"He didn't come inside, Jonny. He apologized for not calling first, for just showing up here and upsetting you. Now he's going to wait to hear from you."

"Where's he staying?"

"At the Holiday Inn near the beach. He has a rental car, too."

They had nearly finished eating. Billy's hand shot out in the direction of his glass and it tipped over onto the table cloth. Claude used his napkin to mop up the spreading puddle of milk.

"Sorry," said Billy, instantly mortified.

Jonquil ran to the kitchen and brought back paper towels to augment Claude's efforts. "It's okay, sweetie. Just a spill. You have to remember to take your time, that's all. Are you feeling okay?" Anxiously, she felt his forehead.

"I'm all right, Mom. My eyes were sore, but they're better now." He yawned loudly.

She hunkered and squinted at each of his eyes. "Sore how?" To her they appeared more focused each day, and the painful headaches had not returned. The fear, though, remained high.

"Not like that. Sore, like the way you missed Margo so much, you said your eyes hurt. When we were in Ireland, remember? My eyes were sore for Grampa but not anymore."

His answer tugged at her heart. Her gaze found Claude and she indicated with a wink that she'd fill him in later.

"Oh, right." Tossing the soiled paper towels in the waste basket, she took her seat again. "You've had a big day, and your birthday's tomorrow. Time for your bath, young man. I'll be along soon to say good night."

Billy rose and pushed back his chair. Affectionately, she reached over as he passed by her chair and let her hand skim his soft buzz cut.

Ranger trotted after him out of the dining room, tail wagging. Seconds later, Billy raced back in and gave Claude a hug. Then he scampered out again.

Claude went down to the Jeep and came back to the apartment with two brown grocery bags which he handed to Jonquil.

"Can you please wrap these up for me? When do you guys typically open your birthday gifts?"

"Oh, you didn't have to get him anything, sweetheart."

She set the bags down on the coffee table. "As for when we open them, we celebrate all day long. Usually, he opens one at breakfast, one after school, and the rest after he blows out the candles on his cake."

"I like that. I'll try to be there."

Peering through the bags, she yawned loudly. "Oh dear, excuse me. Books about baseball. Perfect! I haven't done any shopping yet."

"Why not wrap these up from both of us? Then, you'll only have to get a cake."

"Bake a cake, you mean. Tonight."

"Want me to help?"

She smiled, and he covered her mouth with a kiss.

CHAPTER 54

The Visitor

That night Jonquil dreamed she pushed open a heavy door and was aghast to find herself back in Billy's hospital room. A man with his back to her was seated on Billy's bed. She recognized the shape of his head though he had no business being there. Billy slept undisturbed.

"Joe?" she whispered. As he stood up, Billy sighed and rolled over.

The scene morphed into them sitting in chairs by the window. "What brings you here?" she asked.

"Me? I was called in on a consult and I was just leaving when I remembered your son was here." *No way*, she thought, *your practice is made up of adults exclusively*. "So, without thinking about it," he continued, "I stopped by. He's a good looking kid."

It both jarred and comforted her to have him there. "Why did you really come, Joe?"

He shot her that penetrating look she knew so well. "Come again?"

"What's in it for you?" she asked playfully.

"Nothing," he snapped. "Look, I should be going."

Now the scene shifted to his office at UCLA, though the conversation continued uninterrupted. "Don't you see? Your visit means a great deal to me. It's a gift of your time, Joe, a true gift."

"I see," he grinned and slouched back in his chair. "In other words, you think you have proved me wrong about gift giving using my own behavior as proof. Devious at best, Ms. Bloom." He swiveled round in a complete circle before coming to a halt. "Suppose I was to tell you that my motivation was entirely self-serving? That I get my jollies from visiting the sick? That it's a past-time of mine, like golf or off-track betting. Or, that I do it to gain points with the Lord. Visiting the sick's an act of mercy, remember?"

"I don't believe it, Joe. I think you sacrificed some part of your Sunday to be here for me."

He arched an eyebrow and then flashed his killer smile. "*Touché*, Ms. Bloom. And now you know what Abel knew." The dream dissolved, and she slept through the night. The next morning upon awakening, parts of the dream lurked in her memory. Textbook wish fulfillment, she thought. Except for that one part.

What *had* Abel known?

CHAPTER 55

Gift Counseling 101

Vanessa warmly greeted Jonquil when she crossed the threshold of the Gift Counseling suite. Seeing her face first thing as opposed to Leigh Usher's sour puss was as preferable as a plate of fresh green asparagus to a pile of shriveled up lima beans.

"Morning, Jonquil. How are you today?" was Vanessa's perky opener on Wednesday. Vanessa had on a short sleeve, pink top today under a short-skirted blue jumper and dangling earrings. Hot pink nail polish garnished her slender fingers.

"So far, so good," replied Jonquil walking through to her office to deposit her belongings.

"Would you like a cup of coffee?" she ventured as soon as Jonquil stepped back out to the reception area.

"No, I've had my quota already, but thanks."

"Is Billy happy to be home?"

"You bet. Today's his birthday. He's taking it easy. If you get any calls from the babysitter, please come find me."

Vanessa nodded vigorously. "Sure."

"What a relief! When I think how it could have gone so terribly wrong." Jonquil's face clouded momentarily, then relaxed into a smile.

"Did I tell you his Little League team made a tape for him? His coach dropped it off while he was at Children's Memorial. The whole team participated. The boys told knock-knock jokes, most of them pretty silly, and the girls left him sweet, gushy messages. Then they sang him 'Take Me Out to the Ballgame' at the end."

"That's so cute!" Vanessa giggled and clapped her hands.

"So, what's on my schedule?"

"You have an appointment in ten minutes. Oh, I almost forgot."

Vanessa consulted her note pad while Jonquil waited. "Ms. Egnar called you earlier. Today's executive meeting scheduled for ten o'clock in the board room has been pushed back to eleven. You're...."

Her brow wrinkled with concentration. "Invited? No, that's not how she put it."

"I'm expected to attend?"

Vanessa grinned. "You get the idea."

"Well—"

"Jonquil, Jonquil, I must speak to you." Leigh suddenly loomed behind her. "Right now!"

Before she could react, Leigh herded Jonquil into her office then kicked the door shut. She didn't sit but stood right inside the door panting.

"They're deciding today, Al just told me."

"Who? What?"

"The execs. At eleven. About reinstating me as head buyer."

Jonquil folded her arms. "Leigh, I only just got here. I had to go over things with Billy's babysitter this morning."

Leigh rubbed her hands together and strutted over to the windows. "Sure, sure. I understand."

Annoyed, Jonquil reopened the door, stuck out her head at a gaping Vanessa and said sotto voce, "Please let Ms. Egnar know I'll be there. No calls for now." Then, she shut the door again.

She crossed to her desk, took a fortifying breath and composed herself after taking her seat. She didn't feel at ease being alone with Leigh in this mood but pretended the opposite.

"What will you recommend?" the tall blonde, her back to Jonquil, demanded.

"I don't know," answered Jonquil truthfully.

Leigh whirled around and approached the desk. "Can't you tell me?"

"I just said—"

"I want my job back. I've done my penance, done the scut work for months now. You don't know what humiliation is until you've tried selling shoes to a fussy platinum card holder while in your first trimester. Yech!"

"Leigh."

"What?" The blonde gave her a withering look.

"You threatened to phone the Poppi Blair Show and humiliate me, remember? You tried to turn Mr. Merrill against me. You did everything you could to get rid of me."

"I said I was sorry." Leigh's exaggerated tone reminded Jonquil of a valley girl impersonation. It riled her.

She sat up straight. "You didn't sound sincere then, and you don't sound sincere now."

"Who're you to judge?" squawked Leigh, planting her fists on her hips.

"Oh? And who are you to change my office or my appearance with your fancy scarves?"

"You said you liked what I did to the outer office."

"I'd have liked it more if you'd discussed it with me first!"

They were both shouting.

"Maybe I wanted to surprise you."

"Well, maybe I hate surprises!"

"Yeah, well, I'm not a mind reader. That's your job!"

Jonquil inhaled sharply at the insult. Her lips tightened into a straight line. Then, because the situation now struck her as ridiculous compared with the reality of her life, she sat back in her chair.

"Oh, come now. I trained you better than that."

Leigh cocked her head, not quite done with her grievances. "I thought you'd ruin Clyde's. It drove me crazy. Haven't you ever—?"

She eyed Jonquil up and down and her shoulders slumped. "No, of course not. Anyone with your brains has probably never lost it completely."

Jonquil lifted her chin. "I have so."

Leigh snorted. "I'd have liked to have seen that."

The women regarded each other coolly.

The phone on the desk beeped once, Vanessa's signal that a client was waiting to see Jonquil.

"You have to leave," said Jonquil.

No wiser than when she'd arrived, Leigh executed an about face and marched away.

CHAPTER 56

Lots Going On

Jonquil arrived at the board room minutes before eleven. Sunlight streaming in from two banks of windows warmed the rectangular space. The westerly panorama revealed nearby rooftops, the shimmering ocean and wispy clouds skimming the horizon. Big Al, there ahead of her, was nursing a mug of coffee. He glanced up as she entered and gave her a friendly salute.

"Hi, there. I hear your son's doing well," he said.

She yanked hard on the padded captain's chair on castors across from him and plopped down. "You bet. His first follow up neurology appointment is tomorrow. He's doing so well, knock on wood, he's even reading a little."

Her voice caught. "It's a bit miraculous, Al."

"Wonderful. And did Rita tell me you and Claude are engaged?"

His flashy blue eyes crinkled at the corners. A navy serge suit, baby blue shirt and shiny, striped lavender tie diverted attention from his pockmarked face.

"Ye-ep." She glimpsed her bare ring finger and smiled. Claude had her assurance that she'd love whatever ring he chose.

"Congratulations. You've got lots going on, young lady."

"I'll say," she agreed. *You don't know the half of it.*

Corny Bramson, the personnel director, and Iris Escanaba, the PR director, sauntered in together laughing boisterously, followed by the more sedate Burney brothers. A smattering of hushed greetings and covert sideways glances ensued. Rick Ridgeland wandered in next, sneezing and blowing his nose into a large handkerchief. Sy Saginaw showed up last and slid agilely into a seat seconds before Mr. Merrill strode in, a tense set to his jaw.

"Morning, everyone. Thanks for adjusting your schedules on short notice. I've asked Ms. Egnar to sit in." Surprised, Jonquil scanned the room until she discovered the executive secretary quietly taking notes in a corner near the potted plants.

"Let's begin. We're here to review Leigh Usher's request to be reinstated as head buyer. Jonquil is attending because Leigh spent considerable time in the Gift Counseling department and because it was she who Leigh targeted with her unprofessional behavior. Do I need to review the steps leading up to this point, or can we get started?"

Sy spoke up. "It's fair to stipulate that we have to keep Leigh on board until December. Exactly in what capacity is what we're deciding today."

Rich filled the lull by sneezing rapidly several times in succession. "Sorry, allergies," he mumbled into his handkerchief while some of the others mumbled, "God bless you." Iris

266

pointedly moved her chair several inches away from him causing everyone on that side to have to move down, too.

Corny raised his hand. "I asked the managers of various departments to report on Leigh's contributions or lack thereof during her assignments throughout the store. I've made copies for everyone. Sorry, I didn't have time to staple them."

Mr. Merrill reached for one. "Thanks, Cornell. Let's take a few minutes to review."

Al rolled back his chair and handed copies to Ms. Egnar. She rewarded his thoughtfulness with a wink and a smile. Al rolled his eyes and scooted back to the table.

"Wow," murmured Iris. "I'm surprised to see she found a way to solve that nasty mess in jewelry. Page three." The simultaneous rustling of papers indicated that the group was skipping ahead to the section noted.

"Yeah," said Corny, "but check out page six. She mishandled a customer complaint in linens big time." More rustling followed.

Jonquil set down the sheaf of papers. She pictured the willowy blonde in her office earlier, rubbing her hands together, binding her anxiety. No one else at the table knew that Leigh was pregnant. Had her angst that morning been only about the job? Not likely. And no matter how disagreeable Leigh was, expecting a baby was stressful enough, but going through it without a partner? Jonquil had sadly been there, done that.

"Al, let's begin with you," said Mr. Merrill.

Al dropped his papers on the table. "Sure. I'm opposed to reinstating Leigh and here's why. We must have someone we can trust in that job."

"I don't know," murmured Sy. "Isn't trust a requirement of all store positions? She's proved she's a team player to my satisfaction. After months of hard labor, I believe she deserves a second chance."

At the mention of "hard labor," Jonquil sat up straight in her chair.

"Yeah, Sy," chimed in Iris, "but is the woman sorry for what she did?" She shook her head and tsked-tsked. "Hoity-toity as ever." There followed several grunts of agreement.

"She apologized to me," blurted Jonquil. "Twice even. Or tried to."

They looked skeptical. Even Rich, eyes watering, paused before launching into his next cascade of sneezes, at which point BB1 on his other side, moved his chair a foot away.

Mr. Merrill, however, leaned forward, gestured for the others to be quiet, and directed a follow up question at Jonquil. "When was this?"

"The first time was back in spring when she began working for me. I couldn't say she was sincere, but to her credit, she sought me out, not the reverse. She did it again today." Jonquil colored. "But I didn't accept her apology either time."

"Why not?" Mr. Merrill inquired.

Jonquil glanced around, feeling exposed, until she locked eyes with Mr. Merrill. "I ... I didn't take her seriously."

"See?" said Al.

"Let her explain," Mr. Merrill ordered in a curt manner after again holding up his hand.

Jonquil squirmed in her seat. "No, that's not right. I didn't *want* to believe her. I was still angry." The admission made her pause and reflect. "She asked to be forgiven. Maybe it came out hoity-toity sounding but she tried. With her being...." She caught herself in time. "I mean, I'm not the only one with a full plate. Leigh has a lot going on, too." Nodding toward Al, she murmured, "We all do."

Then she added, more to herself than to the committee, "Maybe I could have been more understanding."

"Wrong," stated Al flatly. "Leigh's been a conniver since day one. I was here. I know."

Rich chose that moment to slowly wind up in his chair like a roller coaster—"Ah, ah, ah, ah," before descending in an explosive—"choo!" sending a couple of papers flying.

As Iris and BB2 grabbed them, Mr. Merrill consulted the wall clock before saying, "We'll end soon and give poor Rich a break. It's my decision, nonetheless, I value your input. Two points to revisit before we vote: 1) trust, and 2) second chances. Ms. Bloom, as you're not a member of the committee, you may leave."

Jonquil withdrew but not before observing Mr. Merrill's face wreathed in smiles.

CHAPTER 57

Texas Bound

Tuesday morning, Jonquil woke up even before Ranger. In less than two months, God willing, she'd be married to the most wonderful guy on earth. Who could sleep? She dressed, gathered her wallet, keys, and the latest issue of the *American Journal of Psychology*, then jiggled Ranger's leash till he came running. A peek in Billy's room found him, thankfully, in his own bed fast asleep.

The "little" birthday, as they called the dinner celebration that took place on the actual day, had gone well. Little, that is, in comparison to the celebration with his friends, and possibly his grampa, that was coming up on Saturday.

Ramon had biked over in the afternoon and the boys had listened to the Dodger-Mets game with Billy's babysitter.

Jonquil left work early and prepared one of Billy's favorite meals—barbeque chicken, corn on the cob, green salad and chocolate milk. Claude came, too. A tempting pile of gifts from

Margo, the O'Keeffes, Annie, as well as those from her and Claude, had accumulated on the dining room breakfront.

When it came time to blow out the candles on his cake, however, Billy hesitated, his eyes tightly shut. Her heart stood still. But Ramon pestered him, "Dude, make a wish already."

Billy popped open his eyes and grinned. And she began breathing again.

Now, barely glancing across the street at Claude's job site since it was early, she and the dog headed briskly to the park. The first day of September was shaping into a breezy, overcast dawn with hints of autumn in the rustling leaves. Ranger seemed to note a change in the air, too, and diligently sniffed every signpost and tree trunk, trying her patience all the way to the park.

She leaned back on a bench and paged through her journal, stopping here and there to scan an article. Woefully behind in her reading, she expected to catch up once Billy got free and clear of treatment. His first follow up appointment that afternoon could be the beginning of the end, she fervently hoped.

But would she ever be free of fear? Would her son?

She'd been invited to join a monthly support group for parents at the hospital to exchange information about living with sudden vision loss. Would they help her live with the fear of relapse?

Her attention moved on to other matters. Mr. M hadn't made an announcement by the end of yesterday, so for all she knew, Leigh's future still was undecided. How had the committee advised the boss on trust versus second chances? Second chances were chancy. Trust, too.

Jack Bloom weighed heavily on her mind. The next move was hers.

Tossing aside the journal, she called to Ranger. "Here, boyo." He came bounding over to her, long ears flapping, and she bent forward to give his neck and back a vigorous rub. "There's a good boy. You've been through a lot of changes, too, haven't you? Staying with Annie wasn't bad though, was it? Did she have any men over? Is she dating Coach Hillman? When she gets this quiet, it usually means...." He licked her face, barked and danced around, indicating he was ready to resume their morning constitutional. She didn't want to dawdle either.

Before returning to the apartment, she stopped at the convenience store in the next block for milk and bananas. A couple of Claude's construction crew emerged as she entered and one tipped his hard hat her way.

That kept a smile on her face as she roamed the short, cluttered aisles. Her shopping done, she stood in line speedreading an abstract in the journal when something caught her eye. She peered around a pillar partially blocking her view at the items spread out in front of the cashier: a submarine sandwich suffocating in cellophane wrap, a jumbo bag of chips, a bag of overpriced Oreo knockoffs, and a Big Gulp. Her stomach heaved. Who in the world would call that a satisfying meal? Curious, she looked up, then realized the obstruction in front of her had an elbow, a shirt sticking out of faded jeans, and, topping everything off, a neon green hard hat.

"Fred?!"

He pivoted, gazed down at her surprised face and grinned. "Oh, hi, Jonquil. How ya doin'?"

"Fine, really great. Don't tell me that's breakfast."

"Heck no," he drawled. "This here's a snack."

Gone evidently were the days of workouts and lean meals under Leigh's tutelage.

She teased, "You're going to share that, right?"

"Well...."

That notion momentarily stumped him. Meanwhile, the cashier slid Fred's items past a bar code laser then stuffed them rapidly into a bag.

A minor tug of war broke out in her conscience. Should she mention Leigh or not? Don't get involved, Claude would admonish her. However, Fred looked pale—now she knew what Claude meant by "off"—and Leigh was miserable.

Plus, there was a baby on the way.

"That'll be $24.46," broke in the bored cashier. Fred handed over two bills and hoisted his bag but after pocketing his change, he waited while Jonquil paid for her groceries. They exited the store together. Ranger strained on his leash to get moving.

"Stay, Ranger, good boy."

"How's Billy?" asked Fred. Two cars turned into the lot and parked next to Fred's truck. Both drivers then scurried into the store.

"Oh, doing much better, thanks. And did Claude tell you we're engaged?" She had to stretch her neck and shield her eyes from the morning's glare to meet his gaze.

"That's nice."

His feeble response brought her up short. "Fred, is everything all right?"

"It will be once I get to Texas." At her shocked reaction, he explained that he'd been hired full time by the firm that Claude had consulted for in the spring.

"I'm gonna tell Claude this morning."

The Lone Star State. She diagnosed his behavior instantly. Fred was running away. Time to be blunt.

"Does Leigh Usher know?"

"Leigh? Aw, heck, a lot she'd care. Jonquil, can I ask you a question? Why would a friend lie? She made me think she was your boss. That she practically ran that joint. I found out later from her sister that she was in hot water and lucky to still be there. The job don't mean squat. She could be a window washer for all I care. But why couldn't Leigh be straight with me?"

"I don't know, Fred." The degree of hurt in his voice told her he was carrying a torch, and not for Leigh's sister. "Sounds to me like she wanted to impress you. Like maybe your opinion of her meant very much. I could be wrong."

As he shifted his bag to his other arm and extracted keys from his pants pocket, the full weight of his attention fell on her like a steel girder. "You really think so?"

"Only one way to find out." She kept her tone light.

"Thanks. I might just do that," said Fred, nodding before he hauled himself into his truck.

Sweet guy, she thought, *vulnerable*. As he drove away, she looked down at Ranger. "Let this be a lesson to you. When you start dating, take time to get to know her before you give away

274

your heart." He cocked his head and lifted one ear and then a paw. She chuckled and they jogged back home.

Rita appeared outside of her office at lunch time, her face flush with excitement. She knocked boldly, then whispered from the doorway. "Did ya hear?"

Jonquil motioned for her to come in and have a seat.

"Leigh quit. She's gone," drawled Rita balancing herself on the edge of a chair across from her former boss.

"Was this before or after Mr. Merrill met with her?" asked Jonquil.

"After. He told her she could have her job back this morning. They met for an hour before the store opened."

"I got here late. I had a lecture on campus this morning."

"I know, sugar. I've been over here three times looking for you. This is all very hush-hush."

"Sorry. Go on." Not for the first time, Jonquil thought how fortunate it was to have Rita for a friend.

"So, Sally, that's her secretary, said Leigh agreed to take back her job. She seemed relieved at first. Then, something weird happened. She got a phone call, a personal call, around ten o'clock. She was on that call for a long time. When she hung up, she ran out of her office crying and laughing, all excited—and told Sally to go find a dozen packing boxes. Leigh then called Mr. M back and cancelled or whatever the agreement they'd just made. Then she packed up her stuff and phffft! She went bye-bye."

"A-mazing." Jonquil had trouble picturing a happy Leigh Usher. She wondered, too, how much Leigh had told Mr. Merrill on that final telephone call or how soon she could get the Fred details from Claude. Rita spoke up again.

"She came and said good bye to me."

"Oh, that was nice of her, Rita."

"We go all the way back. I trained her when she started at Clyde's. You know? I'm going to miss Lady Leigh—not." She giggled. "Sounds like she's getting married."

"Yeah. Wait, what makes you say that?" Jonquil had to be careful about keeping secrets.

"'Cause the last thing she said to me was, 'Rita, I'm gonna beat Jonquil Bloom to the altar.'"

CHAPTER 58

This Old Car

ater that same Tuesday, Jonquil had telephoned her father and they'd arranged to meet that Wednesday, her day off. However, her car's transmission chose that morning to conk out blocks from his hotel. She'd left home in plenty of time, but the delay thoroughly discombobulated her. When she notified Jack Bloom that she'd be late, it galled her to have to be the one to say "sorry" first.

Fortunately, a tow truck arrived in less than thirty minutes. As the spunky, ruby red VW bumped down the street and out of sight, she raised her hand in farewell. She elected to walk the three remaining blocks, attempting to calm down and distract herself on the way by reviewing her many preparations.

Before the meeting, Jonquil had sought advice from those she trusted most: Annie, Rita, Al (who was also a vet), new ally Father Frank Williams, and Claude. They'd each urged her to keep an open mind. Though resources abounded on campus and she might have asked for help as a professional courtesy, she didn't. She debated consulting the Mazz, too, but decided that to take him into her confidence might damage the tenor of their academic relationship.

She wondered about making a list of grievances, then recalled a letter to her father she'd written for a high school project. The rage–filled result frightened her so much, she'd ripped it to shreds and forfeited the grade. She gave up on organizing her thoughts.

The next decision was a meeting site. Big Al urged Jonquil to choose some neutral place that held no special meaning. If things went south and she never wanted to go there again, it wouldn't be a loss. He'd been through two divorces; he'd learned the hard way. Not the beach, then, or Clyde's, or any of her regular haunts. Definitely not home.

Then, it hit her. Why not his hotel? Her father had readily agreed to the site and plan.

What to wear? Something old she could toss afterward? Something to impress? No, she decided shrewdly, something comfortable. She chose black jeans, flats and a pretty tunic top.

Her father was in the lobby of the hotel watching for her. Clad in slacks and a mohair sweater, he looked trim, scrubbed, and distinguished. He wasn't as freckled as she remembered. Soft ginger-colored hair crowned his head, though the rest had gone gray, and a deep tan accentuated his wrinkles. An awkward moment when they might have hugged slipped into history.

Still, walking near him for the first time in decades, she inhaled a whiff of his scent that had always reminded her of a bubble bath. Instantly, she recalled being perched in the crook of his arm while dancing around the kitchen in Minneapolis. She'd have to have been about four at the time. Peals of laughter, the Beatles, her mother fixing dinner, the feel of his scruffy, tweed jacket on her skin flowed out of her memory bank. How tall and powerful he'd seemed then.

Now, they stood practically eye to eye. A kick in the gut reminder of time lost.

She wondered detachedly whether the limp caused him pain as she trailed after him down a corridor to a medium sized meeting room within the hotel's conference center. Grimly, she scanned the space, took in the coffee and cups, pitcher of ice water, fruit and pastries on the side board. A fresh box of Kleenex awaited use in the center of the polished table. The awkward setting made her want to gag, but she told herself for the umpteenth time that this first attempt at reconciliation was for Billy and Margo's sakes. Claude had said, "He's trying, babe."

They chose seats opposite each other nearest the door. Which of them would bolt first? He sat down but she remained standing and set off pacing in the lane created by the chair backs and sideboard.

She stopped at the far end of the table, wetted her lips, and faced him.

"Why did you desert us?"

He sat up sharply, palms pressing down on the table, battle underway. "Wasn't my choice. God knows I was headed home to you and your mom. It took me by surprise. I mean, the cold that day in Chicago. So...." His moving hands seemed to want to express size, but he confused her and said, "So cruel. One step out of that hotel and I was right smack-dab back in Korea."

The resonance of his familiar voice after a twenty-six year absence washed over her like rain soaking a parched cactus. But the catchall phrase about surprise raised her hackles, so she began moving again, her head bobbing in curt nods.

"It took you by surprise, right. Did it have to be on my birthday?" Her resentment smoldered. He grimaced; she'd struck a blow. "But then you were released from the hospital. Why didn't you at least let us know you were alive? It killed Mother, the shame." She almost added, *You were the* only one *who could make her laugh.*

His eyes tracked her, imperturbable. "Correction. I was released to a half-way house. I escaped from there, I was never discharged."

"Right-right. You ran away from there, too," she countered in order to mask her chagrin. None of the reports she'd paid for over the years ever mentioned a half-way house.

He continued, "Before my escape, I called Minneapolis and spoke to a buddy of mine. He told me Pauline had died and that you were in Seattle with Margo. Well, I was still your father, after all, so it was up to me what happened next. I decided you were better off with Margo. I was in no shape to raise you. It broke my heart."

She was stunned. "You admit you deliberately abandoned me?"

He shook his head. "No, I never saw it that way. Jonquil, I was in hell, but I knew you were safe and loved." She continued to stare at him. He rubbed his forehead. "Well, then, I drifted down south in stages. A year in Georgia, couple of years in Miami. The warmer weather helped some, but the flashbacks had done their damage. They wouldn't go away. So, I started drinking. Hard. Like in Korea. Don't remember much about that time but nothing killed the guilt."

She snorted.

"Yes, I felt guilty but there wasn't a damn thing I could do."

"Really?" she taunted, half a question, half an accusation.

"I lived on the streets like a bum. Did odd jobs when they were offered, often went hungry, scared of my own shadow. Shadow man, that was me. Without the help of other vets, I wouldn't be here. But let's get one thing straight. There wasn't a day I didn't miss you and want to be with you." He shuddered and said, "It was the sacrifice I had to make. About killed me."

She shook her head, confused.

"Look, this isn't a competition, Jonquil. You had your pain and trust me, I had mine. Try to understand. They have a fancy name for it now, post-traumatic stress disorder. People say it started with the Vietnam War but we who fought in Korea know better. Shell shock, battle fatigue, it's all the same. Hell, anyone who's seen combat knows the feeling.

"A crippling anxiety is what it is. Comes out in peculiar ways. For me, I could no longer endure cold weather. It isn't something I faked to welsh out on being your father. It had nothing to do with either you or Pauline. I brought this home with me from Korea, never knew it. The cold there, it can't be described in human words." His arms twitched almost imperceptibly.

After a pause, he asked, "Didn't I manage to live in Minneapolis all those winters after the war before I snapped?"

She nodded.

"I had a delayed reaction. That's how this thing works. Out of nowhere, it blindsided me. Afterward, there was no going back home. I was given an ultimatum, like a doctor's order. Move south, or else.

"But more happened on that day in Chicago. I didn't piece it together till later. A horde of Asian school boys arrived at the hotel. They were dressed alike in black jackets, shouting to each other in Chinese. The Chinese fought with the North Koreans in the war, did you know that? It felt like I was surrounded again by the enemy. And they kept on coming! I thought they were coming for me. But they were just kids, Jonquil. I was inside of a flashback."

She struggled to respond. His plight had been much worse than she or Margo had guessed. Her lips quivered, tears sought release. "I coulda joined you in Florida."

"No, you could not. You were just a child. A school girl. You needed to be in a rock-steady home, go to school, make friends, live a normal life. You deserved it. I couldn't take care of you. And you and Margo couldn't have taken care of me. I had to let you go." His gaze fell.

"Your own mother, you couldn't tell her?" she whispered. Her voice sounded hoarse.

His head shot up. "No."

He wasn't looking for sympathy. She felt her emotions zigzagging between rage and respect. Incredibly, something inside her was moving like the first rocks heralding a landslide. She must stop it.

"How'd you find me?" She sniffled rudely before snagging a tissue.

His shoulders relaxed slightly. "I saw you on the tube. My lady friend Nora watches what's-her-face a lot. I called the station after seeing you. They told me zip. Nora got hold of a tape of the show and that's how we learned you lived in California and worked at Clyde's. And that I had a grandson. I phoned the store once, and someone in your office said you were away."

That pink message slip Leigh had filled out. "Jack, from Minneapolis," it had said.

"I was in Ireland then with Billy visiting Margo." She poured herself a glass of water—he didn't want any—and grudgingly slumped down in a chair.

"I've spoken to Mom twice." His brow creased with pain. "Thank God she's still alive." Neither mentioned his father, who'd died before Jonquil's birth.

"When'd you get here?" she asked.

"Roughly two weeks ago. Took time to arrange things back home."

"How long are you here for?"

"Till Saturday."

He'd be gone again in two days. Her shoulders drooped.

"Wish I could say 'for as long as it takes' or change my plane reservation and stay for Billy's party but with the way things are going between you and me.... Anyway, I have to get back." He stood up and poured himself a cup of coffee.

She folded her arms. "What do you want?"

"I want to make amends to you." He reclaimed his seat.

283

She lowered her head onto her balled fists. "Stop it! I have to use jargon at work but I can't stand hearing it from you. Use your own words, Dad. Talk from your heart."

He blinked rapidly several times as she raised her head. "You still do that. You used to do that as a little girl," he added wistfully.

Were those tears? She couldn't be sure so she glowered back at him.

"How'd you hurt your foot?"

His tone flattened. "Oh, I was cleaning one of the boats, hose got caught on a bulkhead, I tripped, fell hard, messed up a tendon."

"Were you drunk?"

He grunted. "No, daughter, I've been sober twelve years. I got that job through a friend in AA. He later asked me to go partners with him, and left me the fleet when he died. Fleet as in seven touring boats."

Seven toy boats in a bathtub floated before her eyes, including one misspelled Dock. The silly image dissolved.

She shook her head. "Twelve years. And in all that time your AA sponsor or Nora didn't once say, 'Jack, why don't you give your poor daughter a call, see how she's doing?'"

"Sweetheart—"

Her face darkened. "Don't you sweetheart me."

His eyes closed briefly then reopened. "You'll never know how much I needed you." He met her gaze. "But I had to stay sober if there was any hope of being a part of your life again. I had a few slips, I was shaky. Sobriety's a great gift, but … it comes at a price. I had to keep away. Quite frankly, I didn't have the guts to face you until now."

His voice was husky with emotion and more. Some deeper truth gave his words heft. It made her veer from the direction she wanted the discussion to go and consider whether she would have wanted him back sooner if it would have meant compromising his sobriety, possibly killing him. He looked healthy, loving, sane, more or less. How was that possible?

Curious, she asked, "How'd you find sobriety? Am I saying that right?"

He nodded. "It found me. I was in the Keys by then. Dying. I was brought to a VA hospital and offered the last rites. Refused 'em. Guy in the next bed started talking to me. Navy chaplain fresh from the Persian Gulf. He knew what I'd been through. He quoted me from Saint Mark. 'What can a man give in exchange for his soul?' Not what *would* you give, but what *can* you give? What can any of us give? So ... I decided to live and find out." He turned his cup around and around in its saucer. "I'm still working on it."

She pictured him near death. A lifeline flung out to him. Him grabbing hold of it. Shuffling down a hospital corridor to his first AA meeting like she'd seen patients do at her practicums. Clawing his way back to life.

That quote about giving from Saint Mark momentarily distracted her. Had she ever heard it before? She certainly hadn't come across it in her research. Which led to her next questions.

"How'd you get those gifts to Billy in the hospital? How'd you even know he was sick or what to get him like that special wristwatch he loves, huh?" She drained the water in her glass, irritated by the tone of her own voice but unable to soften it.

"I flew in the day before Billy got sick. I rented a car and followed you home from work. I followed you when you took Billy to the hospital—"

"That's creepy, Dad. Why didn't you—"

"Let me finish, please. I scanned his chart in the ER when no one was looking. It was serious, I wanted to help. Guy I know has a daughter who's blind. I called him for ideas about presents for Billy. I may have told a few fibs at that kiddy hospital when I showed up at the volunteer office and they were short of help. I actually worked in a hospital in Tampa years ago. Having been a Ranger in the army, I pretty much know my way around bureaucracy."

"That tells me nothing." *Au contraire*, Claude would have remonstrated, it reveals many things, mainly, that he cared enough to take his time approaching you.

Jack sipped his coffee. She regarded him with growing apprehension. Did he know she'd gone down to the ocean that first night? Had he followed her *there*? That frantic plunge down the hospital stairwell still swamped her memory with the least bit of prodding, the frenzy to escape so she could breathe. She could no more have ignored her panic than— Was that what cold did to him? Her feelings were becoming confused.

"What is it? You looked troubled."

"Margo gave me your medals when we were in Ireland."

"Keep 'em."

"Billy thinks you're a hero."

He set down his coffee cup and leaned forward. "And you?"

"I used to. I thought you were *my* hero." She averted her eyes. "Let's take a break."

The restroom was across the hall. Jonquil relaxed when she discovered it was empty. She freshened up, then paced in front of the sinks, hands linked behind her back, in turmoil. Feeling resentful that it fell on her to have to forgive Jack Bloom. Her mother was dead. Her grandmother was in Ireland, and anyway she'd already forgiven him. It wasn't an issue for Billy. Claude, she could tell, was sympathetic to the man, no matter how fair handed he tried to appear.

Something Frank said now kicked in. Forgiveness comes from God. God alone forgives. All manner of evil is done against God. Only God, therefore, is big enough, righteous enough, and tender enough to forgive. Ask for God's forgiveness.

There it was again, she was considering her own need for forgiveness, not her father's.

She'd wanted to believe the priest. But couldn't quite do so. He'd then told her, "Jonquil, don't make it harder than it has to be. Say an 'Our Father' before meeting with your dad. Say just those two words if you can't say the whole prayer."

"Our Father," she now prayed aloud, his Father and my first Father. She scrubbed her hands, touched up her lipstick, and headed back to the meeting room.

CHAPTER 59

Where's a Rocking Chair When You Need One?

W
e searched for you for years, Margo and I," she informed
Jack Bloom coolly when they reassembled.

He listened, his fingertips softly strumming the table. The
tension in the room climbed.

"We had your social security number. And your fingerprints.
We tried the Army, the Salvation Army, the DMV. I put ads in
newspapers in Minneapolis, Chicago, and elsewhere and offered
whatever reward I could afford. Margo and I had your name and
picture added to every missing persons bureau we could think of,
and I also looked you up routinely in criminal records. I hired a
private detective in Chicago. Twice I went there and searched for
you myself. Why couldn't we find you?" Her anger mixed with
dismay flared at the memory of the many dead ends.

"I figured Margo would try to find me, so I went by different
names for years. Got paid in cash, never carried any identification
so the times I was arrested for vagrancy or intoxication, I was a
John Doe. After I got sober, I didn't trust myself. I had the

company put in Nora's name. When a man doesn't want to be found, he finds a way.

"Later, after I'd been in recovery a while, I normalized things. Took back my life, as they say. Paid back taxes. The rest you don't need to know."

It stung her, the idea that for years he hadn't wanted to be discovered.

"I don't understand."

"I didn't want to screw up," he blurted. "Right or wrong, Jonquil, it's taken me till now to be able to have this talk with you." His face contorted.

"Someone in a detox facility told me once that moving to warmer weather helped slow the flashbacks and when that quit working, I fell into a bottle. I still have nightmares, night sweats." He had stopped strumming his fingers and his hands lay still. "Plenty of good men never make it back. It took me years."

His words were getting to her but she continued to resist. "You missed a ton of important things," she accused him. "By the way, how long do we have this room for?" *We*.

"Till noon."

The clock on the wall showed 11:15. She welcomed a time limit. By then, the windowless walls covered with industrial artwork were making her antsy.

"You were saying?" he probed gently.

"You missed so much." Her eyes narrowed. "Mom's funeral which I barely remember. Then, me getting shipped off by 'the aunts' to Seattle 'cause they couldn't handle me." He grunted again. "School stuff, graduations, fun things like father-daughter dances, bad things like when I almost drowned in a pool when I was twelve. Christmases and birthdays."

She shook her head slowly, remembering. "So many things."

"I'm sure Margo—"

"Margo was great but she wasn't you!" Her vehemence felt good.

He seemed to go inward for a moment. "I'm so sorry."

That wasn't enough. She wanted to let him have it then, shout and scream at the top of her lungs, stomp her feet and hurl anything within reach until the hotel staff came bursting in to find out what the mayhem was about.

But visions of him homeless, hopeless, his brave service, his sacrifice, kept intruding. Still, if nothing else, she would make him feel bad for her.

"I earned a full scholarship to UW. Wild, huh? I met my husband there. Gerald Will O'Keeffe, Gerry, a great guy from a wonderful family in Philadelphia. He was an environmentalist. We were married right after graduation. I so wanted a family by then."

Suddenly, her mouth struggled to form words. Too many tears glutted her vision. "You weren't there to walk me down the aisle. You weren't there to hold me when Gerry died. You … you … weren't … when Billy…." She closed her eyes in anguish.

"Daddy, oh Daddy, *where were you?"* she cried and buried her face in her arms.

Tears streaking his cheeks, he levered himself to his feet, limped over to her side of the table, pulled out the nearest chair next to hers and dropped into it.

290

"I'm here now, Gumdrop. I'm so damn sorry. Please forgive me. I love you so." He, too, began to weep as he reached out and caressed her shoulder.

She raised her head, turned toward him and they fell sobbing into each other's arms.

Minutes passed as their tears escalated and then subsided. Jonquil cried hard but not like there was no end to her tears. That had been the feeling when she was a child and no one could comfort her.

Now with him there, some, though far from all of her pain was released. She became aware of them softly patting each other on the back as her composure gradually returned.

They were still together in the same room.

Neither had fled.

The arm of her chair was digging into her abdomen so she sat back and stood up. She reached for the Kleenex and grabbed a few tissues before handing him the box.

The clock indicated it was time to go. Time to choose.

Either to extend this drama for a second or third meeting and prolong the agony before his plane left Saturday. Or walk out without a word and kill his hope of ever achieving a genuine reconciliation. But she knew now that revenge wasn't her goal.

There was a third option.

Forgiveness could begin today. Not totally, of course, that might take years, if ever. She could, however, love him right now without having all the answers, and leave herself vulnerable to come what may.

"We need a rocking chair," he murmured, blowing his nose.

Sniffling mightily, she said, "There's one at home."

He stared up at her questioningly, his eyes red and puffy like hers must be.

"Dad, come have dinner with us tonight. We can talk more another time. I'm too happy to stay mad at you." She broke into a rueful smile. "You can walk me down the aisle *this* time."

"Claude?"

She nodded, beaming. He rose and they hugged tightly. That felt good.

"That's … oh, honey, that's fantastic news. When?" He stepped back.

She laughed and leaned over to grab her purse. "It may sound crazy, but we're trying for Thanksgiving weekend."

"May I bring Nora?"

"Yes, of course. I want to hear all about her, too, but right now I need to freshen up and then see about a rental car."

"Can I drive you anywhere?"

She said she would welcome a lift to the garage where her car had been taken, and where she fully expected a post mortem would be administered.

"Can I buy you a new car?"

She scoffed. "No, you may not. I want much more from you than a car."

She deposited her glass and his cup and saucer on the sideboard.

"A down payment on a house then? For a wedding gift?" He positioned the chair he'd commandeered back into place.

"No, Dad, no house."

He held open the door for her.

"Then what, honey?"

She flattened her hands on his shoulders and peered into his gray blue eyes.

"Be Billy's grampa. That's enough."

CHAPTER 60

Yield

Hours later, ensconced in a teal blue Honda Civic but armed with the happy news that her car would live to see another day, Jonquil sat at a stop light in Santa Monica munching a tart green apple, breathing in the fragrant ocean air as she put the night's menu together. Her dad had driven from the garage back to the hotel so he could take a nap before dinner.

It occurred to her that she hadn't made her grandmother's crowd pleasing John Mazzetti casserole in a long while. It was the Bloom adaptation of a more famous recipe with a similar name. Humble, hearty, it should spark happy memories for her father. Claude was bringing wine and dessert, though tonight they might skip the wine. She'd make one of her inspired salads to augment the main course and ask Claude to add crusty bread rolls to his list.

She started humming as the light changed. The elusive family circle at last would be forming at the dinner table that night. All because a jazzy talk show host named Poppi had invited Jonquil back on television ostensibly to forgive and forget, and her dad's girlfriend happened to be a fan. The serendipity gave her goose bumps.

If only Margo were there.

Forgiveness, what a one hundred eighty-degree difference it made. Three hundred sixty degrees, really, because forgiveness had the power to transform everything.

So much dead weight had been lifted off her shoulders, the lightness could be felt down to her toes. She had cried her eyes out, now she couldn't stop smiling though something her father had said nagged at her. She raked her fingers through her hair trying to remember.

True gifts were free, she clung to her theory as firmly as to an article of faith. But Jack Bloom had raised the noble aspect of sacrifice. Had he sacrificed his personal happiness in hopes that one day it would be restored? She could not fathom such faith.

Perhaps true gifts weren't free after all.

Her mind was racing but getting nowhere. Cars honked behind her and she tabled the intriguing conundrum for later.

CHAPTER 61

It Happened One Night

Jonquil stood at the kitchen sink draining hood noodles and daydreaming. Through the open window, she overheard Billy and Ramon playing down by the swimming pool. Ranger kept them company as well as greeted their neighbors, home from work. She knew from experience that more than one had made a habit of bending down to give the cagey cocker spaniel a good rubbing. That dog's no slouch, she thought with amusement.

The ground pork began to sizzle in the skillet. She put aside the bowl of drained pasta, picked up a knife and started chopping mushrooms and an onion.

Her imagination whisked her away to a future classroom at UCLA where she stood—no, sat—at a round table with seminar students who appeared alert and eager. No, bored. No, a blend of bored and eager. Two men and five women, she counted. Correction, four women and a man. Not many people would take a chance on a new field of study for a career. Those who did, however, would turn out to be the cream of the crop.

"What is the best of all gifts?" she heard herself ask in a scholarly tone. Each semester she began and ended with the same open-ended query. Material things were usually offered initially. Fancy cars, robust health, cash. Intangibles such as virtues came later. The growth in the students' insights, exemplified by their responses the second time around, always gave her a thrill.

Or would one day, if she ever finished her Ph.D.! She would telephone Joe Mazziotti after the wedding and get her project back on track. Tuesday, she had spotted him on campus speaking with the art therapy director so she did not interrupt. But now having met with her father, already she felt less of a seductive pull toward her advisor. Could transference fade so fast? Anything was possible. Ah, but her new understanding would not diminish the very real pleasure of working with the Mazz. Of that, she was certain.

By now the onions were irritating her eyes, still puffy from the morning's watershed with her father. She dabbed at them with a dish cloth, making things worse. They demanded rest. She was adding in the diced vegetables to the meat, when the phone rang. If she were in a seminar at that moment and asked to identify the best gift of all, her answer would be another pair of hands.

"Hello?" she said, after snatching up the receiver and stretching the telephone line so she could turn over the meat.

"Jonquil, hi. It's Georgina Phillips. What can I bring to the party on Saturday?"

"Oh, hi, Georgina, how nice of you to call." The two car pool moms chatted above the racket Jonquil made locating a deep casserole dish in a lower cabinet. The air became redolent with mouth-watering aromas. A glance at the time informed Jonquil that it was going on five o'clock. Fortunately, she had set the table as soon as she came home. The casserole would take less than an hour to bake but she needed to keep things moving. She got off the telephone and heard Billy pounding up the stairs.

"Mom, Mom," he yelled, charging into the apartment, the screen door banging shut behind him. "Is that what I think it is? Can Ramon stay for dinner? He's never had it."

"Sweetie, it's a little late to call Mrs. DeWitt, don't you agree?" What she really thought was, *This is a special night. Ramon can stay another time.*

Billy's face fell. "Aw...."

She removed a can of tomatoes from the pantry and set it on the counter. "Come on now, wasn't Ramon here all day Monday playing video games with you? And he'll be here again on Saturday. His mother will forget what he looks like."

"No she won't. Please, Mom?" He threw his arms around her waist and gave her his wiliest smile. "He'll love John Mazzetti."

She sighed, placed her hands on his forearms, and gently swayed with him to and fro. He'd grown another inch or two over summer and almost reached her shoulder. She was thankful to discover that her son's eyes were shining again. Not a hundred percent like in his portrait in the main room, but enough to make her heart swell with hope. Knowing his grampa would be there for dinner no doubt fueled his excitement.

"O-kay." So the family circle would include Billy's best friend and not Margo. Of *course* not Margo. She sighed again. "You win."

298

"Yes, yes, yes!" He spun around and dashed outside. Ramon and Ranger were soon upstairs and inside. The three scampered down the hall to use her bedroom extension.

"Make it quick," she called. "Clean your bathroom, please."

Where was she? Ah, yes, the best of all gifts. However, by then the seminar students had slipped from her mind. Just as well.

A half hour later, the casserole, covered in grated cheese, was in the oven baking, the tossed salad was in the refrigerator chilling. She'd outdone herself this time with sliced zucchini, celery, carrots, scallions, radishes, a cup of sweet corn, chopped pear for body, pine nuts for added crunch, and mixed greens. It was time to shower. She turned over the job of hospitality to Billy, Ramon, and Ranger. Her crew.

Claude arrived just before six. They had spoken several times during the day, sharing feelings about the talk with her father and the unexpected departure of his foreman. Fred's decision had taken him by surprise but Claude told her he'd manage.

Now, he strolled down the hall in search of her. "Sweetheart?" He rapped on her bathroom door. "Jonny?"

"Coming." She wrapped herself in an old cloth robe before opening the door and found herself enfolded in his arms. "Mmm," he murmured low. They kissed deeply. Instantly, the world began fading. Oh, it was so tempting but not tonight.

She broke away and stared up at him. He looked delicious in a dark suit and crimson tie. He must have come from a business meeting. She asked whether he'd remembered the bread, dessert.

He nodded vigorously and peered down at her. "Your eyes are red."

"I know. I cried them out this morning and chopping onions a while ago didn't help."

"Poor baby. Let me kiss."

"They need cucumbers, hon, not kisses." She pointed to a plate on her dresser.

He nodded as if that made perfect sense. *"D'accord.* Just wanted to let you know that Katie is coming for dessert and to update us on the church." He gave her a parting kiss and left.

Lying down for ten minutes, soothing cucumber slices on both eyelids, she reflected that sore eyes were becoming the bane of the Bloom household.

She missed Jack Bloom's arrival. By the time she returned to the main room, her father was already occupying the rocking chair that Father Tim used to favor, head to head with both boys. Claude, too, was riveted on whatever they were all peering at.

The photo album of the trip to Ireland.

"Well," she said to gain their attention. Her glance took in the autographed baseball, manila envelope containing Jack Bloom's war medals, stack of other photo albums, and camera that Billy had laid out on the coffee table. She considered whether the medals might upset her father. Before she could react, he handed the album to Billy and pushed himself to his feet. "Jonquil, how lovely you look." He took her hands and buzzed her on the cheek. He wore a festive Hawaiian shirt, tan slacks and boat shoes.

After spending the afternoon in the hot kitchen, she'd wanted to create a sweet, fresh impression. Her frizzy hair was held back from her face with twin barrettes. She wore a sleeveless, pink and red plaid cotton dress, pearls and wedge sandals. Her green eyes had benefited from their brief rest and were sparkling. On one wrist was the bracelet Claude had given her for Valentine's Day.

Claude slipped his arm comfortably around her waist and kissed her ear lobe. "Something smells divine ... besides you."

Pleased, she made sure everyone had a beverage before disappearing with Claude into the kitchen. They kissed again.

"What amazing thing are you baking?" he asked.

"One of Dad's favorite casseroles," she replied. "I hope it brings back happy memories. Mmm. You're wearing your smell'ums."

"Special occasion," he murmured, then cleared his throat. "What can I do to help?" In tandem they set out the food and filled the crystal glasses with water. She filled Ranger's bowls, too.

"What do you think, Claude, will it bother Dad if you and I have wine?"

"I asked him before I opened the bottle. He assured me it wouldn't and insisted I open it."

"I'll skip it tonight. What's he drinking?"

"Water for now, coffee later. Regular, black."

"I'll just start a pot then."

He grabbed her hand. "That can wait. Let's eat."

Claude seemed to be in a hurry. She surveyed the table. All was ready.

She smiled serenely and said, "Light the candles, please."

Claude faced her in the chair he occupied whenever he stayed to dinner. Billy was in his accustomed place to her right, Ramon next to him. Jack Bloom sat on her left. The table was square, to be sure, yet in her mind they formed a lopsided circle of Blooms. She wanted to sing.

"Who will say grace?" she asked.

"I will," volunteered Jack Bloom. They crossed themselves and bowed their heads.

"Bless us, O Lord, and these Thy gifts...." Her ears didn't hear anything beyond the word gifts.

When they had finished the prayer, she said, "Ramon, your job will be to take pictures we can send to my grandmother in Ireland. She'd so like to be with us tonight."

"Sure, Ms. Bloom. Want me to start now?" Ramon sprang to his feet, jarring the water glasses.

Claude said, "Don't let your food get cold."

He's famished, she thought. That explains Claude's edginess. "Okay, it can wait until after dinner," she agreed.

Jack Bloom did not immediately recognize the casserole. However, after two bites his face became suffused in smiles. "Jonquil, I remember this dish!"

She grinned and then discovered Claude regarding her with radiant love. It nearly took her breath away.

"Our family recipe," said Billy proudly. "It's the best thing ever." The clatter of forks against plates and accompanying lack of conversation underscored the accuracy of his remark. Ranger padded over and stretched out by Billy's chair, the picture of contentment.

Now, truly, the entire household had assembled.

Toward the end of dinner, Claude began checking his watch every few minutes. He tried to do it without her noticing but that was futile. She gave him a questioning look.

He responded with a grin and shrugged his shoulders. "Wonder what's keeping Katie."

She pushed back her chair. "Let's stretch our legs and hold dessert until she gets here. Billy, will you help me clear the table?"

"I'll help you," said Claude. "Jack, want that coffee now?"

"Sure, Claude, sounds good."

Jack went down the hall to use the bathroom while Billy and Ramon fiddled with the camera. As soon as Jack returned, Billy posed with him for a picture. Then Jack paused for a moment to admire Billy's portrait on the wall before he reclaimed the rocking chair.

Billy handed him the bag of medals. His grandfather opened it and removed the box containing his Bronze Star.

He heaved a sigh.

"Grampa, don't you want your medals?"

"Pal, you keep them for me, okay?"

Ramon, meanwhile, took a few more photos.

"Grampa, we haven't studied the Korean War at school yet. Maybe you can come on Grandparents Day and tell us about it?"

"We'll see. You know, boys, the Korean War is known as the forgotten war but it's still going on. We never did sign a peace treaty. But that's enough about war. Tell me about school."

The boys each answered questions about their favorite subjects and teachers. Claude set a mug of fresh coffee on the table beside the rocker. He glanced at the door and frowned.

By now Jonquil had joined them in the main room and perched on the edge of the sofa.

Jack looked up and said, "Jonquil, I hear you're in the church choir."

Before she could reply, Billy cried, "Grampa, guess what I have! A tape recording of Mom and Margo singing together in Ireland!"

"Well now, Billy, that's something I'd really love to hear."

Billy dashed down the hall. When he returned with the tape however, the portable radio with the cassette player couldn't be found. They searched high and low to no avail. Finally, Claude said, "Jonny, why not sing it for us right now?"

Just then the doorbell rang.

Claude looked relieved, saying as he crossed the room, "Maybe later. First things first." He opened the door, and in walked his sister with Annie Berghoff.

"We have the church!" shouted Katie.

Introductions were made followed by dessert—a tasty assortment of petit fours and coffee. It became evident that Katie and Annie had gotten in touch with each other without Jonquil's knowledge to discuss among other things, a wedding shower. Annie, the maid of honor, had begged to be present when her best friend received the happy news about the church.

Katie started to furnish details but Claude raised his hand. At the same time, Ramon picked up the camera and prepared to snap more pictures but Claude intervened.

"Ramon, can you stop for a minute, *s'i'l vous plaît*? I've got something to say, eh, or rather, to do."

Claude got up from the table and came toward her. Jonquil could not recall ever seeing him nervous before. His voice sounded husky, too.

"This seems like the perfect night for what I'm about to do. Jonquil has already consented. But we're both glad you're here, Jack. Katie dear, you, too."

He then knelt down on one knee before Jonquil and produced a small jewelry box. She gasped. Carefully opening it with steady hands, he said, "Jonquil Bloom, *mon amour*, will you be my wife?"

"Oh!" she moaned, as her hands flew to her lips.

Nestled on a cushion of dark blue velvet was a ring of such beauty, it made her eyes gleam. She knew it well and had shown it to Annie on a visit to the jeweler at Farmers Market in Los Angeles over a year ago.

The rustic auburn colored diamond, graced on either side by rose cut white diamonds, appeared at once both old fashioned and brand new.

Like love itself.

Claude set down the box on the table and took her left hand. He slipped the ring onto her finger and kissed it. "Woman, don't keep me waiting. You know how I hate waiting."

They all laughed. Ranger started barking until Billy shushed him. Claude climbed to his feet.

She could not tear her eyes away from the ring. Yet, she could sense those she loved in the background, watching, waiting with baited breath for her response. Anticipation of all that lay ahead stirred inside of her so deep, it might last, day in and day out, a lifetime. Her heart felt near to bursting with the love that makes new dreams come true. Caught between tears of joy and joy outright she chose the latter.

Jonquil shoved back her chair and jumped to her feet. She kissed the ring too, then flung her arms around Claude's neck.

"Yes," was her answer, "oh, yes, oh, dear God, yes!"

EPILOGUE

What Abel Knew

*W**here's Claude? He should be here by now.*
Jonquil struggled to remain calm as she scanned the arriving parishioners from the back of church, Jack and Billy nearby.

Mild November evening air wafted in from the main entrance. Through the lobby glass doors, she spied the wedding guests sprinkled among the regular church goers: Mr. Merrill and his wife, Rita and Al, Iris Escanaba and her husband, their neighbor, Mrs. Crandon, who had given Billy the dog, the carpool moms, Ramon and his family, Claude's parents and relatives, his friends and business associates, Katie Ryan.

Ed Ryan was inside directing the choir—her choir—and the music. Jonquil's assistant, Vanessa, couldn't make the wedding, but she and her husband would be at the reception at Katie's house. Maid of honor Annie and Coach Bobby Hillman, so cute together, were already seated up front.

Her father squeezed her hand.

"He'll be here."

Claude mysteriously had left town two days ago. In so doing, he'd missed the wedding rehearsal, but he had assured Jonquil he would be at the church in plenty of time for the actual ceremony.

Bewildering to say the least.

What could be so important? she'd asked. A fishing trip in Canada had been his reply. His buddies back home wanted to give him a proper bachelor's send off. Customary. He couldn't disappoint them.

"You must be here for the rehearsal," she'd flamed incredulously. "Your family's coming. Do you really expect me to meet them for the first time without you here?"

"You can do this, babe," he'd said. "They can't wait to meet you. Katie will help you."

She'd shaken her head, not listening.

"Jonny, I wanted to be here when you met my family, eh, but I can't get out of this," he'd replied firmly. "I know it's a lot to ask. Please try to understand. We'll call my folks together. That way you can meet them *par téléphone*."

They'd made the call and yes, it had at least broken the ice, but not like the live hugs and kisses encounter she had envisioned.

The night he'd broken the news to her, she had felt irritable and couldn't sleep. Didn't he know how much family meant to her?

Since becoming engaged, they'd talked practically non-stop, trying to cover the basics of their future life together, from living arrangements, finances, work goals, their Catholic commitment, to future children. He'd seemed so keen on it all.

So now what? Wild imaginings assailed her: He had a secret other family, he had doubts, he was fleeing back to the seminary he'd spent time at in his youth.

He'd hit a raw nerve. She'd once told him she didn't trust love because when those she loved left her, they never returned. And he had responded by saying he'd never leave her.

Although, granted, after a long absence, the first person to leave her *had* returned.

That stark realization induced her to take stock. She faced herself in the bathroom mirror, bleary-eyed, tears trickling down her cheeks.

This was the man she loved, why send him off feeling guilty? Hadn't she had all the wedding trimmings once before? Even Margo had been present back then. And who was it who'd stayed with Billy in the hospital, trusting her to return, on that first night?

This time around things would be different, which was a good thing. After all, Claude was forty-three years old with lifelong friends who naturally wanted to be part of the celebration. Jonquil had felt suspicious because the trip seemed to have popped up from nowhere. *Let it go*, she decided. And as she picked up her tooth brush, the thought struck her forcibly that this is what Abel knew. To give, not by half measures, or grudgingly, but wholeheartedly, and when the occasion demanded it, with wild abandon. Her glum attitude was replaced by the start of a smile.

By the time Claude phoned her from LAX to say goodbye, her tone was upbeat. He sounded surprised and greatly relieved. This was her gift to him, to face both the rehearsal and dinner alone *cheerfully*.

So, when Annie griped about Claude's quirky behavior en route to the beauty salon later that afternoon, Jonquil shrugged. The letdown was forgotten for Jonquil grasped that she, too, had been gifted with a humbling view of her own self-absorption. Annie remarked on her friend's sunny attitude, saying perchance she was crazy in love. They soon got to giggling and time sped by.

She'd gone on to the rehearsal, Annie and Billy with her, head held high. Father Frank and the pastor walked her through the simple logistics. The vows and rings would be exchanged after the homily. Family and friends would do the readings and bring forward the gifts. The Nuptial Blessing would immediately follow the Lord's Prayer. The music for the Mass was out of her hands but she was invited to make a selection for her walk down the aisle.

Jack and Nora had arrived Friday, and they all met at the church that afternoon, including Nora's daughter, Molly, from Tucson. Molly immediately nicknamed Jonquil "Sis" which had a nice ring it.

Dinner followed at a restaurant she and Claude frequented. There, Jonquil and Billy had met the other members of the Chappel clan: his effusive parents, a sister and her spouse from Quebec, and his brothers from elsewhere in the States. Jonquil welcomed them all warmly. If it felt awkward without Claude, she gave no sign, and the evening ended up being a superb success.

The hardest part was not being able to telephone him but the camping trip did not allow for instant communication. What bride would put up with such behavior right before a wedding? But she couldn't revert back to being angry at him. Instead, she prayed for his safe return.

Now, Jonquil glanced down the main aisle toward the altar, relieved that the priests hadn't yet made an appearance. She and Claude had provided the bowers of orchids that graced the sanctuary. Altar girls and boys darted about, lighting the candles, and her pulse began to race. Gingerly, because of the bouquet in her hand, she raised her wrist to check the time. The photographer from Clyde's waited nearby, a generous wedding gift from Mr. Merrill.

Her engagement ring caught her eye and she gazed at it intently.

Back on that September night after Claude had presented Jonquil with the ring, there had been singing, Irish tunes, mostly. Her father had joined in with his rich baritone, followed by Katie, Claude and the boys. Annie, who wasn't much of a singer, had ducked out, saying she had a date. Jonquil hugged her before she left and thanked her profusely for clueing in Claude about the ring.

Jonquil's attention was then drawn to an interaction between her son and her father.

"You can play it when you get home, Grampa," said Billy, handing Jack the cassette. The portable radio and cassette player sadly had remained lost.

Before she could intervene, Billy sealed the deal with, "You're gonna love it."

It wasn't like they listened to the recording daily, true, but it had helped Billy stay calm in the hospital. Moreover, the music was a precious souvenir of their trip to see Margo, its sentimental value priceless. Billy must have felt her eyes on him. He came over to her and patted her arm. "Mom, no worries. Tommy can probably make us another one."

Her face had relaxed. "Of course, sweetie. Even if he can't, you did the right thing. I'm very proud of you." She touched his cheek before he skipped away.

Aside from the ring, the other amazing development that night came from her future sister-in-law, Katie. Jonquil's wish to be married at Saint Monica was going to be granted provided she didn't mind a church full of strangers looking on.

Puzzled, Jonquil asked, "What strangers?"

"Oh," said Katie airily, reaching across the table for another petit four, "anyone attending the vigil Mass on Saturday afternoon that weekend."

"You mean, we'll be married at Mass? I've been to weddings with a nuptial Mass but never a Mass with a wedding."

Katie laughed, thoroughly enjoying her role as the bearer of good news. "Well, it counts. You told me your guest list would be short, Claude's, too, so, because the church is booked solid with other weddings Thanksgiving weekend, the pastor offered this

312

alternative. Most people prefer a private ceremony so it's rarely done. Or, you two can get married on Sunday morning but I thought you might want to slip away Saturday night." She lifted her eyebrow suggestively.

Jonquil and Claude gazed at each other and grinned. Jonquil said, "Katie, we love that idea." Katie urged them to secure a meeting with the pastor the following day for time was short.

The intervening three months since that night had flown by. Now her dad was studying his mobile phone. He showed her something called a "text" from Claude. The word on the screen simply said, "Coming."

Her father suggested they take their seats. She breathed in deeply, exhaled and nodded.

It didn't much matter that Claude wouldn't be there to watch her walk down the aisle. It wasn't going to be a traditional ceremony in that sense.

Nor was she dressed in a wedding gown or veil. Rather, with Rita's fashion acumen and Vanessa's input, she was wearing a vintage, champagne-colored, silk gown with a scooped neckline, empire waist and puffy sleeves. She'd accessorized with new earrings, heels and a sequined hat. The rest of her funds had been spent on Billy's navy suit.

Billy was well! His sight was steadily improving. His medication and follow up appointments continued but no signs of the disease had resurfaced. She lived with the fear of its return yet Claude was there now to share the burden and to pray with her for Billy's permanent recovery.

Billy's beloved Dodgers had struck out that season but you can't have everything. That would be heaven. Making a heaven on earth was the best you could do.

She now looped arms with Jack on one side, Billy on the other and took her place. Katie, watching from up front, gave her husband the signal and a quartet began to play Pachelbel Canon in D.

A ripple of applause greeted them as they walked down the aisle and cameras flashed around the church. They proceeded slowly due to Jack's limp which, Jonquil hoped, gave Claude a little more time.

Be brave, she told herself, concentrate on your blessings.

They settled in a pew near the front. So far, so good, thought Jonquil. Yet, she couldn't sit still.

She winked at the choir, happy they were there. Glancing about, she spotted Fred and Leigh entering a pew behind her, over to the side.

Leigh gave her a quick, showy wave with one hand and patted her middle with the other. Jonquil smiled back at her, inwardly groaning,

Swell, Leigh's here but not the groom!

Her gaze gravitated to the tabernacle on the main altar. Once while visiting their parish church in Minneapolis, her mother had explained to Jonquil that the tabernacle was God's little house inside of His great big house.

She bowed her head and quieted her soul for a fleeting moment. When she looked up again, the priests were on the altar and the congregation stood.

Still no sign of Claude. Instantly, her throat felt dry while the palms of her hands turned clammy.

Beside her, Billy shot to his feet, ready to burst. "You know something, don't you?" she murmured. Her glance shifted to her father who was all smiles.

"You both know something."

She would learn later over prime rib with their guests at Katie's house that Claude, Billy and Jack had conspired on a plan to make the wedding unforgettable. That Billy and Claude had made the telephone call together. That Jack had paid for the tickets and hotel. That Claude, having offered himself as escort, had flown not to Montreal early Thursday morning but to New York City, met the plane from Ireland and stayed the night at a hotel before flying back to Los Angeles. That Jack Bloom had picked them up at LAX earlier to have his own poignant reunion. That the pastor and Frank had been in on the surprise, which was why they'd taken their time getting the Mass started.

That nothing would ever be the same because she'd found the one man who could read her heart.

The choir began to sing "Amazing Grace."

Billy turned around, pointed excitedly and cried, "Mom, look, LOOK!" He then squeezed past her and out of the pew.

Jack Bloom stepped out into the aisle next and beckoned her to join him. When she, too, faced the back of church, her jaw dropped.

Claude was advancing toward her, beaming. On one arm was Tommy Toolan, on the other, her beloved grandmother, Margo, who now stopped to hug Billy.

For a split second, she could not take it in. She gaped at the tableaux before her in sheer awe.

From behind her came the choir's voices:

"... I once was lost but now I am found, was blind but now I see."

The congregation picked up on Billy's excitement and started to applaud. Jonquil ran to greet Margo. After a tight, loving embrace, she gracefully relinquished her grandmother to Jack. Then, brushing away tears of joy, she floated back down the rest of the aisle, arm in arm with her gallant true love.